# THE DARK SPIRIT

*By the same author and artist*

THE CREATURES OF CELTIC MYTH

# THE DARK SPIRIT

## SINISTER PORTRAITS FROM CELTIC HISTORY

BOB CURRAN

Illustrated by ANDREW WHITSON

CASSELL&CO

First published in the United Kingdom in 2001 by Cassell & Co
A Member of the Orion Publishing Group



A CIP catalogue record for this book is available from the British Library

ISBN 0 304 35622 0

Designed by Richard Carr
Printed and bound in Great Britain by
MPG Books Ltd., Bodmin, Cornwall

Cassell & Co
Wellington House
125 Strand
London WC2R 0BB

# CONTENTS

# INTRODUCTION

There is a dark spirit that underlies much of Western history and society, both cultural and political, and which has had a profound influence upon both. It has its roots in the ancient traditions and beliefs of the Celts – those enigmatic people who occupied much of the West in earliest times. So what is this spirit and how has it manifested itself across the ages?

Much early Celtic belief concerned itself with positive things that could benefit society, such as the rituals which caused the crops to grow and guaranteed fertility in both humans and animals. The exponents of these antique beliefs were an integral part of Celtic society: people who could divine the weather or heal illness through the use of herbs. This tradition has continued down the centuries to the present day, as is evidenced by the publication of books on Celtic-based self-improvement and healing. It also finds expression in the activities of 'white witches', who can still be found, often on the fringes of modern-day society. This side of Celtic perception looks towards the 'light' or more positive aspects of the world.

There is another part of the Celtic mind, however, that is fascinated with the negative or darker side of things – those powers and beings that shun the light and lurk in the shadows. Celtic folklore is filled with them. Innocent-looking rocks and trees were sometimes believed to be the physical embodiment of malevolent spirits who were always ready, willing and able to harm those who did not show them due deference. Malignant fairies were thought to lurk at the very fringes of human society, eager to cause evil and misfortune whenever they could. The unquiet and often hostile dead hated the living with a fierce passion and were always ready to strike out against them, and unsociable people who never really 'fitted in' to conventional society acquired dark and supernatural powers which they often used against their neighbours. The ancient Celts also believed in a mystical land that lay just beyond human vision (which they called 'the Otherworld') where such beings dwelt, and from where they could influence human affairs. This negative element, which some writers have referred to simply as 'the night side of nature', has been just as important in the formation of society across the ages.

Down through the centuries, the darker side has had an influence on how men and women perceive both themselves and each other. It intruded upon the political and religious spheres, where dark and monstrous beliefs were used in order to burn old women and children as witches, to brand certain areas as 'unholy' and suspect, and to terrify and awe people into submission. Certain themes have resurfaced time and time again in historical writings, in general literature and more specifically in folklore and folk belief. Such themes as dark witchcraft, vampirism, incest and so on have had a particular effect on how the Western mind perceived the world in general, how it shaped its laws and societal mores, how it formed its prejudices, how it established its social history, how it perceived and treated those who 'did not fit in' to conventional society, and how, in turn, they themselves, perceived and dealt with those around them. The dark spirit affected Western society at its deepest, most primeval level.

Of course, being so deeply ingrained within the social fabric of Western society, the spirit did not confine itself to those lands in which the Celtic peoples initially settled. As the New World was colonized by peoples from western Europe, both the 'light' and 'dark' elements of their legends and mythologies travelled with them. In this way, the darker strand of Celtic folk belief mingled with other immigrant tales and indigenous Indian worship to form a significant part of the rich seam of American folklore. Even in the New World it is still possible to trace survivals of older European traditions that were forged by the earlier Celts.

Arguably the best way to examine these traditions and their roots in Celtic belief is to look at some of the individuals who embodied them. Instances of such exemplars are legion, both in rural and national folklore, and in some historical texts as well. When faced with such a wide choice and with such an intangible concept, it is always difficult to make a selection. So many colourful characters who have made an impact upon both literature and history seem to demonstrate the impact of the dark spirit: David Ritchie, the misanthropic Black Dwarf who influenced Scott's novel of the same name; Moll Anthony and Biddy Early, famous far beyond their native areas of Kildare and Clare as healers and prophetesses and who influenced a generation of Irish writers; the Reverend Polkinghorn, the noted Cornish exorcist and smuggler who may well have been the template for Russell Thorndyke's 'Dr Syn'; and the Faas, the celebrated 'Gypsy Kings' of Scotland, who have left their mark on poetry and song. All of these cry out for further examination and attention. However, such a book would be a massive, uneven and unwieldy tome. So, a rather arbitrary attempt has been made in this book to give at least a flavour of the dark spirit by selecting a sample of those who have been 'in touch' with the underlying Celtic darkness and who have impinged upon literature, history and folklore. There has also been an attempt to achieve a wide geographical location right across Celtic Britain and to give a wide collection of characters who have all, in one way or another, manifested the dark spirit and who have also somehow touched the lives of those around them. Some are criminals such as Coppinger. Some were national scandals, such as Major Weir. Others are tyrants, such as the Wolf of Badenoch. Some, such as Joan Wytt, are simply strange, 'fey' people. Also included within this book are a number of connections between the folklore and mythology of western Europe and that of rural America – the first time that this has ever been done in such a direct way. The collection is arranged loosely in chronological order.

As the 21st century dawns, it is easy to dismiss the contents herein as simply so much superstition and old tales, and yet it may be that something still lurks beneath the surface of what we call 'civilization' – something which stretches back into pagan times, into prehistory. Come, then, and prepare to catch a glimpse of the Dark Spirit.

# THE WOLF OF BADENOCH

'Aweel,' said the Wolf. 'Step forrit Bishop an' show me the land-titles which ye hae brocht.' Bishop Burr looked around him at the towering stone that completely dwarfed his frail human form. The Wolf had placed his chair in the very centre of the pagan stone circle and was holding out a mailed hand to receive the documents. Looking directly at him, Alexander Burr suddenly made up his mind. This was a pagan place filled, it was said, with ancient magic, and even the Church would have no power within its confines. Furthermore, no promise or guarantee given within the stones of Kingussie would have any force in Scottish law – and the bishop had no trust in the Wolf. Clutching the documents tightly to his chest, he took a step backwards. 'Naw!' he declared. 'I'll no come forrit!'

The shadow of a 14th-century wolf dominates much of the folklore of the Scottish Highlands, the associated tales filled with hints of witchcraft, devilry and slaughter. In the Scottish Lowlands, too, the name of Alexander Stewart, the Wolf of Badenoch, has become synonymous with bloody warfare, pillage and evil sciences, his black deeds celebrated in both legend and song. The truth behind the legend, however, is, in many ways, just as interesting as the tale itself.

The ancient lands of Badenoch form part of the southern end of the Spey Valley, stretching through Loch Insh and Kincraig, and lie close to the ruins of Ruthven Barracks (occupied by the Jacobites following the '45 rebellion) and also to the Speyside holiday town of Kingussie. The name Badenoch means 'the drowned land', and the description is an apt one, because the broad, glacial valley through which the River Spey flows is frequently subject to flooding in spring as the winter snows melt further up in the Highlands, and burns and rivers struggle to cope with the excess waters. There is little doubt that Badenoch was also the site of pagan worship in pre-Christian times. There are tales of forgotten and now-lost tumuli and of 'druid's altars' within the locality, and Kingussie itself once boasted a druidical circle of standing stones which reputedly challenged both Stonehenge and Callanish (on the Isle of Lewis) for magnificence and mystery. This circle is no longer in existence and its site has been absorbed into the modern-day village of Kingussie, with its shops, railway station and housing developments. Yet, in the days of the Wolf of Badenoch, it was a wild and lonely place, mysterious, eerie and perhaps more than a little threatening. It was a fitting place for such a dark and sinister man.

Alexander Stewart was of royal blood. In fact, he was one of the three surviving sons of King Robert II of Scotland by his then mistress Elizabeth Mure, and it is in the circumstances of Stewart's birth that we gain our first clue as to his brooding temperament. He was born in around 1343 (certainly before 1344) as the fourth son of an illicit union. His father did not marry his mother until 1347, thus effectively making Alexander and his two surviving brothers bastards for almost four years. Indeed, Alexander was not fully recognized as a legitimate son of the king (and therefore a possible heir to the Scottish throne) until a declaration made in March 1371, immediately following Robert II's coronation. He was 28 years of age before the stigma of his birth was lifted from his shoulders. His fierce nature, honed by years of alleged illegitimacy, made him the most formidable of his father's sons and one who considered himself to be the rightful successor upon the death of the king (Robert II was an old, bleary-eyed man of 55 when he ascended to the Scottish throne).

In an attempt to pacify his brooding son, Robert gave him several titles and responsibilities. On 30 March 1371, he made him Lord of the Lands of Badenoch and Strathspey, granting him the important northern castle of Lochindorb, with the rank of Justiciar of the North of Scotland. This effectively made him the most powerful man under the crown, second only to the king himself, responsible for the administration of justice in an area which stretched from the county of Moray to the Pentland Firth. Furthermore, around 1388, Alexander also made an extremely useful marriage. By wedding Euphemia, widow of Sir Walter Leslie and daughter of the Earl of Ross, he acquired the further title of Earl of Buchan, and took sizeable holdings in Ross-shire together with several other large possessions. The region he controlled was an especially troubled one. Moray was the seat of several families who traced their ancestry back to Macbeth – a former king of Scotland – and who were firmly opposed to Stewart rule. It was the responsibility of the Justiciar to keep them under control. This Alexander did with a ferocious relish, attacking numerous families throughout Moray and driving some of them from their lands, which he subsequently claimed in the name of the Scottish crown.

His main power-base was established in Ruthven, where he built an imposing castle (later to become a Hanovarian barracks in the 18th century), although he had many fortresses and strongholds scattered across the Highlands. The choice of Ruthven was an important one. The abundance of prehistoric tumuli and earthworks in the area, together with the magnificent stone circle at Kingussie, had given Badenoch (of which Ruthven was a part) a rather sinister reputation. There were many tales of old powers, spirits were said to reside in the stones there, and reputedly seven witches dwelt within the district at any one time. The melding of both supernatural and political power served Alexander Stewart well. His castle was built on a pre-Christian mound, which not only gave a commanding view down the Spey Valley but also gave the building a suggestion of pagan, Otherworldly power. Alexander went even further. He used the stone circle at Kingussie as his major court where he heard petitions and from which he dispensed justice. The significance of the site was not lost on the locals. Although technically Christian, much of Scotland still had a healthy respect for the old, pagan ways which had not quite died out, and the influence and mystery of the standing stones gave the king's Justiciar an air of even greater authority. In the popular mind, he was more than a simple magistrate – he was imbued with the powers that emanated from the stones themselves. Of course, such a move was not popular with the Church.

Earlier, in August 1370, Alexander had summoned some of the leading chieftains and churchmen to his castle at Lochindorb, and had promised them his protection should he ever become Justiciar of the North, in return for 'a trifling sum'. It was, of course, protection money, but the nobles paid up rather than face the prospect of the fury of the son of the (then) prospective king. Among those who came to meet with him was Alexander Burr (sometimes given as Birr or Barr), the Bishop of Moray, to whom the Lord of Badenoch promised 'his especial protection'. As soon as he assumed the judiciary, however, Alexander Stewart surrounded himself with a number of Highland caterans (a name derived from the Gaelic *ceatharn*, denoting a troop of warriors, but at the time taken to mean ungovernable Highland bandits or robbers) and almost immediately went back on his word. He was joined, said the venerable Episcoporum Vitae (Boece's 16th-century history of the Bishops of Aberdeen) 'by certain vile creatures [who] drove off all the bishop's cattle and carried away his property, killing at the same time, in the most high-handed way, the peasants'. He divided as he pleased the lands stolen from the church and gave them to be cultivated by certain wicked men who 'had no regard for God or men'.

There was worse, however. Since coming to Badenoch, it was rumoured, Alexander had been consorting with Highland warlocks and carlines (witches) and had learned the ways of Scottish sorcery. In his castle at Ruthven, he was supposed to hold the only known copy of the infamous *Book of Black Earth*, called 'The Wicked Bible' by the later Calvinists, a book of pre-human blasphemy which could only be studied if the brow of the reader was surrounded by a circlet of iron in order to ward off its baleful influence. (The same, incidentally, was said of the *Red Book of Appin*.) This awful volume he had acquired from a witch in the Highlands, and it was the source of his power. He was also said to worship strange, pre-human deities in the great druid circle at Kingussie, so that all who stepped within the megalithic construction would fall under his control. That was the principal reason why he frequently conducted court there, or so legend said. These tales were taken very seriously, not least of all by the Church, and, while they undoubtedly contributed to Alexander Stewart's power and authority,

they also marked him as one of the foremost sorcerers in Scotland.

These rumours were further enhanced by the acquisition of a lonely castle on an island in the centre of Loch an Eilean in Rothiemurchus – the rolling, thickly forested lands which lie between the Spey and the Cairngorms. Loch an Eilean lies several miles south of the present-day town of Aviemore, and its banks provide a magnificent view of the Cairngorm Mountains. It is a wild and desolate spot, and the island is believed to have been the site of pagan worship of a prehistoric entity known as 'Mhor-Ri' (Great King), which, according to Thomas Pennington, was still venerated in remote parts of Scotland as late as the 18th century. Alexander constructed a fortress on the alleged site of this worship, the ruins of which can still be seen. Within its walls, he was rumoured to have called up the Devil himself and to have engaged in perverse and disgusting rites including human sacrifice.

Disputes and disagreements were quickly developing between the Lord of Badenoch and the representatives of the Scottish Church, particularly Alexander Burr, the Bishop of Moray. Lands belonging to the Church had been suddenly seized on the slightest pretext, the authority of the bishops had been flouted and many Church tenants had been put to the sword by the lord's band of drunken robbers. Added to this, the stories that Lord Badenoch openly consorted with demons and fairies both at Kingussie and on the island at Loch an Eilean were now very widespread and were accepted as fact. In October 1380, Bishop Burr strongly protested against the lord's deeds and reputation and, in response, Alexander invited him to attend a meeting at Ruthven Castle (on 10–11 October 1380) to debate the issue. Lord Badenoch had, of course, no intention of listening to the bishop and, after a rather heated exchange, had him ejected from the castle. He then summoned Burr to appear before him 'within the Rathe of Kingussie', bringing the titles to all his lands for His Lordship to inspect. Some versions of the legend say that Burr actually came but refused to enter the druid circle; other versions state that 'he came not' but that he burnt the summons in Elgin 'with due solemnity and in the presence of a great assemblage'. Having openly disobeyed the direct command of the king's representative, the Church lands were forfeit to the crown. The Bishop immediately refused to recognize Badenoch's jurisdiction and appealed directly to the king, Robert II. Alexander's decision was overturned and the bishop's lands were restored to him, but the confrontation led to a deep and abiding hatred between the two men, which was never resolved. From then on, Burr never lost an opportunity to denounce Alexander Stewart for even the slightest misdemeanour – and he had plenty of scope. Not only were tales of Badenoch's alleged witchcraft increasing, but events in the lord's private life left much to be desired as well.

In order to acquire the Earlship of Buchan, Alexander had contracted his marriage with Euphemia of Ross in 1389. He had already seized some of the lands in Ross-shire, but the marriage consolidated and extended his northern empire. Hardly had the ink dried on the marriage contract and the lands been transferred than Alexander abandoned his new wife and took up residence in Lochindorb Castle with a mistress, the beautiful Mariota Athyn. Gleefully, the Bishop of Moray denounced him as an adulterer, urging him to return to his lawful wife and enlisting the support of the Bishop of Ross and, significantly, Alexander's older brother John, Earl of Carrick. This alliance was to signal a family split which would plague the Stewarts for a number of years to come. In addition to this, in February 1390 the bishop switched his protection payments to the Sheriff of Inverness, thus depriving Alexander of part of his revenue.

Angered by the bishop's indictment and by the loss of payment, Alexander took forceful action. Once again he demanded that the bishop present himself at his court in Kingussie and show due entitlement to his lands. Once again, the bishop refused. When Lord Badenoch threatened to seize the lands anyway, Burr replied by excommunicating him; this only provoked Alexander to an even greater fury. In May 1390, he and his men descended on the town of Forres, completely burning it to the ground. The following month, he led an attack on the cathedral town of Elgin, the seat of the Bishop of Moray, destroying many buildings there, the majority of which were Church property. In the process, he burnt the only hospital in the area, putting many sick and infirm to the sword. For this unspeakable action, he earned the title 'Wolf of Badenoch', and tales of his great evil increased.

In his book *History of the Highlands* (1838), the scholar James Brown wrote: 'The sentence of excommunication not only proved unavailing, but tended to exasperate the Lord of Badenoch to such a degree of fury that, in the month of May, thirteen hundred and ninety, he descended from the heights and burnt the town of Forres, with the choir of the church and the manse of the archdeacon. And, in June following, he burnt the town of Elgin, the church of St Giles, the hospital of Maison-Dieu, and the cathedral with eighteen houses of the canons and chaplains in the college of Elgin. He also plundered the churches of their sacred utensils and vestments, which he carried off.'

He escaped the full consequences of his actions because of his royal connections, although he was forced to make submission in the church of the Dominican Black Friars in Perth in the presence of the Bishop of St Andrews and of the monarch, and to repair much of the damage that he had done to Elgin. However, he now had something else to rage about. Throughout the worst of his excesses, the Wolf of Badenoch had always been convinced that he would one day be king. He was, after all, the most forceful and physically ferocious of his father's three remaining sons from his first marriage, and he considered himself to be the future Alexander IV of Scotland. On 19 April 1390, after 13 years of largely lacklustre government, Robert II acknowledged his own ineffectiveness and abdicated from the Scottish throne. On hearing of his father's departure, Alexander immediately set out to claim the throne for himself. He was, however, to be thwarted, for his elder brother John, Earl of Carrick (who had supported the Bishop of Moray against him), had already been named as Robert II's successor.

John Stewart was the most ineffectual of kings. Crippled both emotionally and physically (he had been seriously injured by a kick from a horse four years earlier), he was certainly unfit to take the throne, and throughout his reign (1390–1406) the general complaint was that Scotland was 'nocht governit'. So insecure was he that he flatly refused to be crowned under his own name (in Scotland the name 'John' was associated with tyranny and failure; King John of England had attempted to invade Scotland in the 13th century, and the name was also linked with the puppet-king John Balliol who had been nothing more than a pawn of the English), choosing instead the name Robert, which was connected with the celebrated Bruce. Robert III, as he became, had plenty to deal with. Not only had he to placate his brother Alexander in Badenoch, but he also had to deal with his other brother, the Earl of Fife and Monteith and Duke of Albany (who was actually, and rather confusingly, also called Robert). Although not as physically formidable as Alexander, Albany was, nevertheless, a skilled politician and an extremely devious man who also thought that he should be king. One day he effectively would rule Scotland during the Regency of James I (the period which has been referred to by some Scottish historians as 'The Reign of Robert IV' even though Albany was never officially proclaimed king). Robert III was prepared to leave the Wolf to his own devices in the Highlands, while he ineffectively tried to deal with Albany's intrigues and with the family squabbles his succession had created.

In utter fury, Alexander returned to the Highlands and to Ruthven. There, if tradition is to be believed, he interviewed a series of ancient crones and beldames – all reputed Highland witches – in an attempt to kill and thus depose his weak brother and to take the throne for himself. These exchanges apparently came to nothing, and, although it is said that the Wolf consulted with certain supernatural beings who lived in a sealed fortress, high in the Cairngorms, Robert III remained King of Scotland. His reign, nevertheless, seemed blighted. There was little law in Scotland and there were frequent raids on the Scottish Lowlands by 'wyld, wikkid Heland men, comely in form but unsightly in dress' (organized robbers), and clan feuds reached a new pitch without any form of royal intervention. King Robert seemed more interested in keeping his young and only surviving son, Prince James (then only an infant), out of the clutches of his brother Albany than in governing the country. He was not really up to the job anyway, was continually ill and had become little more than a recluse. Was this ineffectiveness and sickness brought on by the dark magic of the Wolf of Badenoch away in the Highlands? Certainly many of the Lowland Scottish populace seemed to think so.

There seems little doubt that many of the raids conducted by the Highland caterans on the Scottish Lowlands were at the instigation of, if not personally led by, the Wolf. In desperation at the collapse of the country into anarchy, Robert III more or less abdicated his position, and from 1393 until 1399 the land was virtually ruled by the Duke of Albany, acting for the king. Albany proved a reasonably capable administrator and set about bringing the major clans to heel. Yet Scotland had deteriorated to such an extent that he could not restore it to its former peace, and neither brother could rein in the Wolf of Badenoch.

Even so, Alexander was taking less of a part in Scottish affairs. Apart from leading the occasional raid against the Lowlands, he seems to have largely withdrawn from the pages of history. There is only one reference to him after 1390. That is on 3 May 1398, when he was ordered by his brother, Robert III, to deliver up to its former owner the Castle of Spynie which he had seized from the Bishop of Moray (which seems to suggest that the enmity between the Wolf and Bishop Burr and his successors still continued). This gives the error to Duncan Stewart's *History of the Stewarts* (1739) which suggests that he died on 24 June 1394. It is said that Alexander remained in the Highlands, consulting with the witches there, in an attempt to dislodge both his brothers from their positions of power through foul and arcane arts. He is reputed to have frequently consulted 'The Wicked Bible' (which only he could read) and, by doing so, brought about many of Scotland's misfortunes at the time. Even if he was not there in person, the Wolf bestrode the pages of Scottish history like some evil spirit.

By late 1404, even the ineffectual Robert III had to admit that the royal family was in difficulties. His brother, Robert of Albany, was steadily growing in political power and there was some talk that he might join with the Wolf in an attempt to secure the throne for himself, rather than acting as the king's agent. Already extremely ill (it is thought that he was suffering from chronic mental depression), Robert III was not overly worried about his own position but, with his queen dead, he feared for the life of the young Prince James. Taking matters into his own hands sometime in 1405, he decided to get the child out of the country and placed him on a boat bound for France. Protected by the French court, he hoped that the prince would be well beyond the reach of both Albany and the Wolf of Badenoch. As Robert sat down to dinner at Rothesay Castle one evening, a messenger is said to have arrived bearing two pieces of news – one good and one bad. The bad news was that the ship carrying Prince James had been attacked in the Channel by English pirates, and had sunk. The prince himself had been captured. (The pirates, undoubtedly acting under Albany's instructions, conveyed their young captive to Great Yarmouth and from there to the court of the Lancastrian usurper, Henry IV. He would remain in England until 1424 when he would return to Scotland as James I to commence a harsh and intimidatory reign.) On hearing of his only son's capture, Robert III swiftly succumbed to a 'seknes of his person', and died several days later. The piece of good news that the messenger also brought was that his brother Alexander, the Wolf of Badenoch, was finally dead.

Just when the Wolf died is not actually known, but it was probably during the summer of 1405. It *may* have been in the early months of 1406, but nothing is certain. Of course, there are many folktales concerning his end. The most common one was that Alexander sat down to play chess with the Devil, whom he had summoned from the Pits of Hell for an evening. It is known that chess was one of the Wolf's favourite pastimes and that he often wagered on the outcome of a match. With little money at his disposal, he unwisely wagered his own soul – the Devil won and conveyed the wretched warlock down to Hell. Other tales say that the Lord of Badenoch was literally torn apart by a demon which he had brought from the Infernal Regions and which he could not control. The actual circumstances of his demise were probably far less dramatic. Some stories say that he died during a drinking bout with a number of his caterans, and this is a far more plausible explanation. He left no legitimate issue, but had several illegitimate children, the eldest of which – a boy also named Alexander – became Earl of Mar and seems to have had almost as colourful and ferocious a career as his father. An able military commander, it was he who led the forces of his uncle, 'Robert IV', at the Red Harlaw when Donald of the Isles invaded the north of Scotland in 1411. *The Book of Black Earth*, the blasphemous volume which the Wolf is said to have frequently consulted, simply disappeared. Some accounts say that it passed through the hands of several Highland families and that it is still to be found among their descendants; others say that it lies somewhere beneath the ruins of Ruthven Barracks; still others say that it was destroyed, but not before portions of it had been copied into other Scottish grimoires (including the *Red Book of Appin*). It is said to have resurfaced during the 'Killing Times' in Scotland (the end of the 17th century) when it was consulted by John Graham, Earl of Claverhouse, as part of his campaign to rid Scotland of the Covenanters. Because of this, the Calvinists named it 'The Wicked Bible'. Of course, nobody can really tell what happened to it.

The Wolf of Badenoch himself passed into folktale and verse. The foremost novelization of his life, the title of which bears his name, was written in the 19th century by Sir Thomas Dick-Lauderdale, and there is no doubt that his eventful career forms the stuff of literature. He was certainly a cruel and bloodthirsty man, but perhaps no different from other men of his time. Many of the Scottish warlords of the 14th century were equally cruel – the atrocities of the Border Lords, for example, made many of the Wolf's deeds pale into insignificance. It is also worth noting that the epithet 'Wolf of Badenoch' was mainly widespread only in the Scottish Lowlands and only after his raids there, and that in many parts of the Highlands he was known solely as 'Great Alexander – the King's Most Royal Son'. What set him apart from other such warrior-lords of the day was his invocation of the supernatural Otherworld, which fashioned the basis of many legends concerning him. Such stories only added to the awe and terror in which his contemporaries held him and greatly added to his authority in the area in which he ruled. His choice of Ruthven as his principal stronghold, together with the use of the druid circle at Kingussie as the site of his court were probably designed to reinforce this superstitious perception. So too was his construction of a fortress on a pagan worship-site at Loch an Eilean. As to whether or not *The Book of Black Earth* (the Wolf's grimoire) actually existed, there is little doubt that he consulted with witches and cailleachs throughout the Highlands (of which there appear to have been many), seeking out their evil and arcane wisdom. He may also have actively and deliberately encouraged the strange tales which circulated about him: of how he possessed a magic belt that transformed him into the guise of an actual wolf (a common tale about several historical characters); how he was able to call up the Devil at will; how he was able to work frightful spells against his enemies: and how he often conversed with ancient pre-human creatures in remote parts of the Highlands. At a time when the teachings of the Church still had not fully taken hold on the Celtic mind, and the pre-Christian Otherworld pressed close to reality in the isolated and misty Highlands, such perceptions were extremely important. Not only were these perceptions created and fostered by the Wolf himself, they were also fuelled by the Church and in particular by Alexander Burr. As the Wolf confiscated more and more Church lands, so it suited the Scottish Bishops to portray him as a warlock of the blackest kind who consorted with supernatural creatures and unclean sprites. Of course, the lonely and remote area of Speyside and Badenoch which was his power-base did nothing to diminish the legend. The region is still a place of great and terrifying beauty, and a common local folktale says that the Wolf's unquiet ghost is still to be seen hurtling down the valley on a black charger, or standing in the ruins of Ruthven, glowering moodily down the glen. As the sleet and snow of the winter months whirl around Lochindorb and the chilling wind whips up the waters of Loch an Eilean to a madcap frenzy, it is not hard to believe that there is not at least some truth in many of the old legends. Perhaps the Wolf of Badenoch actually did consort with inhuman beings that were as old as the world itself; perhaps he did possess a blasphemous grimoire; and perhaps he did learn dark and arcane secrets around the smoky peat fires of the Highland cailleachs.

# 'BURN THE LADLE' – THE WITCHES OF TAIN

Beneath the oft-times turbulent surface of Scottish history, the notion of witchcraft runs like a dark current. We must remember that Scotland, previously a separate country in its own right, was the only part of the present-day United Kingdom actually to burn its witches with any regularity (following the old Scottish dictum 'Cha tig olc a' teine', meaning 'No evil comes out of a fire') and that, during the 16th and 17th centuries there, ferocious Calvinist ministers denounced the 'limmers and carlines' in their midst on a scale which was quite simply staggering. Old women, living in isolated villages and hamlets or by themselves on remote moors throughout the countryside were often 'suspeck' of trafficking with the Evil One or of using unearthly charms and spells to carry out dark designs against their neighbours.

There is little doubt that many of these folk on the fringes of organized society often did behave in odd and sinister ways, and that they may have even deliberately encouraged such beliefs about themselves. It was, perhaps, the only way in which they could gain any form of reasonable status within a community, particularly if they were old, disabled or extremely frail. There were those, too, who used their dubious reputations as a source of income. They either 'hired out' their allegedly occult abilities or else engaged in a kind of 'supernatural extortion', threatening curses and blights on the community unless they were paid in some way (usually in kind – eggs, milk and so on). These were dark folk who dealt with the cotter in his croft and also with the rich and powerful in their halls and castles and who used such contacts to alleviate their own poverty-stricken situation. The celebrated case of the Witches of Tain in Ross-shire serves as an illustration of this.

During the late 16th and early 17th centuries, Scottish nobles were not above dealing with witches and warlocks. Indeed it was often a routine part of their lives – if they needed to charm a prospective partner or to do harm to an enemy. Although later perceptions of Hibernian witchcraft owed much to strict Calvinism, which viewed witches as agents of the Devil, there is evidence to suggest that earlier nobles looked upon them as integral members of society. This belief, of course, stretched back into Celtic times when the shaman, druid or wonder-worker was a pivotal figure in community life. Every Celtic king both consulted and used the druids for his own purposes and this tradition continued, even in nominally Christian lands, right up until the advent of Calvinist Protestantism. Arguably, nowhere were the dubious services of enchanters more used than in remote Scotland. Here clan feuds and internecine rivalries sometimes demanded the use of 'evil powers' in order to achieve certain objectives. Clan chieftains usually consulted carlines (witches/wizards) on a regular basis and used them to dispose of rivals or sometimes rival claimants to their clan title – brothers or cousins, for instance. This was widely regarded as common and even acceptable practice. The employment of witches and warlocks was particularly suitable to those with enemies or with family difficulties, since many of them were especially skilled with poisons and deadly potions. Indeed, so thorough was their knowledge of such preparations that in Scotland the terms 'witch' and 'poisoner' practically became one and the same. Local (and sometimes national) politics, therefore, was sometimes founded upon the relationship between noble and witch. This allowed King James I of England (James VI of Scotland) to believe that the spells of the North Berwick witches, directed against the queen and the then Prince Charles in 1603 were politically motivated by Catholics. Once again, the Ross-shire illustration contains elements of this locally politicized perception.

The Monros of Foulis – the principal clan of the area – believe themselves to be a family of great antiquity. They claim originally to have been vassals to the Earls of Ross, receiving their lands under Royal Warrant when the former Earls forfeited them to the Scottish crown in 1476. Most of the property that they inherited lay on the northern side of the Cromarty Firth and contained the parishes of Kiltearn and Alness. The clan established its seat at nearby Foulis Castle.

The late 16th century saw this region badly riven with internecine clan divisions. The clan chieftain at this time (the 17th to hold that position) was Hector Monro of Foulis (c. 1540–1603). He had seized the chieftainship from his elder brother Robert in rather suspicious circumstances (Robert had only been clan chieftain for a matter of months following the resignation of his father Robert Mor Monro in 1588, and it was said that he had been bewitched to surrender the lordship of the clan in favour of Hector). Robert died shortly afterwards, and poison was suspected but nothing could be proved. Odd as it might seem, Hector, who was widely regarded as a schemer and as a possible warlock, had initially been studying for the Church. In fact, so able and scholarly was he that Queen Mary I of Scotland appointed him as Protestant Chaplain of Newmore and later of Obsdale. He was then elevated to the high honour of Protestant Dean of Ross, very much against the wishes of the previous incumbent, Alexander Urquhart, who campaigned vigorously against the appointment. The source of this objection was that Hector was regarded as one who trafficked with evil spirits and that he kept sorcerous volumes, including the blasphemous *Book of Elgin* in his castle at Foulis. Nevertheless, Hector took the lofty Church position and remained in it, awaiting the death of his brother. Similar reservations were expressed regarding his intended lordship of Clan Monro but, once again, he chose to ignore these and took over the chieftainship almost immediately.

Much earlier, in 1563, while Hector waited and plotted to become clan chief, a change occurred in his life. The mother of both Robert and Hector was Margaret Ogilvie, who was now dead. Their father, Robert Mor Monro, was still very much alive, and he suddenly remarried. His second wife was Katherine Ross, the daughter of the 9th Chief of Ross in Balnagown. Although she appeared, to all intents and purposes, to be a caring wife, and although she bore him six more children, Katherine

Ross was widely regarded as being 'unchancy for a pious man'. She was well known, far and wide, as an enchantress and for her dabblings in the occult sciences. It is not altogether clear whether she influenced her stepson in the pursuit of the arcane, or whether he influenced her, but soon rumours were spreading that both were practitioners of the black arts and that they were actively seeking out the company of local witches and warlocks. Several people, who had crossed the unholy pair, had suddenly died, or some misfortune had befallen them, and the most common explanation for this was one of darkest witchcraft. It was said that there was a secret room in Foulis Castle where the two of them offered up sacrifice in the Black Mass, instructed by old and evil books, the reason for their sorcery being family business.

It was thought that Robert Monro would die soon, making Hector undisputed clan chief, but also leaving a considerable fortune to his widow. Lady Katherine's brother, George Ross, had married Marjorie Campbell, and it was the death of this lady (together with the speedy demise of Hector's brother Robert) that the diabolical pair ultimately desired. Such occurrences would leave George Ross free to marry Robert Monro's widow, allowing Katherine to get her hands on Robert's fortune and linking the two families even more closely.

To carry out this murderous plan, Katherine Ross and Hector Monro sought the aid of several local witches. The foremost of these was a hideous hag, greatly feared throughout the area. She is said to have lived alone in a tumbledown hut on the edge of a remote moor and, although no accurate description of her exists, she may have been slightly deformed or at least extremely ugly. Her name was Marion (or Marjorie) MacAllister, but she more frequently went by the Gaelic nickname of Loisg na Lodar (literally 'burn the ladle'). MacAllister was widely known throughout the Scottish countryside for her evil spells, especially those involving the *corp creadha* (a clay image which was used to inflict pain and/or death upon her enemies), and for all manner of wickedness against her neighbours. Under the name of Marian MacIngarrath, she had been arraigned at the Cathedral Court at Fortrose on several counts of witchcraft – attempting murder by her 'foulle and diabolick airts' – but had been discharged as no one could be found to testify against her.

It was to this awful crone and her equally disreputable partner, the wizard William MacGillivray, that Lady Foulis and her stepson went and asked for help in disposing of Marjorie Ross.

In response to their request, MacAllister used her tried-and-trusted spell-casting using the *corp creadha*. A clay image of Marjorie Ross was hastily made, shot with 'elf-bolts' and buried in a nearby wood with due ceremony, invoking terrible names including that of Satan himself. For all its alleged 'sorcery' and 'diabolism', this act produced no tangible results, and the Monros now consulted with several other witches. An entire panoply of supernatural means was used to bring Marjorie to her doom. For four shillings, one wizard, John MacMillan, prepared 'fairy arrows' which he attempted to shoot at the unfortunate woman as she rode by his door. This too apparently failed. Marjorie suffered a 'distemper of the stomach' (which might just as well have been caused by something she had eaten) but nothing more. Another witch, Agnes Roy, who appears to have been a doting, elderly woman, 'spoke with the fairies', asking them to slay Marjorie Ross, again without any appreciable results. The lady seemed to be proving eminently and surprisingly resistant to the malefic arts.

In desperation, MacAllister and another witch, Christina Ross Malcolmson, made 'clay pictures' of Marjorie in a 'secret place in the woods' and ritually destroyed them with 'severe incantation'. When this also seemed to fail, MacGillivray tried more direct methods. He procured something called 'witchcraft' (probably no more than rat poison which he bought at Elgin market) and, with the help of Katherine and Hector Monro, he slipped it into the lady's night-time posset, probably accompanied by dark 'spells' and ill wishes. The poison, however, failed to work on its intended target. Perhaps the two accomplices did not fully carry out their instructions, or maybe the poison was not strong enough, but somehow Lady Marjorie survived. Nevertheless, the 'witchcraft' had some effect, because she was stricken by a mysterious illness, which left her a bedridden invalid for the remaining 13 years of her life. A servant who merely tasted the posset with the tip of her finger died within minutes of doing so. Whether there was any similar attempt on the life of Robert Monro at this time is unknown.

The servant's death rekindled stories of the alleged witchcrafts of Monro and Lady Foulis and there was much talk of attempted murder. There was some talk that the clan chieftain of the Monros might be questioned and that Lady Katherine, who was considered 'a foulle beldame', might be burnt. So widespread did the scandal become that Lady Katherine was forced to flee to Caithness where she lived in seclusion for almost a year. When she returned, the authorities were still waiting for her. She was arrested, together with Hector Monro, and arraigned on a charge of witchcraft at the Court of the Quarter Seal at Fortrose on 23 January 1578. The judges included Colin MacKenzie of Kintail, Hugh Ross of Kilroak and Alexander Falcouner of Halkertoun – esteemed gentlemen, all of whom were Monro's own peers. With the accused stood most of the witches whom they had consulted, including MacAllister and MacGillivray. Both MacGillivray and Christina Ross Malcolmson were condemned to be burnt at the stake at Fortrose, but MacAllister (perhaps because of her fearsome reputation) avoided death, although she was probably imprisoned for a time. Lady Katherine and Hector Monro were acquitted. They were local landowners and the jury feared eviction and loss of employment if they were convicted.

In the same year (1578), however, witches seemed particularly active in the area. One report given to a court sitting in Caithness states the following: 'In the ewening George Dunbar in Thane sa and mony main with him ane battell abue them upon ane hill callit Knockbane quhilk did last twa owris and vanist away. It is alegit it was the sche wychthis [she witches].' Another witch, Sarry (Sarah?) Muir, claimed at her trial in Fortrose that she had magically travelled through the air with a great company of witches to the Muir of Ord in order to call up storms and to wreak havoc on shipping far out at sea. Yet another, Elizabeth Stennis, stated at the same trial that she had taken part in another diabolical company near Rosskeen which had been convened by the Devil for the purpose of doing harm to God's servants in the area. Strange cloud formations were also seen above Foulis Castle – great dragons, giants and other monsters, and some even in the shape of giant, hag-like women. The people of Tain took these signs to mean that more evil might be on the way. They were right. Hector Monro was indeed planning further witchcraft.

Shortly after the 'demonic battle' at Knockbane, Robert Monro (Hector's elder brother) died in rather suspicious circumstances. This effectively confirmed Hector as the undisputed chieftain of Clan Monro and Master of Foulis. For a time, he seems to have led a superficially staid existence, acting out the part of a 'country gentleman' and fleetingly seeing to the needs of his tenants. He even seems to have cooled his relationship with his stepmother, who sank, more or less, into the background. Nevertheless, the old, dark sorcerous side of his nature had not gone away. Throughout these 'quiet years', Hector Monro still kept in contact with Marion MacAllister (or Marion MacIngarrath as she now continually styled herself). Late at night, it was said, an old servant woman would make her way to the hamlet of Tain (where the hag now lived) and fetch the witch who would be taken up to Monro's chamber. By the light of guttering candles, the two of them met in terrible conference, concocting spells and incantations. It was further believed that Hector Monro had written down several books of blasphemous sorceries in his own hand and at the dictation of the crone. If these books did indeed exist, they have since been lost or else are in the hands of persons who will not avow ownership of the awful texts.

In 1589, Hector Monro fell ill. The weight fell from his body and he assumed a pale and sickly appearance. He would not eat and, if he did, he could not keep anything down. A physician was brought and he pronounced that the Laird of Foulis was 'like to die'. The prospect filled Hector with terror, for he knew that his badly stained soul had no hope of going to Heaven, and so he was determined to avert death at any cost. He sent for his old confederate Marion MacAllister to see if she had any charm or spell which would put off the evil day. Once the witch had been admitted to his private chamber, Monro dismissed the servant who had brought her.

'Ye hear that I am about to die,' he told her. 'Is there any potion or spell or incantation that ye can cast ower [over] me so that I may live awhile yet and die at a ripe old age?' After looking him up and down, the witch replied that she knew of only one way in which he might be spared. She could not actually prevent his death – no power on earth could turn back the Dark Angel once He had already been sent forth,

she told the trembling laird – but she might be able to transfer the sickness to someone else and so let Hector Monro live. Death would then claim the other person. However, the spell was long and complicated and, if it went wrong, it might have serious implications, she warned.

After a long and sinister consultation, the ghastly pair decided upon a hideous plan. If Monro were to follow the witch's instructions, then he would live but his half-brother, George Monro of Obsdale, would die in his stead. It is said that MacAllister also consulted Lady Katherine as to which of the two men she would prefer to die and the Lady answered that she wished that Hector should live. The witch then is believed to have consulted with the Devil on the very summit of Knockbane as to whether the evil spell would work, and it was said that she had received her Infernal Master's permission to carry it out. The dark work was set in motion by the sorceress running a distance of 'nine rigs' (about one mile). Then she was ready to commence the sorcery.

One dark January night in the year 1590, the witch went to Foulis Castle where she met with Hector Monro. Together they went to a wood near the castle which was alleged to be very badly haunted. Strange sounds, like the wailing of the dead, were said to issue from it at certain times of the night, and it was reputed that somewhere in its overgrown depths lay one of the very gateways to Hell itself. Deep in these woodlands, two baronies met, and it was this point that MacAllister chose as her mystical spot. Being the fitter of the two, she commenced to dig a shallow grave in the iron-hard, frost-bound ground. When it was ready, the witch laid a horse blanket inside it and motioned to the Lord Foulis to lie down on it as if he were asleep or dead. In all these proceedings, no word was spoken in case it broke the enchantment. Foulis did as she signalled. Over the top of the now prostrate Laird, Marion MacAllister placed withes (willow branches), and over these she placed a thin layer of turf, making a makeshift final resting place for her evil confederate. Then she spoke for the first time, beginning the 'witches' roon', a grim spell used by Highland witches to call down the darkest powers and to bend them to her bidding. The ancient wood rang with strange and sinister invocations – some, it is said, in a foul, prehuman language – commanding the Dark Angel to turn away and find someone else to carry away to the Country of the Dead. Soon the ritual was complete and Hector Monro returned to Foulis and Marion MacAllister to her tumbledown croft in Tain.

Within a matter of weeks and in defiance of all those who had prophesied otherwise, Hector's health began to improve. Everybody, including the doctor, was astonished. As the laird grew well, however, the health of his half-brother George went into a sudden and inexplicable decline. In April 1590, a few months after he had been taken ill, George died. No one could account for his sudden demise, and the old rumours of witchcraft began circulating in the countryside once more. Accusing fingers were again pointed at Hector Monro and Lady Katherine, and gradually the servants related the story of how they had been sent to fetch the witch MacAllister and of how she had been brought to the laird. All suspicions seemed to have been confirmed and the increasing rumours could no longer be ignored.

In the summer of 1590, Monro and Lady Katherine were once more summoned by the King's Advocate, David MacGill, to present themselves before the court at Fortrose where, on 23 June, they were duly charged with 'witchcraft, incantation, sorcery and poisoning'. The charges against them were dismissed for lack of evidence, but MacGill's court did claim one witch. Along with the two landowners, Marion MacAllister (charged under the name of Marian MacIngarrath) was also tried, and this time she was found guilty. She seems to have confessed to a catalogue of heinous crimes under torture, which was carried out at the express request of MacGill himself. Perhaps the King's Advocate wished to rid the neighbourhood of Tain of the taint of her vile witchcraft for ever. She was tied to a large stake just outside the gates of Fortrose and her body daubed with tar and set alight. Legend states that the sky above the town turned black – almost like an eclipse – as the Devil came for his own. It was a darkness that was added to by the black smoke that poured into the air from the burning woman on the pyre. Soon it was all over and the evil had apparently passed.

Late in 1590, an Enactment of the Scottish Parliament required Hector Monro to produce a surety of 10,000 marks towards his continued good conduct and against that of his clansmen, even those living well away from Foulis on other clan holdings. The requirement seems to suggest that the Scots monarch and the judiciary were keeping a persistent and watchful eye on his activities. In response, Monro seems to have become a solid citizen and was even granted a commission by King James VI of Scotland to hunt down the Earls of Huntly, Errol and Angus who had been implicated in the murder of the Scots Regent, the Earl of Moray, some 20 years earlier. This was a task which he carried out with particular enthusiasm and relish. Nevertheless, despite his new-found respectability, the taint of witchcraft and evil magic still hung about Hector Monro like a dark cloak. He frequently seemed uneasy and nervous in his ways, as though he believed that something monstrous was following him, and that he hourly expected it to leap from the shadows and savage him. Much of the time he kept close to Foulis Castle and did not venture far. Locals said that his library of ancient books (including those that he had copied from MacAllister's dictation) protected him from whatever it was that he feared. He died in 1603 (the same year that James VI of Scotland also became James I of England), a haunted man, wary of his neighbours and surrounded by lawyers. His heir, John Monro, inherited the lands of Foulis but died intestate shortly afterwards.

The noxious air of witchcraft which Monro and MacAllister had generated lay heavily on the countryside around Tain for many years after. In 1727, for example, the last judicial execution for witchcraft in Scotland took place at Dornoch in Sutherland – not terribly far from the hamlet of Tain. The accused was one Jennet (or Janet) Horne who was described in the indictment as an 'infamous witch and shapeshifter'. She was indicted for 'having ridden upon her own daughter whom she transformed into the guise of a horse which was then shod by the Devil', and was tried before the Judicial Bishops of Caithness. Found guilty, she was condemned to be executed by fire. Even as late as 1790, records show that the relatives of Janet Horne were still being shunned by credulous locals.

In 1750, the Parish of Tain found itself having to deal with three men who, one night, had dragged a local woman and her daughter out of bed, laid them on the floor and, while two of the men held them down, 'scored and cut their foreheads with an iron tool calling them witches'.

The practice was a very ancient one, commonly known as 'blooding a witch' or 'cutting above the breath', and was supposed to take away the sorcerer's supernatural powers. It was reputedly extremely common in Scotland, especially in Ross-shire at the time during which Monro and MacAllister were operating their vile magic there. The culprits of 1750 made the frightened women promise not to identify them. However, the two did not honour their word and the men were discovered and rebuked in front of their respective congregations at Alness and Rosskeen. It transpired that one of them was suffering from consumption (tuberculosis) and believed himself to be bewitched. A wise-woman in his own locality had named the two 'witches', saying that their bodies were inhabited by the malignant spirits of Marion MacAllister and Lord Foulis.

In 1607, two unnamed men were brought before another court, sitting at Fortrose, and charged with witchcraft. They were accused of causing the only cow of a woman neighbour to sicken and die when she refused to sell it to them. It appears that they had also made threats against her, telling her that she would 'follow her coo tae the grave'. Both men, however, were discharged 'for want of evidence'. If indeed there were other charges of alleged witchcraft in the Tain district, they appear to have gone unrecorded. Maybe the influence of the two evil sorcerers had finally dissipated. Maybe not.

There is no doubt that Hector Monro was a greedy, ambitious and scheming landlord who would stop at nothing to achieve his own, selfish ends. This included dabbling in supposed witchcraft himself, and consorting with local carlines. There is no doubt either that his activities left a dark blight upon Tain, and the region around it, which may not have been truly eradicated even to this day. Was he really, however, the dark wizard that folklore has made him out to be, or is his reputation solely based on his credulous contemporaries? Who can say? Certainly many of the events which occurred as a direct result of his so-called 'arcane arts' were too 'close to the mark' to be dismissed as mere coincidence – for example, Hector's own recovery from a terrible and wasting illness and his half-brother's concomitant submission to the very same illness, and then the mysterious death of his brother, just as Hector wished. Perhaps there actually was something in the spells and incantations that he and Marion MacAllister performed in their closed chamber in Foulis Castle. Also, what happened to the books he is alleged to have written from MacAllister's dictation? A number of people have tried to find them, but they seem to have vanished. Are they still somewhere in Scotland awaiting discovery? Are they true spells or simply the outpourings of a malignant and disordered mind?

Hector lived in a time when belief in the black arts as a way of interpreting certain events was very common. The people of such a remote area as Ross-shire held firmly to the old Celtic view that, just beyond the tangible, mortal world, another sphere existed where magic, fairies and baleful powers were the order of the day. Practitioners of witchcraft formed a living bridge between that world and this, bringing the forces of the former into the latter for their own evil ends. At least that was what conventional wisdom said. There seems little doubt that, on some level at least, this belief may even continue down to the present time. The Witches of Tain may have been long consigned to history, but the timeless evil which they unleashed in the hearts and minds of individuals may bubble beneath the surface of society, even today. The Celtic Otherworld is probably not as far away as we think.

# THE DEVIL AND THE DOCTOR

Folklore from many parts of the United Kingdom is littered with tales of Faustian deals between ordinary mortals and the Evil One, many of them coming from a time when concern for one's immortal soul was paramount. In former ages, the Devil was thought to be very near, ready to snatch away any hope which individual men or women might have of Paradise in return for a short period of temporal pleasures. Many of the early Christians (or example, the saints and the Church Fathers) were, of course, impervious to such blandishments, but some less hardy souls succumbed to the (false) promises of the Father of All Lies. In Ireland, the Devil and the fairies (who were construed by the Church to be agents of the Infernal Master) continually tempted righteous souls in a nefarious attempt to lure them away from the religious path. The souls of clergymen were most in jeopardy, and only the most religious of men could resist. In the north of the country, especially, where Protestantism was deeply rooted, the Devil was believed to go about his work with great enthusiasm.

The area of the island that is now Northern Ireland had been largely planted and settled by both Anglicans (partly during the reign of Elizabeth I) and later Presbyterians (many fleeing the imposition of Anglicanism in Scotland). The majority of these later arrivals were weavers and spinners who became involved in the burgeoning Northern linen industry and settled along the banks of the major rivers there – the Bann, the Lagan, the Braid and so on. Many of these Presbyterian settlers were fundamentalist in their religious beliefs and revolutionary in their political ones. Great sections of them hated and despised the Anglican Church, which had driven them from their lands in Scotland; they also disliked its doctrines which they considered to be but one step away from the Papacy of Rome. Many of the landowners, however, belonged to the Established (Anglican) Church, having been granted their lands under the first Elizabethan plantation or under the later Jacobean one. If the landowner involved was both an Anglican and a member of the Anglican clergy, then he was doubly damned in the eyes of the Presbyterians, many of whom might be his tenants. This inherent dislike of both religion and status was sometimes expressed in folkloric terms. The individual concerned had surrendered his soul to the Devil since it was considered that he belonged to an Apostate Church in any case, and was therefore extremely vulnerable to the Evil One's temptations. If the landowner concerned flaunted his Anglicanism (which was, after all, the Established and recognized Church in Ireland), then the fury of the Presbyterians knew no bounds. They did not stint at ascribing the blackest sorceries to that particular individual. His soul was invariably damned and was certainly in the possession of the Enemy of All Mankind.

Nowhere is this thesis more apparent than in the story of Dr Colville, who owned lands around the village of Galgorm, near the town of Ballymena in mid-Antrim.

Galgorm (which still exists as a village today) has enjoyed an often turbulent history. During the 15th and 16th centuries, it was a stronghold of the MacQuillan clan, who erected a large stone castle around which the original village grew. The MacQuillans themselves were an old Norman-Welsh family who, from around the early 14th century, held the title 'Constables of the Province of Ulster'. Their original forebears were believed to have come north from Dublin with John de Courcy who had been given the lands of Ulster to tame by King Henry II in 1171. It has been suggested that these original MacQuillans were the illegitimate sons of William de Burgo, former Viceroy of Ireland. Their name had been taken from the Welsh by the Irish who called them 'MacGwillem' (the sons of William) which was later Anglicized to MacQuillan. With Norman backing, the family soon made itself into one of the most important dynasties in Ulster, building castles right across the northern sector of the Province and taking most of the major political posts in that region for themselves. At one time, they controlled an area known as 'The Route', which stretched from the North Antrim coast to the valley of the Sixmilewater, south of present-day Antrim town. For the MacQuillans, Galgorm Castle was a principal and strategic stronghold that gave them mastery of The Route.

In the early to mid-1500s, their dominant position in Antrim was to change. Since the end of the 14th century, other families had been making their presence felt throughout the area – the principal one being the MacDonnells whose power-base lay in Islay and Kintyre in Scotland. The MacDonnells had originally settled in the Glens of Antrim, which they had acquired by marriage, but had begun to spread out across the surrounding countryside, seizing MacQuillan lands as they did so. The English, who were also starting to settle in the North of Ireland, seemed powerless against them. By the 1550s, the most feared man in North Antrim was James MacDonnell of Red Bay who, together with his younger brother Sorley Boy, raided in the North from Carrickfergus to Ballymena and beyond. Part of the lands in The Route which James and Sorley Boy took from the MacQuillans included Galgorm, which was given to another of their brothers, Colla. He turned it into a MacDonnell fortification, building a fine, new castle on the site, which was architecturally 'in the Scottish manner' and which still stands to this day.

MacDonnell power in Antrim was finally broken in 1565, when James and Sorely Boy were defeated at the Battle of Glenstaise (near the town of Ballycastle) by the forces of Shane O'Neill, the great Earl of Tyrone, acting on behalf of the English government. Their lands in The Route were confiscated by the Crown. For years, the English disputed with both the MacDonnells and the MacQuillans regarding ownership and, in 1604, Edward MacQuillan (then 104 years old and completely blind) travelled all the way to London to petition the new English king, James I, to return the lands of Galgorm to his family. After promising that he would, the king promptly broke his word, and handed the castle and its estates to the incoming English Colville family. Galgorm suddenly changed its name to Mount Colville.

The most famous (or infamous) member of that family to live at the castle was the 17th-century cleric, the Reverend Alexander Colville, an extremely learned scholar and an Anglican minister. Little is known regarding his actual history, as the doctor appears to have been a relatively secretive man who kept a distinct distance between himself and the majority of the locals (all of whom were Presbyterian). Much of his 'history' is merely superstition and rumour, although there are one or two definite facts concerning him. He had been ordained into the Church in 1622 and had subsequently held the Vicarage of Carnmoney (near Belfast), the Prebend of Carncastle and the Precentorship of Connor. He also possessed considerable wealth, though nobody could say for certain how he had obtained it. Dr Colville's own story was that he had sold land in England, but there were others who claimed that he had used black arts to procure whatever money he had.

A portrait of Alexander Colville, allegedly painted around 1630, shows him to be a portly man with a certain arrogant air about him. This arrogance seems to have infuriated his neighbours, for the doctor was a firm believer in the supremacy of the Anglican Church above all other forms of religion. Furthermore, he was an extremely educated and learned man and is believed to have written a series of pamphlets, rather pompously dismissing the fundamental beliefs of other Churches when set against his own. He owned an extensive library which reflected his alert and enquiring mind. It may be that such a collection included books which were not altogether appropriate for a clergyman to own, or it may be that his neighbours, jealous of, and annoyed by, his not-altogether-impartial learned writings, began to attribute certain volumes to his library which were not there at all.

Whatever the reason, stories began to circulate that much of Dr Colville's library was composed of books on witchcraft, devilry and blackest sorcery. It was even said to include: a handwritten copy of the infamous *Book of Black Earth* (or 'Wicked Bible') which had been reputedly penned by the Wolf of Badenoch under the tutelage of a Highland cailleach (see The Wolf of Badenoch); a copy of the *Red Book of Appin*,

which was so blasphemous that it could only be read by a man with his brow encircled by a protective iron band; several ancient works dating back to both Greek and Roman antiquity; and the works of the darker medieval scholars. Rumours of such abominable tomes reflected the strict Scottish Presbyterian background of Colville's neighbours, and only served to scandalize the entire locality around Galgorm. Furthermore, whispers went round the countryside that the doctor himself was a warlock and that he was, in fact, the Devil's foremost vassal in Ireland. Many claimed to have seen him fishing on the banks of the River Braid, surrounded by fairies and evil sprites with whom he seemed to be conversing freely and quite happily. If the doctor himself was aware of these rumours, he gave no sign and paid them no heed.

In the late 1630s and early 1640s, according to popular legend, complaints were laid against Dr Colville by the Presbyterians, accusing him of being a Devil-worshipper and of leading members of the local community astray with his wicked ways. So seriously were these allegations taken that the Synod of the Presbytery of Belfast commanded the doctor to appear before it and give an account of himself. Dr Colville showed the ultimate contempt by ignoring the summons and on the appointed day he went fishing, a pastime which appears to have been one of his chief hobbies. In his absence, he received a stern rebuke from the Synod, but no further action against him appears to have been taken. Stories concerning his diabolical behaviour, however, continued to circulate. There were tales, for instance, that he roamed the countryside in the shape of a huge and hooded crow, spying upon his neighbours and finding out ways in which he could blackmail them to his will. He was also said to travel through his lands invisibly, stealing items even from the poorest tenants so that they could not afford to pay their rents and he could evict them. He was reputed to have a magical mirror somewhere in the depths of the castle in which he could both witness and influence events happening in faraway places, even the Royal Court in London. It was also said that he commanded legions of dark and evil spirits who brought sickness, misfortune and even death to the district.

The most famous tale concerning him, however, was that he had sold his immortal soul to the Devil and was therefore certainly to be considered a witch and a heretic. As the story began to expand, it was said that Dr Colville had actually cheated the Infernal One, making him an even greater deceiver in the eyes of local people than the Enemy of Mankind himself. Over the years, the story became more and more elaborate and eventually took the following form.

Dr Colville was extremely fond of gambling and, despite having started out with an immense fortune, he soon frittered it away on idle wagering. Almost bankrupt and having nothing of value to barter with, he resolved to sell his soul to the Devil in return for gold. Now the doctor was shrewd enough to know that his spirit, stained and corrupt as it was, would be of little interest to the Evil One. Satan certainly placed a high value on the souls of ministers and those of Godly men, but the shabby shade of a rascally Episcopalian clergyman was no more than a passing thought to him. However, Dr Colville was a wily old reprobate and he soon came up with a plan. Taking down one of the larger books from his infernal library, he commanded, through incantation, that the Devil appear before him and, within the moment, the Infernal Master stood in the doctor's secret chamber in Galgorm Castle. If Dr Colville had expected an enormous shaggy creature with horns and burning eyes, he was sadly mistaken, for the Prince of Darkness appeared as a small, pallid man dressed in black, peering over old-fashioned half-moon spectacles at the end of a long and pointed nose. Indeed, he looked more like a lawyer or a Presbyterian minister than the Father of All Lies. Under his arm was a large, ironbound ledger in which he recorded those souls that were damned.

'Well?' he demanded irritably. 'Why have you disturbed me when I am extremely busy enumerating the souls that I have harvested for myself throughout the year?' The doctor told him of his proposal – namely, the sale of his soul for an agreed sum. Opening the ledger, the Devil scanned the pages, running an ink-stained finger down the lines until he found Dr Colville's name. Looking up, he gave the anticipated response.

'All souls are of interest to me,' he said smoothly and with a thin smile. 'Nevertheless, some are worth more than others. I'm sure that a man of your undoubted education will appreciate the distinction. Some are fresh and unblemished – those of maidens, saintly men and tiny children for example – while some are so stained and filthy with inherent evil as to be almost worthless. I'm afraid, dear Dr Colville, that yours is among the latter kind and, while I'm certainly prepared to negotiate a price with you, I'm afraid that it will not be very high.' He laughed a trifle unpleasantly. The doctor merely gave a wintry smile, and said that he was prepared to accept a low figure for the surrender of his soul if the Devil would merely fill his old top boot with gold coin right away, and seven years later similarly fill his old soft hat. Then Dr Colville would be well satisfied. The actual surrender of the soul, the doctor suggested, should take place 20 years hence on 25 December. The Devil, however, suspected a trap, since 25 December was, of course, Christmas Day, the birthday of the Saviour Jesus Christ, when traditionally he had no power in the world. After some thought, he suggested that the date of the surrender should be the last day of February, 20 years hence; after some haggling, the doctor agreed.

The Devil then requested to be taken to the doctor's top boot which was to be filled with golden coin as specified. The boot was standing upright against a wall in the scullery of the kitchen, as though waiting for the requested coin, and Dr Colville insisted that the Evil One fill it to its brim straight away. Snapping his fingers, the Devil caused a shower of twinkling coin to fall into the open mouth of the boot and instructed it not to stop until the footwear was completely filled to the brim. This took some time; the gold continued to flow, but the level of money in the boot never seemed to increase. What Satan did not know was that it stood over a large hole in the floor of the scullery which led directly to the cellars of Galgorm Castle, and that the wily doctor had cut away its heel, allowing the golden shower to tumble down into the vaults where his servants were shovelling it into great piles. Too late, the Devil realized that he had been tricked, but he was bound by his word and there was nothing he could do about it. He had to stand by and watch as the gold poured endlessly into the cellars below. At length the vaults were full to bursting and the old top boot itself was filled to the brim as had been stipulated. With an angry howl, the Devil disappeared in a puff of sulphurous smoke, promising that he would have his vengeance on the doctor in seven years' time. Dr Colville merely smiled and stated that he would look forward to their next meeting.

For seven years, Dr Colville was said to live in Galgorm Castle in the lap of luxury. He wanted for nothing and spent incredibly freely. However, his disposition towards his tenants did not improve with his new-found wealth, for he was still as cruel and heartless as ever. He continued to evict many of them from their cottages and to confiscate their lands for his own use, and he continued to practise the black arts against those who crossed him. At the end of seven years, the Devil came again, as agreed.

This time, suspecting another trick, the Infernal One refused to meet Dr Colville in Galgorm Castle but chose an old lime-kiln, midway between Galgorm and the village of Broughshane, as their meeting place. This time, he came in the guise of a tall, muscular, sooty blacksmith in a leather apron, his arms and face covered with the clinker and smuts from his forge. In his right hand, he carried a mighty hammer. When he appeared at the kiln, he found the doctor already there and waiting for him with an old soft-felt hat in one hand. This he required Lucifer to fill with gold coin as he had been promised seven years earlier. With a snap of his fingers, the Devil caused another shower of gold coin to fall into the hat. Despite his precautions, however, he found that he had been cheated once more, for there was a thin slit in its crown and the gold continued to pour right through it and into the lime-kiln below. Bound by his oath, Satan could not stop the flow of gold until the hat was filled; once again, this took some time, and was extremely expensive because the kiln was very deep. Again, Satan departed with a snarl, promising to collect the doctor's soul at the end of the remaining 13 years.

Dr Colville continued to live like a lord, adding to his castle and making improvements to it here and there. He added a walled garden, a sundial, and attractive walks which had never been there in the time of Colla MacDonnell. He bought the finest clothes and the finest wines and brandies, and he gorged his portly frame on only the finest of foods. All the while, his neighbours went hungry, and he never lifted so much as a finger to help them, even though he was supposed to be a clergyman.

At the end of 20 years, the Devil came to collect his side of the bargain. This time he came as a tall, black-skinned man, wearing a huge, green travelling cloak. When he arrived at Galgorm Castle, he found the doctor in the old church that stands beside the castle itself. The so-called clergyman was apparently absorbed in reading the Bible by the light of a single candle mounted on the pew beside him. The Devil demanded that he made himself ready and accompany him to Hell where a special place had been prepared for him.

'Wait a minute,' replied the doctor. 'Let me just finish this piece of Holy Scripture. Promise me that you'll wait until this candle completely burns down so that I may read the Sacred Word.' The Devil gave his agreement. In fact, he could do little else since no fiend or fairy can approach an open Bible. With a loud cry of triumph, Dr Colville snuffed out the candle and placed it between the pages of the great ironbound Bible, which he then slammed shut. 'Then it will never be completely burnt down,' shouted the doctor, 'for it will never be lit again!' Of course, for as long as it was held between the pages of the Bible (God's Holy Word), the Devil could not touch it. Once again, the wily doctor had outwitted him and he vanished in another cloud of reeking smoke.

Here, the story splits into two distinct versions. In his book *Irish Witchcraft and Demonology* (1911), the Reverend St John Seymour states that the Bible and candle were buried with Dr Colville in his tomb at Galgorm. However, another, more persistent version states that the candle was later accidentally burnt down by an old woman who was doing some cleaning in the doctor's study while he was away. Wanting a light, she found the stub of the old candle and, removing it from the Bible, lit it. 'He will not mind me having this wee bit of light on such a dark evening,' she said. As soon as it had completely burnt down, a demonic laugh echoed through the castle. When Dr Colville returned and heard what had happened, he went completely white and began to tremble violently, as though stricken with illness.

'You have damned my soul to Hell,' he told the old woman as he dismissed her from his service. However, the doctor was a resourceful man and soon had devised a means to deal with the situation. From that day onwards, as the end of February approached, he became very religious in his ways. On each 28 February, he was always to be found in prayer, singing hymns or religious psalms, or reading from God's Word. As long as he was engaged in such religious pursuits, the Devil could not even come near him to carry him off. As soon as the date had passed and 1 March had come around, however, he was back to his old ways and was as cruel and heartless as ever – until, of course, the next 28 February, when he became pious again.

Finally, when one 28 February had passed (the great clock in the hall of Galgorm Castle had just struck midnight), the doctor was relaxing in an upper room with some of his friends whom he had invited for a morning's gambling and wagering. In his hand, he had the largest glass of brandy that he could pour, and he seemed very pleased and relaxed. 'I declare that I've never enjoyed a 1st of March so much,' declared Dr Colville, taking a long swig from the glass. His companions looked up in astonishment. 'But it's not the 1st of March yet,' said Mr Spence from Broughshane, who was sitting across the table from him. He always kept an almanac close by him. 'It's the 29th of February – this is a leap year.' At his words, Dr Colville paled and sat forward. 'What?' he cried, searching for the Bible that he had so recently discarded. 'A leap year? It can't be!' Rushing around the room, he searched for the Bible but could not find it. Where had he put it?

By then it was too late anyway, for there was a hammering on the doors of Galgorm Castle that sounded like thunder. When an old servant opened up, there was a great dark man in a green travelling cloak standing outside. Ignoring the servant's protests, he strode into the castle and marched straight up to the room where Dr Colville sat quaking. 'It's time that our bargain was completed!' he boomed. Throwing wide the cloak, he swept the doctor into his embrace. The pair vanished from the middle of the room in a whiff of foul-smelling smoke. Neither was ever seen again. If such a story is true, say the doubters, then who lies in the ancient tomb in the now-ruined Galgorm Church beside the castle – a dark and foreboding place even on the brightest day? Maybe the influence of the evil doctor still lingers on there.

The story of Dr Colville is a fine tale indeed, and one which was reputedly used by the Irish novelist, J. Sheridan Le Fanu, as the basis for his celebrated and often anthologized ghost story 'Sir Dominick's Bargain' in which a local landowner cheats the Devil but makes exactly the same mistake regarding the date as the doctor, and suffers the same awful fate. In fact, the character of the story's protagonist, Sir Dominick Sarsfield, is allegedly based upon the persona of Dr Colville himself.

Although the above might seem to be little more than a quaint Faustian tale, it serves to demonstrate the underlying animosities that existed between the Anglicans and Presbyterians in the North of Ireland during the 17th and 18th centuries, and also how those animosities found an expression in local folklore. Dr Colville, being a High Anglican, was certainly dismissive of (and perhaps even cruel towards) his Presbyterian neighbours, many of whom had flooded into the Antrim countryside to avoid the perceived tyranny of the Anglican Church in Scotland. It was only natural, then, that, because of his personal nature, his religion and the nature of his office within the community, Dr Colville should become associated in the popular mind with the dark sciences and with the Devil himself. It is also only natural that, because of his allegedly nefarious and insincere ways, he should try to cheat even his Infernal Master as well. After his death, he was buried in a dark vault in Galgorm Church situated near the altar. The place is now dilapidated, overgrown and dangerous to approach, and has an air of menace about it. No date is given for his demise (although some understandably differing accounts cite the late 1600s) and it is said that his ghost still haunts the precincts of the ruined place, continually tormented by the Fiend whom he sought to cheat. Other accounts, however, place him in the beautiful gardens which he constructed around the castle and have him looking wistfully at the ornate sundial as time passes.

Dr Colville's reputation survived him and even stretched beyond Ireland. Some time later, according to Robert Law's *Memorialls*, a servant-girl at house of Major-General Montgomerie of Irvine in Scotland was brought to court on a charge of stealing some silverware from her employer. In admitting the theft, she declared that she had been forced to do this after raising the Devil by witchcraft. She then detailed an elaborate method of summoning the Evil One which shocked everyone present by its explicitness. Asked where she had learned such abominable witchcraft, she replied that she had learned that particular branch of the black arts when formerly employed in Ireland, at the house of a certain Dr Colville, 'who had habitually practised it'.

Galgorm Castle still stands – a square, solid fortress built in the Scottish tradition. The garden with its sundial and elaborate walkways which Dr Colville created are also still there (a place where the doctor's ghost can still be seen consulting the timepiece at certain times of the year), and the doctor's portrait still hangs in the castle's main hall. A persistent and widely known tradition says that if this picture is removed, for any reason, then some terrible calamity will befall both Galgorm Castle and the nearby village almost immediately. The long shadow of Alexander Colville, whether as Anglican minister or as dark warlock, hangs over the Antrim countryside like a funeral shroud, even today.

# WEIR THE WAERLOCK

> Dougal was glad to see Steenie and brought him into the great oak parlour; and there sat the Laird his leesome lane; excepting that he had beside him a great ill-favoured jackanape, that was a special pet of his; a cankered beast it was, and mony an ill-mannered trick it played – ill to please it was and easily angered – ran about the haill castle; chattering and yowling and pinching and biting folk, especially before ill weather, or disturbances in the state. Sir Robert ca'd it Major Weir after the warlock that was burnt, and few folk liked either the name or the conditions of the creature – they thought that there was something in it by ordinar – and my gudesire was not just easy in his mind when the door shut on him and he saw himself in the room wi' naebody but the Laird, Dougal MacCallum and the Major; a thing that hadna chanced to him before.
>
> (Sir Walter Scott: 'Wandering Willie's Tale' from *Redgauntlet*)

Arguably, no sorcerer is so well known in Scottish folklore as the Edinburgh wizard, Major Thomas Weir, after whom Sir Walter Scott named old Sir Robert Redgauntlet's hideous jackanapes. Perhaps it was the duality of Weir's nature – outwardly incredibly holy and religious, inwardly depraved and corrupt – which has so fascinated the Scottish mind. It is a theme which appears in that other Caledonian classic tale *Dr Jekyll and Mr Hyde*, by Robert Louis Stevenson, and it reflects the strange ambivalence which lay at the very core of ancient Celtic belief.

For the Celts, the gods and spiritual beings that dominated their world were capricious and untrustworthy entities. Weather spirits, in particular, manifested both the bright and dark sides of supernatural power. They could provide periods of calm and bring gentle rains which would provide their followers with ample crops for the coming year, or they could send devastating gales and wind-storms which destroyed all that grew and brought famine and pestilence in their wake. If they were not shown proper respect and worship, they could punish entire communities with floods and drought. Other spirits, such as hunting gods, would ensure that there was plenty of game to be hunted, or that there was no game at all. In many ways, they were like small, spoilt children who had to be bribed or cajoled into fulfilling requests. The terms 'good', 'evil', 'beneficent' and 'hostile' did not really apply to these early Celtic deities, since they embodied elements of both.

The ambivalent and capricious nature of the gods often transferred itself into the human practitioners of what might be termed the 'arcane arts', and who dwelt in many communities. Many of us are familiar with the concept of the 'wise-woman' or 'cunning man' – the healer, the seer, the finder of lost or stolen objects – who usually lived at the edge of a village but who was often an integral part of that society (see also The Magician of Marblehead). It was to such a person that the locals went in times of illness or distress in order to seek cures or to protect themselves from the onset of disease, to help with the birth of a child or to prepare a corpse properly for burial, to find the whereabouts of a lost article or to locate a thief. These were good and 'community-spirited' activities. However, like the ancient deities, such people had their darker side as well. With a single word they could sometimes bring sickness and misfortune upon those who crossed them. Besides dispensing healing balms, they issued potent curses, they blighted their neighbours with awful diseases and they caused great evil to descend on the houses of those to whom they took exception. This was, of course, the 'dark' side of their power – that side which was used for malign purposes.

Christian religion made the distinction between 'light' and 'dark' all the more stark, and diluted the ambivalence of power that had existed since the former Celtic times. If one was not 'good' (within rigidly specified terms) then, logically, one must be 'evil'. Since religious leaders determined what was to be considered 'good', those who opposed them or who deviated from their dictates must assuredly be 'evil'. 'Them that are not for us,' ran the thinking, 'must certainly be against us.' In Scotland, the strict Calvinist thinking, brought from Geneva by such preachers as Wishart and Knox, added fuel to the fire by imposing a rigid demarcation between 'saintly' and 'diabolical' behaviour. The Doctrine of the Elect which such teachings exemplified divided the world into 'saved' and 'unsaved' and placed the followers of the more ancient Celtic beliefs (many of which were centred in the Calvinist-abhorred Catholic and, to some extent, Anglican faiths) firmly within the latter category. Such rigid Calvinism strongly opposed anything that smacked of the old (pagan or idolatrous) ways, which were now looked upon as 'witchcraft' and 'devilry', and strove mightily to suppress them. As religion in Scotland took on a more political tone during the late 1500s and early 1600s, through the activities of such groups as the Engagers and the extreme Kirk Party, more radical theologies came to the fore and more 'moral' codes of conduct were introduced, as political figures at all levels strove to outdo one another in terms of 'holiness' and righteousness. Old women, who had acted as 'cailleachs' or 'wise-women' within their communities and who had formed an integral part of that society, now found themselves publicly denounced as 'agents of the Devil'. Many were executed, and it is worth noting that Scotland was the only part of the present United Kingdom to burn its alleged witches as heretics (in England they were hanged as malefactors). Those who denounced such people had to be themselves of impeccable character and standing. Yet, beneath the veneer of religion, many still sympathized with and even followed the old Celtic ways – even those who set themselves up as judges and arbiters. Many of those who served as the 'pillars of society' were, in many ways, far below the perfection they claimed for themselves, and there are few better examples of this brand of societal hypocrisy than Major Thomas Weir. It is this 'moral duality' which has given him the reputation of one of the foremost black magicians in Scottish history.

Whatever crimes Weir committed, abominable though they were, he was no warlock. In fact his crimes had little to do with the supernatural at all. Yet the stories that grew up around him condemned his 'rank sorcery'. He was burnt on several charges, one of which was enchantment, and his name is so heavily connected with witchcraft that for many years (even into the 19th century) no decent Scotsman would utter it, far less write about him in any detail. 'I decline in publishing the particulars of this case,' wrote Hugo Arnot in 1785, for Weir had 'exceeded the common depravity of mankind', while William Roughead lamented the problems when dealing in print with 'a veritable monster'. Even Robert Louis Stevenson, who had written about the Edinburgh body-snatching trade, refused to comment upon Weir, describing the case as 'happily beyond the reach of our intention'. When Sir Walter Scott became intrigued by the major and thought of writing 'a popular romance' concerning him, or at least of making him a leading figure in one of his novels, a friend bluntly retorted that Weir was 'a disgusting fellow – I could never look at his history a second time. A most ungentlemanlike character.' At first Scott thought that he might rescue the character of Weir in one of his prose works, but the stigma of witchcraft and evil ways was so persistent that he eventually conceded that such a novel would be 'too strong meat' for the majority of his readers. The warlock cast far too long a shadow. He contented himself therefore by making Major Weir the devilish jackanapes in a portion of *Redgauntlet*. Just who was Weir, however, and why was he branded the 'most abhorrent and depraved sorcerer that ever stalked the Edinburgh streets'? The answer is an extremely complex one, embracing elements of fact, fiction and superstition.

Thomas Weir was the son of a small Clydesdale laird – Weir of Kirkton – who held some lands in the parish of Carluke. Although his family claimed at least some noble connections, through a fairly distant relationship with Lord Somerville, they were people of relatively modest means. The estate was sold off by his parents in 1636 (this may have been to meet some debts) and Thomas went to Edinburgh. There, he took up with and eventually married a widow woman, Isobel Mein, who had previously been married to a fairly prosperous Edinburgh merchant named John Bourdon. For Weir, the marriage was a socially favourable one, for it brought him free admission as a burgess of Edinburgh and as a Guild Brother of the city. These honours were in return for his marrying and providing for the widow of a former burgess. At this time, Weir was also strongly attracted to the Covenanting faith – a more extreme form of Presbyterianism – and was becoming deeply and actively involved with other like-minded religious radicals in and around Edinburgh.

In 1642, rebellion broke out in Ireland, and the new plantations in the north of the country (many of which included Scottish Calvinist traders and merchants) came under threat from the Catholic Irish. As the death toll among the Scottish planters rose, repeated calls were made to the Scottish Parliament for an army to come over and aid in putting down the rebellion (over which the Irish commanders were rapidly losing control, allowing unbridled anarchy to reign). A Covenanting Army, made up in the main of Presbyterians and under the command of Major-General Robert Monro, landed at Carrickfergus in County Antrim early in 1642, and among them was Thomas Weir. His rank was that of a captain-lieutenant in the company of Colonel Robert Home – thus he was the lieutenant in the company commanded by the regiment's colonel. This company had been raised in 1640 and had already seen some active service in southwest Scotland during the Second Bishop's War. Weir may already have been a serving soldier at that time, but this is not certain.

It was in Ireland that he was said to have acquired his famous walking-stick – cut from an Irish tree. Trees were important to the Irish and many of them were believed to have supernatural attributes. In the early 1650s, according to a popular legend, a troop of soldiers under the Cromwellian Captain Thomas Preston rode into a strange circle of trees in the north of County Kerry, the gnarled barks of which appeared to form the shape of old men's faces. The grove had allegedly been used for terrible and blasphemous practices in druidic times, and the evil which had been carried on there had apparently imbued itself upon the trees themselves. The men were incredibly disconcerted by the place and Preston, a devout Puritan, ordered the wizened growths to be burnt. As his men put them to the torch, the trees screamed with awful, nearly human voices. It was from a tree such as these that Weir was alleged to have cut and fashioned his famous staff, which was said to have maintained a life of its own, independent of its master. The head of the stick was carved with the heads of satyrs, and the major permitted no one to hold it save himself.

The notion of the eerie staff is also very important, since such an artefact was usually the symbol of authority of the pagan druids, the holy men of the Celtic world. Such staffs were also imbued with magical powers; they were, for example, lowered into wells so that cattle could drink, and they could also be used to conjure up storms. In Christian times, the staff or 'bachall' could also detect malefactors or liars in the community, although now they were no longer associated with druids but with early Christian saints. At the ruined church of Ardclinis on the east Antrim coast, for instance, alleged malefactors were required to swear their innocence on a bachall placed in the west window of a ruined church and dedicated to the mysterious St McKenna. If the person swore falsely, some terrible supernatural harm would befall them. A similar practice was carried out on a staff – widely known as the Bachall of St Dympna – which had been placed in the ruins of a convent in County Monaghan, where if the accused swore falsely their mouths were supernaturally twisted out of shape (thus ever after marking them as liars). Again the bachall was carried into battle by several ancient Irish kings in order to ensure victory – the Bachall of St Columcille was carried by the Dalriadic Scots when they made war against Ivar II, Norse king of Dublin in 914. Gradually, the 'druid rod' metamorphosed into three other representations of power and authority: the king's sceptre, the bishop's crozier and, significantly, the magician's wand. Acknowledging the importance of such ancient staffs, small wonder then that such attention was paid to the major's ornate walking-stick as he strode about the Edinburgh streets.

Thomas Weir did not remain long in Ireland. Records show that by May 1643 he was back in Edinburgh, and had made a rather modest financial contribution towards a fund that had been set up to maintain the army in Ireland in which he had recently served. Nevertheless he appears still to have been interested in a military career and to have had sufficient military connections to enable him to pursue it. In June 1644, he was back in active service, this time as a major and second-in-command of a regiment, raised by the Earl of Lanark for the Scottish army which had intervened on behalf of Parliament against Charles I during the English Civil War. His military service, once again, seems to have been prematurely cut short. In an attack upon Newcastle-upon-Tyne in August 1644, Weir was captured during a sortie by the Royalists and was quickly taken as a prisoner to Newcastle Gaol. He was freed when the Scots stormed the town in October, and was returned to his regiment. He seems to have had enough of fighting, and quit the army early in 1645. For the purposes of arrears of pay, he was credited with a total of 19 months in Ireland and 12 months with Lanark's regiment. This also marked the full extent of the military career of Major Thomas Weir – a career in which it was alleged that he cared more about receiving money for service than about leading his men into battle. In fact, throughout his entire service, he is said to have avoided conflict of any kind whenever he could.

Weir was also becoming more and more deeply interested in religion. Once back in Edinburgh, he became peripherally involved with a group of extreme Presbyterians operating in the City's West Bow where he was now living. The group was both highly religious and politically active so they may have proved attractive to Thomas Weir by offering a way in which he could show his radicalism without any military involvement. The year 1645 was a significant one in his life. His wife died and his sister Jean (also known as Grizel) became his 'live-in' housekeeper. Previously she had 'kept a school' in Dalkeith but now gave that up in order to look after her widowed brother full-time. In that same year, he was appointed Commander of the Edinburgh Guard, a position which made him responsible for the peace of the city and entitled him to raise the local watch forces (police) if need be. His reputation as a military officer coupled with his standing as a Covenanter probably secured him the post.

Weir proved himself to be an ardent supporter of the extreme Kirk Party, which came to power in Scotland in 1648, following the fall of the Engagers under James Hamilton, and was given the task of guarding the fledgling government as it established itself. When the captured Marquis of Montrose was imprisoned in Edinburgh awaiting execution in 1650, Major Weir was responsible for guarding him. It is said that he showed the great Royalist general 'only the basest contempt' and that he treated him like an animal. The new religious government of Scotland did not last long. In 1651, it split into two warring factions and Weir predictably supported the Remonstrants, the more extreme of the two. However, as the extremist religious and political forces in Scotland began to crumble, and as the country was first made subject to the rule of the Cromwellian Parliament and then to that of the restored Charles II (together with a restored Episcopacy), Weir and those like him became increasingly marginalized and disappointed. Together with other radical Presbyterians, he formed a tight religious grouping which met at his house in the West Bow. The Anglican nobility of Edinburgh (and others) scathingly referred to this sect as the 'Bowhead Saints', because of their excessive holiness and their exclusivity. Nevertheless, the city further increased Weir's local status by allowing him to collect on its behalf, and as one of their senior enforcement officers, all import duties on goods brought in from England.

Major Weir had also become something of a preacher, albeit only among the Bowhead Saints. He ranted and raved against the Episcopalian Church, now making advances across Scotland, and questioned the morality of its ministers and indeed that of the king himself. By all accounts, he was most eloquent in his exhortations. Yet there were a number of queries being levelled, even among his own followers, against the conduct of the major himself. For a start, there was his Irish walking-stick with its queer, carved, inhuman heads. Such an artefact was, by common consent, something which no Godly man should possess. There was also the matter of his attitude towards members and ministers of the Episcopalian Church, whom he appeared to hate with a passion bordering on paranoia. He would often go out of his way to meet with certain Episcopalian clerics on the street, and would scowl and mutter as he passed them by, as though fervently cursing them. Several of these venerable ministers attested to smelling a faint whiff of brimstone from him as he accosted them, and it was suggested that the major might not be as Godly as he seemed. Even his style of worship among the Bowhead Saints drew whispers from several quarters. It was noted, for example, that Major Weir never knelt while praying and that, though exceptionally wordy and devout in his public religious displays, his private prayers did not seem overly long. Some of the other Bowhead

Saints had begun to question his commitment and dedication to the holy cause. There was also another unfortunate rumour concerning him that would not go away.

In 1651, a horrified Lanark parishioner reported to her equally horrified minister that, while going about her business, she had seen a man travelling through the parish commit 'ane act of the greatest indecencie' with a cow in a lonely field. Soldiers were immediately despatched to apprehend the villain, but when it turned out to be the Godly Major Weir his outraged protests of innocence were readily accepted. In fact, the woman who had brought the complaint was whipped through the streets of Lanark for making such a terrible allegation against the pious man. Nevertheless, there were still some who wondered if there were not something to the accusation.

The major continued to live in the West Bow and his situation was comfortable if not lavish. Jean continued to keep house for him and acquired something of a reputation for herself among the good wives of Edinburgh as a spinner and seamstress. The couple seemed wholly unremarkable, if a trifle over-religious and slightly eccentric.

Around 1670, Thomas Weir, now well advanced in years but still noted in his own circles for his piety, began to display instances of alarming behaviour. Today, with a wealth of psychological knowledge, we would probably describe him as a man on the edge of a nervous breakdown, but in the late 17th century his actions seemed inexplicable. He began to show distinct and utter terror at the very mention of the word 'burn', as though, said some, he was afraid of burning in Hellfire. Even the most accidental or casual reference reduced him to a shivering wreck. A friend who mentioned a local 'burn' (stream) sent the major running back to his house in paroxysms of fright, a situation which was repeated when Weir discovered that one of the sentries on the Nether Bow Port was called Burn. Shortly afterwards, during one of the Bowhead Saints' prayer meetings, Weir broke down completely and what he confessed profoundly shocked both his listeners and the entire city of Edinburgh. For years, he told his incredulous and terrified congregation, he had conducted an incestuous relationship with his sister Jean, a relationship which had begun when they were both children. The affair had been well known to several members of his own family but had been 'hushed up for decency's sake'. Now he could bear it no longer.

When Jean was about 16, another sister, Margaret, had discovered the existence of the relationship and had reported it to their mother. The liaison was immediately broken up by sending Jean away from home. Her sex and age must suggest that she was the less guilty of the two, but there was also a paramount need to protect the integrity and reputation of the family heir – Thomas. In his astonishing confession, the now-distracted penitent further admitted to another incestuous relationship with his stepdaughter, Margaret Bourdon, and stated that he had married her off to an Englishman when she became pregnant by the major. (In 1649, Thomas Weir was referred to as the tutor and protector of the children of John Bourdon.) He also stated that, for many years, he had conducted an adulterous relationship with a servant, Bessie Wemyss, prior to Jean returning from Dalkeith, when he eventually abandoned the servant and resumed his incestuous relationship with his sister. In addition to this, he stunned his listeners with further admissions of many sexual 'relationships' with various animals throughout the countryside, including the molestation of several cats which his sister had brought to the house in the West Bow. Small wonder that the minds of his hearers were reeling in disbelief at the seemingly unending catalogue of vileness and perversity.

Weir's confession, although displaying depraved and seemingly insatiable sexual appetites, contained no hint of the supernatural or of witchcraft, nor was it initially perceived in these terms. That was soon to change. The Provost of Edinburgh, Lord Abbotshall, just as horrified by the filth of the revelations as anyone else, sent a number of physicians to examine the major at his home. Their brief was to determine his mental condition and to ascertain whether he was, in fact, insane, and was perhaps making up the entire story. They concluded that Weir, though wracked with guilt and utterly terrified of burning in Hellfire, was in fact quite sane. In the religiously charged atmosphere of 17th-century Edinburgh, there was only one other explanation for the obscene outrages he had committed – Thomas Weir was in league with and was guided by the Evil One. Perhaps in a rather pathetic attempt to portray himself as a 'victim' of Satanic influences, Weir went along with this explanation. He claimed that he had never actually seen the Devil but that he had 'often felt his presence in the dark'. If he had hoped that this plea would somehow resolve the situation, he was very much mistaken. There was both a religious and political interest in making the most out of his confession. A new regime in Scotland which rejected the tenets and dogma of extreme Presbyterianism saw the case as good propaganda in its efforts to repress those who still remained loyal to the Covenanting cause. Moreover, groups such as the Bowhead Saints had always presented themselves as pious folk. They were people, they claimed, who were trying to live a Godly life in the face of intense persecution by an inherently corrupt and heathenish establishment. Now a prominent dissident had been shown to have used his outward piety as a cloak for unparalleled, filthy appetites and depraved behaviour; and he had confessed to being in league with the Devil himself. Who were these so-called 'pious people' to sit in judgement on the Episcopacy or the Royal Court when members of their own sect themselves engaged in unspeakable debauchery? What right had they to denounce the Episcopal Church as 'heretical' when one of their leaders was, by his own admission, colluding with the Father of Sin? As one commentator put it, what was wrong with a little 'honest fornication' when set beside the dark sins of Major Weir? Thus a sustained 'whispering campaign' began to circulate throughout Edinburgh, hinting at the major's witchcraft and sorcery. Even his own sister contributed to these supernatural fears in her own way.

When she was arrested as the major's accomplice in incest, the elderly Jean Weir made a series of full and utterly damning confessions. These contained several points of witchcraft in which she implicated both herself and her brother. Her first testimony, however, had nothing to do with Thomas but related to the time when she had taught school in Dalkeith. On several occasions there she had been visited by a strange man whom, upon pious reflection, she now knew to be the Devil. He had taught her to spin yarn, and she attributed her great skill and reputation in this area to his malign intervention. At the time, she claimed, her spinning wheel had begun to spin the yarn by itself and without her aid. Her later confessions were then widened to implicate the major. She had, she asserted, found the Devil's mark (an insensitive area of skin where the Devil was allegedly supposed to have touched a witch, and a certain mark of witchcraft) upon his shoulder; she knew that Thomas had dealings with the Evil One and was jealous of them. She had driven with her brother to Musselburgh in a fiery carriage, drawn by six demonic horses, and there the Devil had foretold the defeat of the Scots army, which followed soon afterwards. She now made reference to his Irish walking-stick which, she averred, contained a spirit so that the staff was able to move about the house of its own volition, 'wheresoever it listed'. This was the actual source of all her brother's evil powers, she told her interrogators.

In the light of his sexual control over her, the phallic imagery of the walking-stick is obvious, and this was seized upon by the establishment of the day. Major Weir, it was imagined, had long been in league with a demon which he had brought back with him to Scotland, following his time in Ireland. There seems little doubt that the suggestible Jean Weir was now being manipulated by her interrogators to make further terrible allegations against her brother, and that her mind was slowly giving way under their questioning. Her various 'confessions' added to a frenzy of ghost-story telling concerning the major and his diabolical practices. Lights were now seen at the grimy windows of the empty house, and noises were also heard as though the stick itself were roaming the abandoned rooms of the place. There was, too, the sound of Jean's spinning wheel, constantly spinning away, even though the house was known to be empty. Townspeople vied with each other to relate stories of sorcery and mystery: the major had conducted a Black Mass within the walls of the old house; he was responsible for the disappearances of several young children in the West Bow; it was even stated that weird, beast-like shapes were seen coming and going to and from his front door. The house was soon shunned, as the tales became more and more fanciful. It was even related that the major's stick was seen going and coming along the High Street and that the anguished faces of Edinburgh citizens who had recently died were frequently to be seen peering down from the windows of his house.

Weir himself seemed to be in a state of intense despair. Convinced of his total damnation and seemingly assured of Hellfire, he refused to let ministers pray with him. No prayers, he said, could help him now:

'Trouble me no more with your beseechings of me to repent, for I know my sentence of damnation is already sealed in Heaven. I feel myself so hardened within that I could not even wish to be pardoned if such a wish could save me – I find nothing within me but blackness and darkness, brimstone and burning to the bottom of Hell.'

At his trial, the jury was unanimous in its 'guilty' verdict; he was found to have committed sorcery and incest, although neither the crime of bestiality nor a formal charge of witchcraft were brought forward. He was sentenced to be burnt for his odious crimes on Edinburgh's Gallow Hill. Too weak to walk, he was dragged on a sled to the place of execution, and was there strangled at the stake before being burnt. Even at this final time, his black mood did not lift and he died convinced of his own damnation, declaring loudly that he was bound for Hell.

His sister Jean was hanged the following day. Like her brother, she had sunk into a deep and morbid mood, and although she claimed to be penitent she failed to convince those who saw her of any real contrition. Much calmer than the major, she nevertheless declared that no punishment was too great for the sins she had committed, and that she believed that she deserved a fate far worse than that to which she had been condemned. Yet, from the scaffold, she berated those who had come to see her die for their lack of support for the Covenant and for their lax morality. Her poor mind had already collapsed. Following these outbursts, she tried to throw off her clothes, so as to die naked, but was restrained, pushed off the ladder and hanged before she could do so. Commentators have suggested that this was an act simply to shame herself even further.

Although the Weirs were both dead, the stories concerning their witchcraft continued to grow, like some rank weed, on the streets of Edinburgh. The major himself was frequently seen, or so it was widely claimed, standing in the doorway of his now-empty house with the horrid stick in his hand. Hideous and unearthly laughter issued from behind its closed doors, and the sound of a spinning wheel clacked ceaselessly in its depths. So widely was it believed to be haunted that the place stood empty for almost a century until at last, in 1878, it was completely demolished and its site left vacant. Even so, the very ground on which it had stood was allegedly plagued by an apparition of Major Weir, galloping back and forth on a fiery black horse. Sir Walter and Lady Scott became so fascinated by the legend that the Lady (with her husband's approval) nicknamed his walking-stick 'Major Weir', as it had a tendency to get lost rather often, as though possessing a life of its own. The sorcerous tradition of the major still persists in Edinburgh to this day.

The tale of Major Weir is interesting not only because it reflects (to some extent) aspects of early Celtic morality but also because it shows how, when faced with behaviour with which the normal conventions and sanctions of society cannot adequately cope, even 'sophisticated' people sometimes resort to the notion of spirits and witchcraft, just as their Celtic ancestors did. Even in the relatively enlightened era of 17th-century Edinburgh, ancient notions of sorcery were still rife.

The behaviour of Thomas Weir followed certain old notions of Celtic morality. In their small and tightly controlled communities, it might be argued, the Celts did not uphold or follow the same rigid moral notions that we do today. In some regions of the Celtic world, for instance, a period of trial marriage – an institution which was not necessarily for life – was observed, a union which was known as a 'handfast marriage' and which lasted for a year and a day. It is quite possible that some Celtic tribes were also polygamous, and there may well have been instances of incest among some of them as well. Indeed, some hints and suggestions of incestuous behaviour are to be found in a few old legends concerning important Celtic heroes. (In the early stories regarding the Irish hero Cu Chulainn, for example, there is a suggestion of incest between the King of Ulster, Conchobhar MacNessa, and his sister.) Doubtless, people who possessed the same heroic blood in their veins could produce heroic offspring through their union. There do not seem, therefore, to have been the same sexual prohibitions or taboos among the early peoples. The coming of formalized Roman Christianity, however, brought some degree of change to the religious and social orders of the Celtic world. Following the Synod of Whitby in 664, Roman dogma and behavioural mores began to have an impact upon Celtic thinking and behaviour, although old ways only died out very slowly. Incest was frowned upon and certain limitations were placed upon this common behaviour, and restrictions were placed around families. There was a logical explanation for this, because the Church probably recognized that same-blood relationships passed on not only heroic qualities but inherent weaknesses and deficiencies as well. Nevertheless, the path was a slow one and, as late as 1101, one of the issues considered by the great Synod of Cashel was the continuing of same-blood marriages, especially between brother and sister, in certain areas of Irish society. These relationships were treated with abhorrence and yet they continued into medieval times in some of the more remote regions of the Celtic world. The Christian abhorrence, through which they were viewed, still continues today, and has become the nightmare of social services everywhere, as well as forming the basis of some of the grittier television dramas.

Faced with such revelations of perceived depravity and lewdness, the stolid citizens of Edinburgh evoked the age-old explanations of sorcery and witchcraft. As has already been noted, Major Weir's crimes, perverse though they were, contained no real element of the supernatural. Yet he is widely remembered as one of Scotland's foremost sorcerers. Perhaps it was the confession of his sister which fanned the flames of witchcraft paranoia by claiming that an evil Irish spirit was dwelling in her brother's staff and that he 'bore the Mark of Satan' upon his body. The folkloric accretions of ghosts, bestial figures and the constant reek of brimstone that hung about the major's empty house were based upon this perception, and only added substance to the overall legend. Once again, as we have seen, there are Celtic connections with the notion of the 'rod' or 'stick' which was the symbol of authority for the druid or holy man (as well as being the Freudian sign of male sexual dominance). Furthermore, certain mystical trees were thought to co-exist in both this world and the supernatural Otherworld – a domain of demons, fairies and enchanters – and conveyed occult powers between both places. Was it, in fact, one of these trees that Major Weir found in Ireland, and from which was fashioned his strange, satyr-headed walking-stick? Certainly such perceptions would only add to the air of mystery and witchcraft which seemed to have formed around his name.

There is no doubt that his name continued to exercise a fascination in both the Celtic psyche and in Celtic-influenced literature. Weir's case may have formed the basis of James Hogg's *Private Memoirs and Confessions of a Justified Sinner*, written in 1824; and, as has been already mentioned, the jackanapes in Scott's 'Wandering Willie's Tale' (a supernatural portion of *Redgauntlet* and a fine ghost story in its own right) was named Major Weir. Charles Kirkpatrick Sharp, too, was fascinated by the legend, but was shrewd enough to leave out the supernatural elements of Weir's history in his celebrated piece of doggerel which formed a scandalous mock-prologue to Byron's 'Manfred' (which was published in 1817 and which itself contained hints of incest):

Most gentle Readers, 'twill appear,
Our author fills this scene
With what betided Major Weir,
And his frail sister Jean.

He freely here his faults avows,
In bringing not before us,
The Major's Cats and Mares and Cows,
Assembled in a chorus.

But by and by, he'll mend his Play,
And then the World shall see,
That incest only paves the way,
For Bestiality.

'Sir Robert in the midst of a' this fearful riot, cried out wi' a voice like thunder in Steenie Piper, to come to the board-head where he was sitting; his legs stretched out before him and swathed up with flannel, with his holster of pistols aside him, while the great broadsword rested against his chair, just as my gudesire had seen him the last time upon the earth – the very cushion for the jackanape was close to him but the creature itself was not there – it wasna its hour it's likely: for he heard them say as he came forward, 'Is the Major not come yet?' And another answered: 'The jackanape will be here betimes the morn.'

(Sir Walter Scott: 'Wandering Willie's Tale' from *Redgauntlet*)

# THE WOMAN WHO TALKED WITH THE FAIRIES AND THE WITCH OF HELSTON

The idea of a 'wise-woman' living in the community and practising many of the ancient Celtic ways has already been mentioned (see also The Magician of Marblehead). Such women were often an integral part of practically every rural community across the Celtic world. Some of them (for example the Irish wise-women Biddy Early and Moll Anthony) often drew clients from well beyond their own areas, demanding cures for illnesses or glimpses of the future – such were the reputations of these women. From what source, however, did these females draw their power, and how did they go about effecting cures or making prognostications? Were they simply herb-doctors, or did they embark upon elaborate and mysterious rituals in order to create an air of the occult around their healing and divination? What, too, about the curses they are known to have uttered – were they the 'dark side' of the powers they possessed, and whence did they come?

The Church frequently argued that such 'wise-women' had made some sort of pact with the Devil or some other evil spirit. Undoubtedly, some of the women encouraged such a perception. Perhaps it encouraged other people to be more respectful of them and to give them what they asked for (such females were usually either single or widowed and were often dependent upon the goodwill of their immediate neighbours); perhaps it increased their status within the community. Those who boasted dark powers were often treated with awe by their peers, and this was perhaps the only way in which old women could acquire some sort of communal standing. Others may well have been plainly cantankerous and took some kind of perverse delight in terrifying those around them. Some may well have been just plain evil.

The 18th-century Cornish crone, Madgy (or Madge) Figgy, popularly known as 'The Witch of St Levan', who headed a gang of smugglers and wreckers, was certainly believed to have drawn her dark powers from the Devil. In an area, known locally as Ted-Pedden-Penwith – a place where cubical masses of granite were naturally piled on one another – she was believed to use the stones as a chair-ladder in which she would sit to call down awful storms in order to wreck passing ships. Her power over the elements had been granted to her by her Infernal Master and could only be used to create death and disaster. However, she frequently levelled curses at those who crossed her, and for a fee would sometimes issue cures to those who sought her out. Nevertheless, she was widely regarded as being inherently evil. Doubtless, her criminal activities and disposition added greatly to this belief.

Another Cornish 'wise-woman', Dorothy (or 'Dolly') Pentreath, who died in 1777, acquired her reputation through the fact that she was one of the last-known native speakers of the Cornish language. From local accounts we know that she sold fish at the market in Castle Horneck, near her native Mousehole, doubtless picking up her stock from the Newlyn fishermen, and it is also believed that she had a fierce temper. Those who crossed her were greeted with a verbal explosion in Cornish, which must have seemed to many like an arcane and mysterious language. It must have seemed as though the old crone was cursing those whom she despised or with whom she was angry. Mr Daines Barrington, brother of Admiral Barrington, who had met Dolly, writes of her in 1773: 'Dolly Pentreath is short of stature and bends very much with old age, being in her eighty-seventh year, so lusty, however, as to walk hither to Castle Horneck, about three miles, in bad weather, in the morning and back again. She is somewhat deaf, but her intellect seemingly not impaired; has a memory so good that she remembers perfectly well that about four or five years ago, at Mousehole where she lives, she was sent for by a gentleman, who being a stranger had a curiosity to hear the Cornish language which she was famed for retaining and speaking fluently and that the innkeeper where the gentleman came from attended him.' (The gentleman was Barrington himself, who had met with her earlier.)

Another account, given by a Mr Blewett, who came from the same area as Dolly and who knew her well, describes her thus: 'She was dirty about her person and habits and very coarsely spoken when she chose. She had a base (illegitimate) child, of which no further information could be given. As regards Dolly's age at decease, this was certainly not the reputed 102 years; it was probably less than 90 years.' This description tallies with others of many alleged 'witches' or 'wise-women' from all over the Celtic world. Barrington further states that she lived in a mean hut beside a very 'narrow lane' faced by two houses which were much grander than the hut. In the door of her hovel, she would sometimes berate passers-by in the Cornish tongue, much to the amusement of her elderly neighbours who knew the rudiments of the language but could not speak it. The celebrated Cornish folklorist William Bottrell describes her as 'a kind of half-witch' and a 'seeress' in the Celtic style (though whether she claimed any actual powers or even practised her 'art' to any great extent is open to question). Her knowledge of an unfamiliar and unused tongue partly gave her this reputation. (Although she is often given as the last Cornish-speaker, it is thought that there were at least two others who survived her. She, of course, may have been the only one to use Cornish as a first language.)

On her death, she was buried in the parish of St Paul near Penzance, and an epitaph was written for her in both Cornish and English by a Mr Tomson of Truro (who could both speak and write Cornish – Dolly could not write – and may have been one of the last actual speakers of the language):

Coth Doll Pentreath cans ha Deau;
Marow ha kledyz ed Paul plea:
Na ed an Egloz, gan poble bras,
Bes ed Egloz-hay coth Dolly es.

(Old Doll Pentreath, one hundred aged and two,
Deceased and buried in Paul parish too:
Not in the Church with people great and high,
But in the Churchyard doth old Dolly lie!)

Such an inscription was never placed on a tombstone for none was erected to her. At the time of her death in 1777, another Cornish-speaker, John Nancarrow of Marazion, was also living, aged 45. Like Dolly, he was regarded as something of a 'wizard' or 'conjuring man' who could perhaps achieve mysterious feats (though whether he himself laid claim to such powers is unknown).

The supernatural reputations of both Dolly Pentreath and John Nancarrow stemmed from their specialized linguistic abilities, but there were others who traced their abilities to more occult traditions. It may be worth looking at the lives and careers of two further Cornish 'witches' and trying to determine how they both sourced and used their alleged powers. Although records of Cornish 'wise-women' remain scanty, there are accounts of a couple of relatively famous females, Anne Jeffreys and Tamsin Blight, whose powers can be traced to different sources.

The earlier of the two, Anne Jeffreys, was born in St Teath (a tiny village near Camelford), north Cornwall, in December 1626. Her father was a poor labourer and quite possibly had a rather large family which he could not afford to keep; consequently, Anne was 'farmed out' to the nearby Martyn family, who looked after her. At some stage of her development with them, she realized that she could both see and converse with the fairies that thronged invisibly round the Martyns' cottage. She grew into a dreamy and listless teenager, more at home with her supernatural friends than with human ones of her own age. This peculiar affinity drew the attention of several worthies in the district, and it is as a result of this interest that we know so much about her.

Most of our information about Anne Jeffreys comes from an account of her life published in a document by Moses Pitt of London. Pitt was a publisher who had heard of Anne's unique abilities and had asked his nephew, who was a lawyer, to interview her. At the time of the interview,

Anne had been unjustly imprisoned by the notorious Cornish magistrate, John Tregeagle, himself the subject of much folklore, especially those tales concerning pacts with the Devil. Pitt's nephew did not interview Anne personally but sent his brother-in-law, Humphry Martin, to see her instead. Martin reported that Anne was extremely reluctant to speak of her experiences with the fairies, whom she claimed were the source of any supernatural power she had. At the time at which she was first interviewed (September 1691), Anne was in her mid- to late 60s and appears to have been in rather frail health. By this time, she was married to William Warren, a herdsman. She spoke about the fairies unwillingly, fearful that people might 'make books or ballads of it', which was contrary to the fairy wishes. Furthermore, having been the victim of injustice because of her belief and consequently having been confined in the notorious Bodmin Gaol, she was frightened that she might be arrested again if she gave such printed testimony.

Two years later, Pitt wrote to Martin again, asking him to try to interview Anne once more, and on 31 January 1693 received a letter saying that Martin had seen her. Her mind was wandering slightly, as she seemed more concerned with the fact that everybody whom she had known in St Treath was now dead, except one Thomas Christopher, a blind man, than with co-operating with her interviewer. Martin contented himself with collecting some folklore and half-remembered stories about Anne, and it is from these that our picture of her emerges.

Anne's period with the Martyn family seems to have been a relatively happy one. She grew into a healthy and rather sturdy teenager, lively in her ways but, said some, a bit introverted in nature. At the age of 19, she was sitting in an arbour near the Martyn home when she suddenly became aware of a number of small people close by. She estimated there were about six of them, all dressed in green, coming through a hedge opposite and talking animatedly among themselves. She rushed in and told the family what she had seen and they, thinking that she had become unhinged, put her to bed. As soon as she had recovered from her fright, she sat up in bed and cried out: 'They are just gone out of the window! Do you not see them?' However, nobody could see anything else within the room, or in the garden beyond.

Grave concerns were now expressed for Anne's health, which seems to have deteriorated after this incident. Around April 1646, she had become so ill that she 'could not stand on her feet' and had become 'even as a changeling'. Even after she was able to get up and move about, albeit holding onto chairs and the edges of tables, she would often fall into fits and 'continued in them for so long that [those about her] were afraid that she might die in one of them'. Gradually Anne began to recover, and was latterly able to pay a visit to the parish church in St Treath in order to give thanks to God for her safe deliverance from whatever had ailed her. However, around that time, she became aware that she possessed some sort of supernatural gift which seems to have centred around psychic healing.

One afternoon, Anne and Mrs Martyn were alone in the house; the men were out in the fields for the harvesting. Mrs Martyn was anxious to obtain flour from the local mill so that she could ask her maids to bake fresh bread. She could not really leave the house, since she feared that Anne might set fire to the place, for she was still very weak and emotionally unstable at the time. She persuaded Anne to come out and sit in the garden while she walked to the mill for the flour. She then locked Anne out of the house.

On her way to the mill, Mrs Martyn stumbled and fell on the uneven road, badly twisting her leg. Unable even to get up, she was found by a passing horseman who lifted her onto his steed and took her home, still in great distress. When the reapers arrived home, the pain in Mrs Martyn's leg still had not eased, and a servant was dispatched to fetch a Mr Lobb, a surgeon from Bodmin, to attend to her. Soon after he had gone, Anne came in from the garden and without any prompting told Mrs Martyn the entire circumstances of her accident (which had not been fully disclosed to anyone) and asking to see the injured leg. She took the leg upon her lap and then proceeded to stroke it, asking Mrs Martyn if she found any ease in the exercise. Mrs Martyn admitted that she did, whereupon Anne asked her not to send for the surgeon for she herself could, by the blessing of God and His servants, cure the injury. She continued to give ease by stroking the afflicted part of the limb. Mrs Martyn believed her and recalled the serving man, allowing Anne to continue touching the leg.

During the time that the two of them were in the room together (the serving men having withdrawn), Anne confided to her guardian how she came to see the fairies. She said that sickness and fits had frequently come upon her (this was borne out by Mrs Martyn) and had left her slightly simple. The sickness was caused by small people, living in the hedge near to the house, who had been trying to communicate with her and had left her rather weak and light-headed. They had continued to appear to her, usually in even numbers, and she had been able to strike up conversations with them. When she had been shut out in the garden, the fairies had appeared and asked if she had been put out of the house against her will. When Anne replied that she had, they became extremely angry and declared that Mrs Martyn would not fare well because of it, and at that very instant her guardian had fallen by the roadside injuring her leg.

Reports of the curing of the leg, coupled with the stories about Anne and the fairies, soon spread like wildfire across the countryside. People from all over Cornwall and beyond, with all manner of illnesses and injuries, came to consult with her. They came from as far away as Land's End, Wales and even parts of England, and they were of every age from very old people to babies. Anne took no money or reward from any of them. Nor did she use salves or medicines to effect her cures as some other healers did. From the day she treated Mrs Martyn's leg, however, Anne ceased to eat with the household – in fact, she ceased to eat very much at all. The only time she broke her self-imposed fast was on Christmas Day (when, traditionally, the fairies had no power), when she ate good quantities of roast beef at the family table. Anne could also inform the family if people were coming to see them days before these individuals arrived. She was also able to state, to within five minutes, the time that they would be arriving.

However, there were inconsistencies in Anne's behaviour. One of the sons of the house reported that he had gone up to speak with Anne in her bedroom and, finding the door locked, knocked very loudly. Anne replied: 'Have a little patience and I will let you in presently.' The boy had then knelt down and, squinting through the keyhole, had observed Anne eating, presumably from a secret hoard which she kept somewhere in her room. When she had finished, she continued to stand by her bedside and appeared to give thanks. When she opened the door, she told him that she had been 'communing with the fairies'. Later, she was challenged about the food, and she declared that it had been fairy food which her supernatural friends had brought her. Although a search was made of her bedroom at her insistence, no secret hoard of food could be found.

Another mysterious event occurred shortly afterwards. One Sunday evening, a neighbour called to speak with Anne and, told that she was in her bedroom, went straight up to speak with her. On entering the room, he found it to be completely empty, and although he searched high and low upstairs he could not find any trace of her. He came down to alert the family to Anne's disappearance, but then Anne walked out of the bedroom behind him. She told the astonished neighbour that she had been there all the time but had been invisible to him, due to her fairy powers.

On yet another occasion, Anne gave Mrs Martyn a beautiful silver cup, which held about a quart, as a present. She said that she had obtained it from her fairy friends, and the good woman became so alarmed that she refused to have anything to do with it. It was a fairy thing, after all! The cup subsequently disappeared just as mysteriously as it had appeared. However, the incident was widely reported and began to draw unwelcome attention towards Anne.

Local magistrates had been aware of her alleged powers and her reputed contacts with the fairy world for quite some time. Together with some local ministers, they paid a visit to Anne in her home and proceeded to question her most rigorously. What was the fairy world like? Anne refused to say. She had been forbidden to say anything about their world. What did the fairies say to her? She could not remember. Were they, in fact, agents of the Devil? Anne did not know, but she did not think so. By this time, she had made a full recovery from her illness and was well able to argue her point. A priest was brought, and he tried to persuade Anne that she had actually been conversing with the Devil or with Infernal Sprites masquerading as friendly fairies. Anne listened gravely but said nothing. When the magistrates and ministers had left,

she suddenly turned to Mr Martyn (who had been with her throughout) saying simply: 'They call now!' She was referring to the fairies. She repeated the statement twice more, then rushed to fetch a large Bible which Mr Martyn always kept in the house. She was gone for a long time before returning with the book, stating that she had been with the fairies in the interim and that they had spoken to her thus: 'What! Hath there been some magistrates and ministers to you? And have they dissuaded you from coming any more to us, saying that we are evil spirits, and that it is all delusions of the Devil? Pray desire them to read in the 1st Epistle of John, chapter 4, verse 1, "Dearly beloved, believe not every spirit, but try the spirits whether they be of God".' (This was of great interest to everyone, since Anne was illiterate.)

This was the only time that Anne ever reported what was said in her conversations with the fairies. However, she continued to meet with them, close to the Martyns' house, and she performed further cures and foretellings. The magistrates had not gone away, however, and were keeping a close eye on her activities. At last, John Tregeagle, a Justice of the Peace, issued a warrant for Anne's arrest on suspicion of witchcraft, and had her confined in Bodmin Gaol, even then widely regarded as a notorious hellhole. There she was kept 'for a long time' (although we do not know just how long, since the gaol records are missing). On the day that the constable came to arrest her, Anne was milking the cows, and witnessed his arrival with the eye of prophesy. In desperation, she asked the fairies if she could hide among them, but they refused her request. With the case obviously fixed against her, Anne was sent to prison. It was alleged at her trial that the Martyns had secretly brought her food in her room and that they had benefited financially from her 'powers' – allegations which were never proved.

After Anne had languished in gaol for some time, Tregeagle had her removed, and kept her at his own house for a while. Here he deliberately starved her to see if the reports about her not eating were true. It was said that, while in gaol, she had not eaten a bite of human food for six months but that she believed she had received sustenance from the fairies. At last, when she was finally discharged in a weakened condition, Anne was not allowed to live with Mr Martyn or his family. Instead, she went to live with Mr Martyn's sister, a Mrs Frances Tom, a widow who lived near Padstow and who took her in. However, she still continued to cure people and sometimes foretell the future, although she was now more circumspect and even more secretive about her 'powers'. At some time during the latter part of her life, she seems to have married, but little is known about her husband. It is also not known exactly when she died.

Anne seems to have been an inoffensive creature – a little dreamy and 'distant', perhaps – who claimed to have spoken with the fairies around her house and who used whatever 'powers' she obtained from them for the good of the community. She may have 'made up' certain aspects of her 'fairy relationship', but she appears to have done no harm. Why, then, was she arrested and subjected to the indignities of Bodmin Gaol? Part of the answer at least was found in the 1930s. While searching for some manuscripts in the Bodleian Library in Oxford, the author and scholar Hamilton Jenkin came across some manuscripts which relate directly to Anne. They were in the form of letters dated February and April 1647:

> I can acquaint you with 'news' of a young girle which foretells things to come and most have fallen true. She eats nothing but sweetmeats, as Alemans (almonds) comfited and the like, which are brought to her by small people clad in green and sometimes by birds. She cures most diseases, the Falling Sickness [epilepsy], especially broken bones, only with the touch of her hands. She hath been examined by three able Divines and gives a good accompt of her religion and hath the Scriptures very perfectly, though quite unlearned. They are fearful to meddle with her for she tells them to their faces that none of them are able to hurt her. At present she is in Bodmin, at the Mayor's house. She says that the King shall enjoy his own and be revenged on his enemies.

The 'girle' can be none other than Anne Jeffreys, and it is the last sentence which gives us our clue as to her arrest. The letters were written after the Civil War, when Charles I had been defeated by the Puritan Parliament. He would be publicly executed in January 1649.

Anne's prophetic utterances that he should 'enjoy his own and be revenged on his enemies' – an overtly political statement, given the unsettled context of the times – counted as sedition and treason against the new Republican Government. In fact, she was quite fortunate that she was not executed herself, given the climate of the times. However, it gave the notorious Cornish witch-persecutor John Tregeagle the chance to have her examined for witchcraft and have her confined to Bodmin Gaol. It would also explain Anne's later reluctance to speak to publishers' agents in her later life. She must have finished her life as the frail, secretive woman that she had been in earlier days.

The second 'sorceress', Tamsin Blight, was quite a contrast to poor, dreamy Anne Jeffreys, and traced her uncanny 'powers' to rather different sources than the fairies. Despite her being one of the best-documented Cornish 'witches', there are still questions and disagreements concerning her, not least of all her actual name. Her surname is sometimes given as 'Blight', and at other times as 'Blee' (which is a Cornish word meaning 'wolf'), while her Christian name is rendered as 'Tamsin', 'Tamson' or sometimes even 'Thomson'. The folklorist William Bottrell called her a 'witch', but most accounts describe her as a 'pellar'. Pellars were an interesting phenomenon. They were not exactly witches or wizards but they had supernatural powers. The word, which is peculiar to Cornwall, is a contraction of 'repeller', meaning a person who repelled evil spirits and forces. Sickness, disease and ill luck were believed to have been caused by malignant forces working against individuals in the community, and the pellar was able to drive these forces away and effect cures and create well-being. They had the power to detect dark witches within the community and to counteract their evil designs, if need be. Although such people were not unique to Cornwall (see the example of Huw Llwyd, in Wales, in The Demon in the Church), they seem to have been granted a special status within the region. Of course, many pellars claimed wider powers than simply tracking down witches or repelling evil sorceries; some claimed the power to curse or to work evil for themselves. All pellars were therefore treated with respect, deference and sometimes fear. Such a person was Tamsin Blight.

Tamsin (Tammy) Blight was born in Redruth around 1798. Her family seems to have been a poor one, but we know virtually nothing about either them or her early life. However, it was frequently stated that she had 'true pellar blood', as her mother had been a seeress of some distinction. We suspect that for part of her life she may have been no more than a single woman living alone and plying a 'pellar's trade' of issuing charms and conjuring. This was a relatively unsafe thing to do in early 19th-century Cornwall since the pellar's craft was often viewed with suspicion, and even hostility in some remote areas. Even during the mid-19th century, newspapers carry accounts of pellars, conjurers and cunning men being attacked in their houses because their neighbours greatly feared their reputations. There are no details concerning this period of Tamsin's life, although it is thought that she was steadily acquiring a reputation for her powers throughout Cornwall.

In 1835, at the age of 38, she married a widower James (or 'Jemmy') Thomas. Like herself, he was not wealthy, and appears to have been employed at a pumping station at a local mine. Pumps were critical to prevent the mines from flooding, and Jemmy's occupation is given as 'boilerman'. Marriage to Jemmy would have given Tamsin the stability and relative respectability which she needed in the Cornish community, and his employment would have given them a regular source of income – few pellars relied on their craft alone to maintain themselves. Jemmy was not slow to capitalize on his wife's undoubted reputation, which had become widespread in the area, even going so far as to claim that he had occult powers himself. The two of them lodged in a cottage near Illogen, although later they moved to Helston. It was at Illogen that she acquired an even greater name for herself, due to one particular incident.

Tammy was apparently in the habit of picking 'cherks' (half-burnt cinders) for her fire from the stacks of ash outside the door of the boiler house where Jemmy worked. On one occasion, an overseer at the mine spoke to her in the most derisory fashion and accused her of having stolen some pieces of timber that had gone missing. Although Tammy denied this, the overseer heaped abuse on her and sent her packing. The next day, the men came to start the pumping engine, which had been shut down to allow for some routine repairs, and found that it would not start up again. The mine quickly started to fill with water and the situation threatened to become an extremely dangerous one. In desperation, the overseer, suspecting some form of supernatural retribution at work, sent for Tammy and asked her if she had put a spell on the machinery. The pellar neither confirmed nor denied that she had, but offered to remove the spell provided that the overseer would apologize and that she would be handsomely paid. Both these demands were fulfilled, and with great relish she removed the spell, allowing the pump machinery, inexplicably, to start up again. The incident was widely reported and greatly added to Tammy's reputation which now extended almost as far as Wales.

Some time after this, both Tammy and Jemmy moved from Illogan to Helston, and it was here that the pair of them enjoyed their greatest successes. Nevertheless, there was a bleaker side to this move, for the couple split up and began to pursue separate careers. Tammy continued to enjoy her fame as a pellar while Jemmy (now acting as a 'conjurer' and claiming increased occult powers for himself) began to acquire a rather unsavoury reputation. One account of him states that he claimed to be able to perform 'dark magic', by which he could contact demons and spirits in the manner of some of the Renaissance 'high magicians'. (It is possible that Jemmy had a smattering of 'book learning' with which he could impress his clients. The term 'conjurer' was usually applied to someone who had a 'magic book' or who used 'magic formulae' in their charms.)

Tammy's fame throughout Cornwall, meanwhile, continued to grow. Several tales connect her to another famous Cornish character, Matthew Lutey of Cury. According to tradition, turned into written legend by William Bottrell, Lutey captured a mermaid and, in return for releasing her into the sea, was rewarded by receiving the occult powers of a pellar, not only for himself but for his descendants as well. It was suggested that some of Lutey's powers had somehow been transferred to Tammy Blight, and that she may have been connected to him by blood. An account of the time states: 'There are hundreds alive to testify among those who yearly consult Tammy Blee and J. Thomas. This worthy couple of white witches seem to be equally successful in the exercise of their art, though many say that the former only is of true old pellar blood.'

Despite his own relative fame as a 'wise-man', there seems little doubt that Jemmy's activities did much harm to his former wife's reputation. He does not appear to have been the most honest of men, and he also seems to have been frequently drunk. He performed elaborate rituals for which he charged large fees. There were other 'scandals' as well; Jemmy also appears to have had homosexual leanings and, as part of the spell, demanded to sleep with some of his clients. Although he claimed that this was an 'essential operation' in the overall charm, it was generally regarded as a satisfaction of his own lusts and laid him open to all sorts of homophobic attacks. At some stage, Jemmy appears to have left Helston and returned to Illogan where he continued to practise as a 'conjurer'. His dubious practices there reflected upon Tammy. In writing about him, Robert Hunt (quoting newspaper sources) states the following:

> During the week ending Sunday last, a 'wise-man' from Illogan has been engaged with about half a dozen witchcraft cases, one a young tradesman and another a sea-captain. It appears that the 'wise-man' was in the first place visited at his home by these deluded people at different times and he declared the whole of them to be spell-bound. In one case he said that, if the person had not come so soon, in about a fortnight he would have been in an asylum; another would have had his leg broken; and in every case something direful would have happened. Numerous incantations have been performed. In the case of a captain of a vessel, a visit was paid to the seaside, and, while the 'wise-man' uttered some unintelligible gibberish, the captain had to throw a stone into the sea. So heavy was the spell under which he laboured and which immediately fell back upon the 'wise-man' that the latter pretended that he could scarcely walk back to Hayle. The most abominable part of the incantation is performed during the hours of midnight, and for that purpose the wretch sleeps with his victims and for five nights following he had five different bedfellows. Having no doubt repaid a pretty good harvest during the week, he returned to his home on Monday; but, such was the pretended effect produced by the different spells and witchcraft that tell upon him from

> his many dupes, that two of the young men who had been under his charge were obliged to obtain a horse and cart and carry him to Hayle Station. One of the men, having had two 'spells' resting on him, the 'wise-man' was obliged to sleep with him on Saturday and Sunday nights, having spent the whole of Sunday in his diabolical work. It is time that the police, or some other higher authorities, should take the matter up as the person alluded to is well known, and frequently visited by the ignorant and superstitious.

The 'wise-man' was, of course, Jemmy Thomas, and there is no doubt that he was acquiring an 'unwholesome press' through using superstition to obtain sexual gratification – a 'press' which was starting to reflect on his wife and other pellars in Cornwall. The *West Briton* under the headline 'Gross Superstition at Hayle' details:

> A correspondent has furnished us with the following particulars relative to the antecedents of the pretended conjurer. He states that James Thomas, the conjurer from the parish of Illogan, married some time since to the late celebrated Tammy Blee of Redruth, who afterward removed to Helston and carried on as a fortune teller, but parted from her husband, James Thomas, on account of a warrant for his apprehension having been issued against him by the magistrates at St Ives, for attempting to take a spell from Mrs Paynter, through her husband, William Paynter, who stated before the magistrates that he wanted to commit a disgraceful offence, absconded, and was absent from the West of Cornwall for upwards of two years. His wife then stated that the virtue was in her not in him; that she was of the real 'Pellar' blood and that he could tell nothing but through her. His greatest dupes had been at St Just and Hayle, and other parts of Cornwall. He had been in the habit of receiving money annually for keeping witchcraft from vessels sailing out of Hayle. He slept with several of his dupes recently, and about a fortnight since he stated that he must sleep with certain young men at Copperhouse, Hayle, in order to protect them from something hanging over them, one being a mason and the other a miner, the two latter lately from St Just. He said himself this week at Truro that he had cured a young man from St Erth, and was going on Saturday again to take a spell from the father, a tin smelter. He caused great disturbance among the neighbours, by charging some with having bewitched

> others. He is a drunken, disgraceful, beastly fellow and ought to be sent to the treadmill. One young man is thoroughly ashamed of himself to think he has been duped by this scoundrel.

There can be no doubt that, with reports like this circulating throughout Cornwall, local pellars were now being treated with suspicion. As his former wife, Tammy was now among those who were being highly ostracized, perhaps even viewed with outright hostility. Jemmy seems to have continued his unsavoury practices until the 1870s. On 26 February 1874, under the title 'Death of a Wizard', the *West Briton* gives the following account:

> On Thursday last, at Park Bottom, in the parish of Illogan, John Thomas, better known as 'the wizard', ended his mortal career. Rich and poor for miles around have honoured him with a visit (in times past) and contributions poured upon him must, if report be true, have been considerable. Every species of ailment which afflicts the human family, he was supposed to cure. If swine were possessed of unnatural propensities or took to dying in an unceremonious manner, John could tell their owners all about it, or if cows misbehaved themselves, adopted vicious tricks or refused to do the correct thing the wizard brought them to their senses. Among horses, he was indeed a host; a kicker might as well be a dead horse, as far as kicking went, after John had worked his will on him and as to stopping blood, if an arm was lopped off, no blood would flow if John cried stop.

This 'John Thomas' was Jemmy, who sometimes used the name John for his own devious purposes. By this time (1874) Tammy was dead – she died in 1856. Following her death, Jemmy's reputation ironically had improved and it was considered that part of the 'true pellar power' had somehow passed from her to him, giving him increased community status. If he continued his scurrilous practices at the expense of his clients, this was not reported, although there is a suggestion that the adverse publicity he had previously received might have counted against him when it came to obtaining employment. At the time of his death, his occupation was registered as a 'copper miner', although whether or not he was actually employed in the mines is open to question.

Strangely, too, at the time of her own death, Tammy's reputation had also started to revive somewhat. Indeed, so successful had she become that she was able to set up her own pellar's business in a little house in Meneage Street in Helston. Here, she received clients and, taking a leaf out of Jemmy's book, began to sell powders and written charms which could be renewed at various times. The best time to have a charm renewed, according to Cornish lore, was during the spring, when the returning sun gave spells, amulets and talismans a boost. It was also during the spring that the pellar's powers were believed to be at their height, and so this was the time when Tammy did most of her trade. Bottrell states that many of her clients travelled great distances to see her, from St Ives, the Scilly Isles and even Swansea, and it was said that many Cornish sea-captains would not put out until they had their amulets and charms renewed by 'Tammy Blee'. There is even a suggestion that Jemmy and Tammy may have worked together for a time, with Jemmy occasionally acting as a kind of 'manager', although there is certainly no evidence that they resumed as man and wife. Jemmy's reputation would have precluded that. However, Bottrell does give a hint that they may well have lived together in the same house for a while, possibly also with another, older relative (of Jemmy's?). There can be little doubt that, when Bottrell advises a friend who is having a run of bad luck to visit 'the wise man J.T. at his abode in or around Helston', he is referring to Jemmy, and that he was back there and living with Tammy.

Tammy's spells and charms were becoming more and more elaborate, probably as a result of Jemmy's influence. Many of the 'amulets' she dispensed were little more than pieces of paper with supposedly mystical words written upon them. Many of the words had been copied from books relating to the magic of the High Middle Ages and had more in keeping with Crowley than with a Cornish 'wise-woman'. It is doubtful if either Tammy or Jemmy even knew what they meant. Some charms bore elaborate and enigmatic symbolism (Bottrell refers to a creation like 'a headless cherub' or 'a brooding angel or bird' drawn on one side of the paper) which was probably largely the pellar's own invention.

These were adorned with words such as NALGAH, TETRAGRAMMATON, and so on, written either in pencil or in cheap crayon. On the reverse of many of Tammy's charms were the words JEHOVAH, JAH, ELOHIM, SHADDAY, ADONAY or HAVE MERCY ON A POOR WOMAN, together with a hotchpotch of esoteric (and indecipherable) symbols. Bottrell (from whom most of the descriptions of the charms come) probably bought many of these amulets himself, and most of them appear to have been partly derived from volumes of medieval magical lore. These had probably been obtained through mail-order from dealers in London, as had some of the rings and pendants which Tammy also sold. These were supposed to be 'blood stones, snake stones and stones of esoteric origin from the Orient'. Tammy and Jemmy claimed to have fashioned some of these themselves under occult conditions, although the same 'talismans' were to be found in cheap shops in the East End of London. Tammy's 'snake stones', in particular, were in great demand. These were blue stones often set into a ring, in which some fancied they saw the shape of a coiled adder, and which supposedly were guaranteed to 'keep the owner safe from any member of the serpent tribe and that man or beast, bit and envenomed, being given some water to drink, wherein the stone had been infused, would perfectly recover of the poison'.

Besides selling amulets and talismans, Tammy also worked as a curer of ailments and injuries. In times when the services of doctors were extremely expensive, the poor in country areas relied on such 'healers'. In one story, a woman, living at Breage, suffered from a 'severe sickness' which prevented her from moving her limbs and forced her to lie in the same position day after day. A neighbour who called to see her suggested that the illness might be the result of someone 'ill-wishing' her or casting an evil spell on her. At her own request, the woman was taken in a dog-cart to see the pellar, Tammy Blight, at Helston. As soon as Tammy saw her, she declared that she had indeed been bewitched by a neighbour's maliciousness, but that she could lift the spell. She made several incantations and then told the woman to go home again. She further informed the invalid that, soon after she was in her own house, the one who had ill-wished her would arrive at her door enquiring after a little black cat. The woman doubted the truth of it but the dog-cart carried her home once more. Hardly was she indoors and laid down than an old woman who lived in the neighbourhood and whom she barely knew arrived at her door asking if she had seen a little black cat. With a sudden burst of strength, the sick woman got up from her chair and, taking two pitchers, went to the well and drew water. Thereafter, the illness left her and she was as hale and hearty as ever, although the old woman who had 'ill-wished' her was troubled greatly with pains.

Some friends of another woman, who appeared to be seriously ill and who was confined to bed, went to Tamsin and asked if the lady in question might be cured. 'Give me sixpence,' said Tammy, 'and I will tell you all about it and will lift whatever ails the woman.' The friends looked at each other. 'We have no money to give you,' said one. But Tammy only smiled. 'Oh yes you have!' she retorted. 'Put your hand into the left pocket of your apron and tell me what you find there.' In doing so, the woman found a sixpence at the very bottom of her apron pocket. It had been placed there some time ago when she had gone to the Copperhouse Fair and had forgotten to spend it. It had lain in the bottom of her apron pocket since. She handed the coin to Tammy, who spat upon it and said a few words to herself which none present could make out. 'Go home, my dears,' she told them. 'Your neighbour is all right and in full health again. By the time you all arrive home she will have baked a cake for your tea.' They didn't really believe her, but set out anyway. When they arrived home, they found their friend up and about and cutting a heavy cake which she had baked in their absence.

In her heyday, Tammy appears to have been a shrewd business-woman, and was probably one of the most expensive pellars in Cornwall. Her 'medical' consultations (for the curing of various ailments), although cheaper than visiting a doctor, were certainly quite costly, while her consultations on other matters were said to be the dearest in Cornwall. When under Jemmy's 'management', she was said to charge somewhere in the region of £2–3 per consultation (although this was later dropped to around £2 when she operated on her own), which was a considerable sum for a working person at that time, bearing in mind that wages in late-Victorian times were roughly ten shillings a week. In some cases, such as in one tale where she was called in to locate a lost treasure (which she failed to do), the charges would probably have been even more, successful or not. She could have been one of the wealthiest women in Cornwall, but most of the money appears to have gone on drink, to the disreputable Jemmy or to buy drugs in order to develop and expand her trade. In later years, Tammy seems to have gone into another line of the supernatural – the calling and raising of spirits. In this line, drugs were essential, particularly hallucinogens. However, herbs and drugs, which were not readily available, were expensive and perhaps only yielded scant results. Nevertheless, Tammy's reputation was widely considered to be infallible all across Cornwall.

Even in her later years, when she was more or less confined to bed, Tammy's powers did not diminish. People suffering from various illnesses, some barely able to walk, were still brought to her and were laid on stretchers by her bed as she pronounced spells over them. After a few minutes with her, even in a weakened state, they were able to rise and go downstairs themselves. Once, according to many stories, a farmer came a long distance to see Tammy, who was extremely ill at the time. He had a horse that was sick and was likely to die. As this was his only animal, the poor man was in great distress and pleaded with the ailing Tammy to do something for him. The pellar was far too ill to be moved but she called her little boy to her (Tammy may have had a very young son at the time, by Jemmy, or perhaps by someone else) and touched him, whispering certain words into his ear. Then, turning to the farmer, she said: 'If you carry my child to where the horse is, his touch will cure it, for I have passed on my power to him for this occasion.' The farmer took the child to the horse and, when the infant had touched the animal, it was immediately cured. Nor was this incident an isolated one, for there are many other tales of Tammy curing at a distance, even from her bed at the height of her final sickness.

Tamsin Blight died in the middle of the 19th century, but such was her fame that her name lives on, even to this day. Many refer to her as a 'witch', but few know the exact circumstances of her profession or of her powers. Nonetheless, the very remembrance of her serves to demonstrate the power such people had over the collective consciousness in Cornwall.

Both Anne Jeffreys and Tamsin Blight represented, in different ways, the power of the 'wise-women' in a largely rural area, and in doing so they demonstrate the importance of such people within Celtic perception. Anne certainly drew her 'powers' from a mystical Celtic source – the fairies who lived in the hedge close to her house – while Tammy combined the Celtic viewpoint with that of more formalized high medieval magic. Nevertheless, in a sense, both women kept alive the old Celtic views and beliefs which lingered well into the age of rationalism, and which may indeed yet linger on, somewhere at the back of the Celtic mind.

U S A

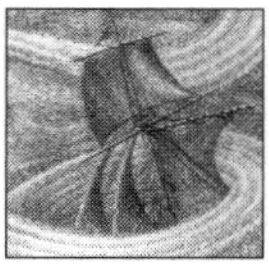

# THE MAGICIAN OF MARBLEHEAD AND HIS GRANDDAUGHTER

Between the 17th and 19th centuries, many parts of the present-day United Kingdom experienced a general exodus for the American continent. The earliest emigrants were mostly seeking religious freedom for themselves in the New World; others were fleeing the Highland Clearances and poverty in Scotland, as well as the horrors of the Irish Potato Famine. All of them, in various ways, served to mould and shape the continent to which they travelled, both politically and culturally.

There is no doubt that with these emigrants went some of the inherent belief systems and cultural perceptions of the lands they had left behind. Seventeenth-century English Puritans carried their fears and insecurities regarding dark and supernatural practices which eventually culminated (in part) in the witchcraft outbreak at Salem Village, Massachusetts, in 1692. Scottish and Irish settlers brought their awe and wonder concerning Highland 'spae-wives' and 'fairy doctors' which still find echoes in tales of the 'granny-women' and 'pow-wow doctors' of Tennessee and Kentucky.

It was, however, in New England – one of the first areas of America to be settled to any great extent by the English – that many of these inherent beliefs took their deepest root. Notions of cunning men, the walking dead (see The Vampire Lady of Rhode Island), ghosts and witches gripped the minds and imaginations of the Founding Fathers as they strove to establish themselves on an inhospitable and alien shore. Like an underlying connecting thread, such thoughts percolated down through the generations of settlers, long after the atrocities of Salem had passed. Much of the mood of such tradition was encapsulated in the American 'Devil Books' which were produced around the 17th and 18th centuries – works such as Cotton Mather's *Wonders of the Invisible World* or Robert Calef's *More Wonders* – volumes that can rank with many of the European books on witchcraft and devilry. As such, whether acknowledged or not, the early beliefs of the pioneers formed at least part of the foundations of modern American culture. Such underlying nightmares resurface from time to time in the works of such writers as Edgar Allan Poe, Nathaniel Hawthorne, Robert Bloch and most importantly H.P. Lovecraft. It was Lovecraft who perhaps best of all caught the brooding menace which lies at the heart of New England society, a menace which had its origins in the Otherworld of Celtic belief. His notions of creatures living invisibly alongside settlers, of arcane and secretive religions practised in remote areas of New England and of 'witches' and 'sorcerers' whose influence lingers within the landscape all convey a sense of the subconscious Celtic-American past. Perhaps, too, there is still something in these 'not quite forgotten' influences.

Marblehead is a quaint and peaceful fishing town on the northern Massachusetts coast, lying close to the important industrial city of Lynn. Although relatively unassuming, it is famous for a number of things. It is, for example, regarded as being 'the birthplace of the American Navy' and the 'yachting capital of the world'. Nearby Lynn is equally famous as the 'cradle of the American shoe industry' and both the writer Eugene O'Neill and the industrialist Lydia Pinkham were either born or lived there for a time. The region has another claim to fame, however. In the years around and immediately following the Salem Witch Trials, Marblehead was the centre for mystics, fortune-tellers and 'sorcerers' of many descriptions. The most celebrated and perhaps the most controversial was the so-called 'Marblehead magician', John Dimond, whose name, together with that of his granddaughter Molly Pitcher, was widely famed across the growing American continent during the 18th and 19th centuries.

Edward 'John' Dimond was a tall, moody man who lived in a large colonial home at Little Harbor, Marblehead, during the early days of the 18th century. Of his childhood, little is known – even the date of his birth is something of a mystery, although it is thought to have been around the time of the Salem Witch Trials in 1692 – but as a young man he was known to go into deep trances which would sometimes last for days. During these trances, he would neither speak nor eat, but would emerge from them fully refreshed and with a curious knowledge of events which were happening well beyond his own community. So startling were these comas that his parents were greatly feared that John was in the grip of some strange sickness.

When his father died, John inherited a small amount of money from his estate (his father had apparently not been a very rich man) which he used to buy some land. Controversially (and perhaps extremely significantly) the ground which he chose to buy was a section of dense woodland surrounding the town's Old Burying Hill. It was not known why he should show a great interest in this stretch of relatively undesirable property, but there were hints and suggestions regarding occult motives. This was a period just 28 years after the notorious Witch Trials in Salem and Concord, and the people of the region were still highly superstitious and given to imaginings about the occult. There were persistent whispers that John Dimond was a wizard and that he was practising black magic in the dense thicket beside the old cemetery. There were even some rumours that he was secretly digging up bodies for use in terrible experiments which he carried on deep in the woodlands. Certain people claimed to have heard him speaking with the Devil along the leafy tracks which ran down from the Burying Hill and into the woods. A generation earlier, John would almost certainly have been accused and tried as a witch but, following the barbarity and outrages of the Salem witch-hunt, most New Englanders were more cautious and circumspect. They tolerated John Dimond and his eccentric ways. Besides, some of his trances now appeared to be useful to members of the locality.

When a certain Widow Brown, a poor and elderly woman, had some firewood stolen, she consulted John Dimond, complaining that the cutting of the kindling had taken her long hours of painstaking work and that it was her only fuel for the long winter months ahead. Dimond immediately went into one of his famous 'trances' and was able to name the thief. On the widow's behalf, Dimond then confronted the culprit, and, when the man denied it, 'so charmed him that he was forced to walk the streets of the town all night with a heavy log on his back'. Dimond probably insisted that he return all the wood to the Widow Brown's house under cover of darkness. Following this incident, John Dimond was frequently called upon to recover lost or stolen articles in Marblehead and in other townships in the area. Although he did not have a perfect record, his powers of detection and recovery were extremely impressive. Some of these, however, may have been little more than elementary powers of deduction in the style of Sherlock Holmes. In small, tightly knit communities, acute observation, local knowledge and powers of logical thinking served much better in detecting criminals than supernatural intervention.

Dimond appeared to have other powers as well, however. For instance, he could predict the uncertain weather around Marblehead with an uncanny degree of accuracy. Before a storm hit the New England coast, John Dimond would climb up through the woodlands to the Old Burying Hill where his presence would alert his neighbours to the approaching squall. It was also widely reported that on such occasions he conferred with the dead, who lay beneath the tombstones, regarding events far away. He must have made a strange and alarming sight, mumbling and whispering as he walked between the serried headstones – indeed, he must have seemed almost like a ghost himself! As the wind increased in intensity, so the wizard's voice would rise. Soon those who heard him began to realize that he was calling to ships far out at sea. 'Captain Jasper MacClelland of the *Elizabeth Anne*, do you hear me?' he would roar to the leaden skies over the old cemetery. 'Keep four degrees to starboard, run true until you reach the Halfway Rock.' He would pause and look around him. 'Captain Benjamin Rowe of the *Hetty*, hear my words. Move six degrees to port or you will founder on a shoal!' For hours, he would roar and shout to the wind, giving commands to one skipper after another and calling each of them by name. Some of them were known to him, and some were not; but each one seemed to be an

actual seaman. Several of the Marblehead captains claimed to have heard Dimond's voice while far out at sea, guiding and encouraging them towards safety. On a couple of occasions, they claimed that his directions had actually saved their vessels in the midst of storms.

There was another side to Dimond, however. If he took a dislike to any captain in the fishing fleet, he would condemn them in the middle of the storm from his place among the gravestones. 'Captain William Orne of the *Plymouth Lass*, hear what I have to say! I curse you from this appointed spot, both you and your brother Jacob, master of the *Charlotte Rose*. May neither of you see port again! May both of you perish with your ships in the storm that is coming! This is my earnest wish and my most fervent prayer!' None of those boats whom he cursed, nor their captains, ever returned to port.

A famous row broke out between Dimond and a certain Captain Micah Taylor of the *Kestrel*, in which the seaman called upon the Marblehead wizard to 'do his worst, for he had no fear of him'. On a clear, calm morning, the *Kestrel* set sail from Marblehead harbour. There was no hint of bad weather at all, but, just the same, the Wizard Dimond climbed up to the top of the Old Burial Hill and began his chant among the gravestones. Slowly the sky started to blacken and dark clouds began to gather from the west. A gale suddenly blew out of nowhere and lashed the New England coast. The *Kestrel* never returned to Marblehead harbour – she was lost at sea with all hands. Other skippers hypnotically followed John Dimond's voice through the worst gales and steered their ships to safety. Death or survival appeared to depend upon the whim of the Wizard of Marblehead.

Dimond also seemed to possess a vivid knowledge of events which were occurring many miles away. This was an era in which men did not really travel very far, nor were there newspapers or continental communications of any kind. If news did travel between settlements, even those which were close together, it usually took some time. While in his trances, John Dimond seemed to travel many miles beyond Marblehead to see what was going on in other parts of the country. For example, while sitting on the top of the cemetery hill, he was able to witness a house fire in Concord through his alleged powers of telepathy, and was able to name those who stood about watching the blaze. When news of the fire reached Marblehead, many people already knew about it through Dimond.

Whether or not John Dimond had extra-sensory powers is open to question. If he did, then the majority of his paranormal accomplishments were for the good of the community. Some people around Marblehead actually liked the queer, gangly man, but most feared him. It was thought that the corpses which lay in the Old Burying Hill actually listened to the sound of his voice. Some people claimed that he had power over the elements, while others believed that his spirit could leave his body and travel to faraway places to watch what was going on there. His reputation was widespread. Nevertheless, he is all but forgotten in the region around Marblehead today. There are still some reminders of this peculiar man, however: a local Marblehead sports team is named 'The Magicians' and there is still some talk in the town when a storm blows in from the sea that 'The Wizard Dimond is up on his hill again'.

John Dimond's granddaughter Molly was born at 42 Orne Street, Marblehead, in 1738. She was born in a timber-framed house which stood directly opposite a narrow path leading up to the Old Burying Hill. Shortly after her birth, her parents suspected that she had inherited certain 'abilities' from her peculiar grandfather. Almost as soon as she could talk, she could repeat complicated conversations she had overheard. When she went to school she could, upon returning home, repeat word for word, conversations which her mother had been having with neighbours, even though she (Molly) had not been there at the time. It was believed that she could also read the thoughts of her family and of friends who came to visit – thoughts that she would repeat out loud, much to the embarrassment of her parents. Soon people started avoiding her home like the plague. As a very young girl, she is credited with predicting the War of Independence and the American victory over the British. By doing so, she earned the enmity of many influential Marblehead traders, all of whom were pro-British Tories. She grew up to be a remarkably plain girl; she had a long, sad face with a slightly hooked nose and thin lips, together with an overly large head that seemed out of proportion to the rest of her slender body. She may also have had a slightly 'wry' or crooked neck. Not many of the local young men showed much interest in her or came forward as suitors (perhaps the majority were put off not only by her looks but also by her weird reputation); however, at the age of 22, Molly married Robert Pitcher of Marblehead. Shortly after the marriage, the couple moved to Lynn, in around 1769.

By the early 1770s, Molly Pitcher's fame as a clairvoyant had spread throughout Massachusetts and beyond, and many people were coming great distances to the Pitcher household, nestling at the foot of Lynn's famous 'high rock', in order to see what the future held for them. Robert Pitcher was extremely proud of his wife's strange abilities and probably acted as her agent, boasting to friends of her miraculous powers and of the accuracy of her prophesies.

Just how accurate Molly's prophesies were is uncertain. Probably they were no more correct than those of the other so-called 'mystics' and 'prophets' of the time and relied on a certain amount of guesswork mixed with local knowledge. As with some of the so-called Irish seeresses (for example, Biddy Early in Clare, or Moll Anthony in Kildare), conversations between those waiting to be seen by the 'prophet' were carefully monitored by his or her confederates, and much information was thereby obtained. This information was then relayed by the 'prophet' to the astonished client. Molly's prognostications, however, were often accompanied by awe-inspiring trances which greatly added to the eeriness of the occasion. Some of those who came to see her were the Tory merchants who had formerly denounced her, mainly to ascertain if business ventures in which they were engaged would come to fruition. Like her grandfather, too, Molly could unfailingly tell whether their ships would return to port. In the days of fierce storms, and when pirates lurked along the New England coast, such knowledge was vital to the success of any enterprise. Molly would not spare any of her visitors, either, for she was, by all accounts, an extremely serious woman. If a seaman came to see her (and many did) to find out if he would return from a voyage upon which he was embarking, Molly would tell him 'straight', without any frills or apology. She never humoured her clients. If she beheld a ship in difficulties at the time or in the future, she would say so. She earned a reputation for 'plain speaking' which was valued among the stolid New Englanders. Those who went to consult her 'for a lark' were frequently told unpleasant, but accurate, intimate details about themselves and came away suitably chastened and with extremely serious faces.

It was not only seafarers and people who had lost valuables, or even star-struck young ladies anxious to find out whom they would marry, who made their way to the frame house in Lynn. Law enforcement officers did too. The business of upholding the law in early New England was still a pretty ramshackle affair, although it was slowly taking on form and organization, and most lawmen still relied on local knowledge, gossip and rumour rather than proper detection methods in order to solve crimes. Following a rather famous murder in Concord, officers made their way to Molly Pitcher's house to see if the mystic could shed some light on the subject. Without any prior knowledge, Molly revealed not only how the crime had been committed but also named three possible suspects (all unknown to her) who were being considered as possible felons. In the end, she actually named the guilty party while in one of her trances. The man later confessed, the police were astounded, and Molly Pitcher's standing as a clairvoyant was greatly enhanced. From time to time, she is thought to have aided the New England authorities with other cases, particularly those involving theft and smuggling. Some of her 'mystic declarations' may have been based on supposition, and on rumour and gossip that she picked up within the community, but some of them may have drawn upon her own supernatural abilities. In any case, an admittedly rather dubious tradition states that they were all unfailingly accurate and that, through her work, a number of criminals were brought to justice.

Like her grandfather, too, Molly Pitcher was known to issue curses against those whom she did not like or who had crossed her in some way. Again, as with her grandfather, these curses always seemed to work, particularly if they were directed against sea-captains and their crews. It is said that certain schooners never left port on the Massachusetts North Shore for the want of a crew once Molly had hurled an imprecation against it. This, coupled with her other mystical and predictive abilities, made her a feared and respected member of the community. By the time she died in 1813, at the age of 75, her reputation as a 'wise-woman' (some might have been tempted to say 'witch') had spread all over the developing east coast of America. Her name even prompted the American poet John Greenleaf Whittier to write a long poem dedicated to her amazing powers of prediction in 1832. There is no other memorial to Molly Pitcher and, almost two centuries after her passing, her name is all but forgotten in New England, again echoing the fate of her own grandfather.

Both John Dimond and Molly Pitcher belonged to a tradition which, although flourishing in the fertile soil of the New World, undoubtedly had its roots in the Old World. Celtic belief placed great emphasis upon the seer, wise-woman and cunning man, and this idea seems to have crossed the Atlantic with the emigrant ships. Among the settlers, such powers ('healing', 'far-seeing' and especially prognostication) were often passed along family lines from one generation to the next. Indeed, in many country areas throughout the Celtic world (especially in Ireland and Scotland), communities actually came to rely upon such people in order to warn them of storms, to find lost property or stolen goods, or to foresee events that would have an impact on the community or on individual activities. In all these aspects, John Dimond and his granddaughter fulfilled the ancient traditions: they both forewarned of gales and winds and guided ships through hurricanes; they both located property and detected criminals; they were both consulted by the elders of the community (and, in Molly Pitcher's case, by leading Massachusetts merchants). Most importantly, both were seen as characters who were integral to the community as a whole, despite their weird ways and abilities. The dark side of their 'power' (the ability to curse and, to some extent, call down storms) was overlooked, and they were mainly regarded as benign 'wizards', rather than evil witches or sorcerers. Their tradition also still continues in the area, to an extent. Many people around Marblehead (and in other parts of Massachusetts) still claim what are today termed 'psychic powers'; indeed, some of today's inhabitants are even relatively famous for their strange abilities.

# THE WIZARD EARL

In Celtic mythology, the 'wise-woman' or 'conjurer' often had a special affinity with nature. Usually they had a wide-ranging knowledge of the powers found in the natural world – in plants and herbs from which they could create potions, salves and balms which cured almost every illness. They could often determine the future by the movements of animals and birds or by looking at the new moon reflected in a pool or basin of water. Many of them were said also to have a close relationship with woodland sprites – fauns and fairies – who frequently revealed to them secrets of the world, not usually given to mortals. The great Clare wise-woman Biddy Early was said to play cards occasionally with the fairies, and it was from a fairy man that she reputedly won her famous blue bottle through which she could effect her cures, foretell the future and work her spells and curses.

Fairies were often in the business of revealing certain of their secrets to mortals whom they trusted or who respected the natural world. Many 'conjurers' boasted bottles or stones or other oddments which they had acquired through interaction with fairy peoples. Others simply received magic words or tunes which they sometimes used in their incantations, but all these came from a supernatural source. Of course, such knowledge often came with a price.

The words and artefacts that such 'wise-people' acquired did not sit easily with the Church. Soon the notion of receiving anything from the fairy world became equated with a consorting with demons or minor devils, and the 'gifts' which they offered were to be shunned. Nevertheless, certain people still continued to seek and receive such gifts. One of the most famous was the Scottish fisherman, Alexander Seaton (or Seton) who dwelt on the coastline near the Firth of Forth during the late 16th and early 17th centuries, and another was Gerald Fitzgerald, the 16th-century Irish Earl of Desmond and Kildare, known as the 'Wizard Earl'.

Alexander Seaton was believed to have received a certain magical 'dust' or powder from the Selkies (seal people or sea-fairies) which had the power to turn any base metal into pure gold. The 'dust' was witnessed by several worthy people, including a Dutch sea-captain named Hausen who invited Seaton to visit him in Amsterdam. Here Seaton performed many miracles, using the fairy powder, a portion of which he gave to Hausen himself. It appeared that Seaton habitually met with the Selkies and could obtain an almost inexhaustible supply of powder from them.

During his stay in Holland, the Scotsman performed many demonstrations of the miraculous dust both in Amsterdam and Rotterdam in front of a number of interested scientists and lay scholars who had come to see him. His claims were examined under the most stringent conditions and small samples of the dust were taken away for further investigation. These samples defied analysis. Although many declared that somehow this fisherman had found the fabled Philosopher's Stone (which turned metal into gold) for which many alchemists had been searching, Seaton stuck to his story that the 'dust' had been given to him by the Scottish Selkies or by fairies, earning him the reprobation of the Dutch Church. Others also took an interest in him.

As his fame grew, he was invited to perform his demonstrations in Germany and Switzerland by the 17th-century German philosopher and arch opponent of alchemy Wolfgang Deinheim. Probably Deinheim intended to expose him as a charlatan and, in doing so, strike a blow against alchemical teaching and thinking. However, Deinheim was more or less converted to the alchemical viewpoint, and then championed Seaton's case in Europe. Seaton now claimed that he could 'manufacture' the 'dust' from a mystical formula which had been given to him by the fairies, but that he could only manufacture it in very small quantities and that no other mortal must see him doing so. This he appeared to do and produced more quantities of the powder, which continued to turn metals like copper into flawless gold. Attention on him increased, and eventually became his downfall. Christian II, the youthful Elector (Prince) of Saxony had heard stories about Seaton and was anxious to meet him and to view the magical 'dust' for himself. He invited the Scotsman to come to Saxony and be entertained at his court. Seaton, who had just married a German girl, declined the invitation but sent his apprentice and assistant, another Scotsman named William Hamilton, in his stead. He gave Hamilton a small portion of the 'fairy dust' but told him not to part with it or to discuss its manufacture with anyone. Using only a fraction of the sample, Hamilton was able to perform transmuting feats for the astonished prince – all metals which were brought in were turned to gold. The method Hamilton employed was the same as that of his master: he demanded a glass of wine, into which he put a small portion of the 'dust' ('no bigger than to cover half of a thumb nail') and mixed it into a viscous potion. Into this, he placed a dull coin, usually made of copper, making sure that it was immediately immersed, and this turned to gold as soon as it was lifted out. Christian had several goldsmiths standing by and they pronounced the transmuted metal to be gold of the highest quality.

Suspecting some sort of trick, Christian asked for the transmutation to be repeated under the most stringent conditions. This Hamilton did, with the same result. Eagerly the Elector asked about the composition of this miraculous 'dust', but Hamilton was unable to tell him anything – how to prepare the powder was known only to his master and had been revealed by Scottish fairies. Greatly angered and now even more anxious to meet with Seaton personally, Christian issued a new invitation for the Scotsman to come to his court – an invitation he could not decline on pain of death. Leaving his new wife in Munich, Seaton set off for the Saxon court at Dresden. He would be extremely sorry that he had not simply gone back to Scotland.

It soon became clear that it was not actually him that Christian wanted to see – the Elector only wanted the secret of manufacturing the 'fairy dust'. The young prince wished to extend his Saxon boundaries and an unlimited supply of gold would enable him to buy the finest mercenaries from all over Europe. Alexander Seaton had become caught up in the unstable world of 17th-century European politics. The Elector initially attempted to wheedle the secret from the Scotsman by flattery and bribery. Seaton stoutly resisted such blandishments, but he did so in rather conflicting ways. Firstly, he told the Elector that he had obtained the powder itself from the fairies, and that he really had no idea how it was made (although he had claimed that he could make it himself), and could not therefore reveal the origins of the compound. When Christian did not believe that, Seaton changed his story and then said that he had made the powder himself, but that he had learned the formula directly from the fairies and could not possibly pass it on to anyone else. Lastly, he admitted that he had discovered the secret of the powder himself through the alchemical arts but thought that this discovery was under the direction of the fairies and stated that he could not pass it on. He further cited the high moral principals of the art which forbade him to disclose his knowledge for the proposed purpose of warfare. Christian was unimpressed, and, when he could not obtain the secret by diplomacy, resolved to take it by force. He had Seaton arrested and thrown into a prison-tower in Dresden, refusing to release him until he had parted with his secret. Forty guards were posted to watch the alleged alchemist day and night, and he was continually pressed to reveal his secret and so earn his freedom. When Seaton once again refused, the Elector suggested that he might yield to torture and had the Scotsman placed on a rack. He was roasted over a slow fire, and he was whipped and scourged, but still he refused to divulge the secret of the powder. 'My body you can destroy,' he is alleged to have told his torturers, 'but, if I were to tell you the secret, my immortal soul would become the property of the fairy kind. They do not take lightly to their secrets being passed on to mortals.' After this, he was submitted to the thumbscrews and the rack once more and a hot branding-iron was applied to his bruised flesh. Nothing, however, could loosen his tongue, so great was his professed fear of the fairies.

During his captivity, Christian allowed other alchemists to visit him, perhaps in the vain hope that he might disclose the secret to one of them. Michael Sendivogius, a Moravian chemist, was fascinated by

Seaton's story and resolved to help the Scotsman, desperately trying to prise the secret from his lips – not for Christian but for himself. He bribed the guards with money that he had raised from the sale of some property, and bought lavish food and drink for the rest of the soldiery. While they were sleeping off the effects, Sendivogius broke into Seaton's cell to free him. To the Moravian's consternation, the other could barely walk, let alone run, and so he was forced to carry him past the sleeping guards. Pausing only to collect Seaton's wife and the remaining quantity of the magic powder, they set out for Poland where they settled down to rest and recover in Cracow.

To the alarm of Sendivogius, Seaton still resolutely refused to divulge the secret, still saying that it was a fairy gift. Christian II, unwilling to allow his forces to enter Poland and provoke conflict, issued an offer that, if Seaton were to return to Saxony and divulge his secret, he would be well rewarded and 'looked after'. Seaton admitted that he was tempted, particularly as his stock of fairy powder was by now running low and he appeared to be in no condition to make any more, even for himself. However, he eventually declined and remained in Poland, in no fit state to travel any distance. Within two years after his escape from the Elector's court, Alexander Seaton was dead, with only a handful of the magic powder left and leaving no formula by which to make any more. In desperation, Sendivogius married his widow, in case he had passed on the secret to her. It was a vain hope – the widow knew no more than he did himself. The marriage, however, gave the Moravian access to Seaton's papers, which he went through with the assurance that he would find something which would profit them both.

Find something he did. Among general papers on alchemical lore, Sendivogius found a pamphlet entitled 'The New Light of Alchymy', which was partly written in a strange and esoteric language that he firmly believed to be the tongue of the Silkies. However, he could not read the greater part of it. This did not stop him putting his own name to what he could read of the document and passing it off as his own. Furthermore, using some of the directions he found within it, he tried to reproduce some of Seaton's experiments, with some success. In fact, although he was unable to reproduce the magic power, he was able to encourage a number of European investors to sink money into his 'experiments' in the hopes of great returns. One of these was said to have been King Sigisimund of Poland, from whom Sendivogius acquired a small country estate. There he lived, still trying vainly to formulate the fairy powder (his reserves of which were by now completely exhausted) and trying to swindle more and more money out of his backers. He lacked the style and panache of Seaton and only brought discredit on both himself and his art. He died in Parma, aged 84, still trying to make sense of the strange manuscript (the original of which disappeared shortly after his death) and still no closer to finding the secret of the fairy dust than he had ever been. Soon the memory of Seaton's miraculous powder had all but vanished from Europe as other scientists took the public attention and imagination.

Even though he seemed to be no more than a simple fisherman, it is quite possible that Seaton was an accomplished alchemist; some stories concerning him suggest that he might have been educated in Edinburgh, and he could certainly both read and write. If he was, then he certainly appears to have found something that continues to elude scientists even today – the ability to turn base metals into gold. However, he was also extremely well known around the Firth of Forth for his wide knowledge of and his contact with the supernatural powers which characterized the ancient Celtic world. He was widely regarded as a 'fairy man' who talked with sprites and goblins, and was sometimes consulted by those who were ill or who were in some sort of misfortune. There is no doubt that his alleged 'powers' pulled him into the turbulent and often messy world of European politics, demonstrating a shift from the old Celtic communal way of thinking to a more individualistically and politically centred milieu. Magic, science and politics were fast becoming intertwined during the 16th and 17th centuries as European society made a hesitant way towards the Age of Enlightenment, and the 'wise people' were often becoming victims of that transition.

Although Alexander Seaton is now relatively unknown and has left virtually no permanent folkloric legacy behind him, other 'alchemists' have sometimes cast a long shadow across the centuries. Like Seaton, some of these have become the victims of political propaganda in their own time. Like Seaton, too, many of these have had their powers denounced by the Church (in Seaton's case, both the Catholic and the emergent Protestant Churches condemned him for consorting with fairies) and by their political enemies. Which brings us to Gerald Fitzgerald, Earl of Desmond and Kildare in the 16th century.

In Fitzgerald's time, much of Ireland was in upheaval with great and powerful families (some of whom were backed by the English government which was trying to consolidate its position in Ireland) competing for land and status. The chief conflicts in the southernmost areas of Ireland were between the Fitzgeralds, Earls of Desmond and Kildare, and the Butlers, Dukes of Ormond and North Tipperary. Much of the propaganda concerning various individuals in both families was spread by members of the other family (for instance, that they were involved in internecine murders, or that they practised witchcraft) and has become part of overall Irish folklore. It is very possible that Fitzgerald was an early scientist; but, in an age where old Celtic superstitions had not yet died out and where enemies such as the Butlers were prepared to use any whisper of suspicion, such a pursuit was an extremely dangerous one. The Church accused him, like Seaton, of consorting with fairies, and, worse, with demons from the Pit of Hell itself. This reputation has followed him down the years, providing the base of much of the folklore concerning him, and touches all sites which were connected with him, as the following account illustrates.

Even though history will tell you otherwise, it is well known that the great Gerald Fitzgerald, the Earl of Desmond, still lives with his entire household in his castle at the bottom of Lough Guir in County Limerick. It was not always this way, for, at one time long ago, the castle stood in all its grandeur on a tiny island in the middle of the lough. This island was joined to the mainland by a narrow causeway over which horses and carriages came and went. Indeed there was not so fair a place in the whole of Limerick than Earl Desmond's castle – a mighty keep with high turrets and battlements and pennants flying from its towers. There was not a magician in the whole of Ireland that was as powerful as Earl Desmond himself. It is still widely reported among the oldest people in the area that there was a tower – the highest in the castle – in which the earl conducted dark sciences and called up strange beings and spirits from lands far beyond this mortal sphere to do his bidding. It is also said that he had a mirror, given to him by a demon, in which he could observe events which were happening in places far away (in other parts of Ireland, in France and even in distant China) and in the lands under the seas and among the highest mountains; he had strange potions and salves which enabled him to fly through the air like a bird, to take on different shapes or to become invisible. There was no end to the things that he could do. He could call creatures from other worlds or ghosts from beyond the grave simply by his whim. There was no doubt in anyone's mind that he was a great and mighty sorcerer.

At last Earl Desmond got married, and he brought his new bride home to the castle in the lough. She was a beautiful girl, one of the most beautiful in Ireland, but she was cursed with an insatiable curiosity. She wished to know everything about her new husband, including his fascination for the dark sciences. Every day, she would prevail upon the earl to take her to his workroom, high in the sinister tower, so that she might see the wonders that he worked there. Each time, Earl Desmond gently put her off. 'Show me the fierce demons that you can call forth from beyond the mortal world,' she would beg, but he merely shook his head. 'I can summon a demon more ferocious than any in the Netherworld simply by striking you across the face!' he told her. 'Then let me talk with the ghosts of the dead!' she pleaded. Again, he shook his head. 'Each man talks with the dead every day,' he said, 'for we are all bound for the grave from the moment of our birth.' Then he changed the subject and would say no more. The girl became more and more impatient, for she was used to getting her own way, and the more he refused her the more determined she became to see his sorcerous workroom.

The interior of the castle, however, was a maze of twisting corridors and stairways which seemed to go on forever and to lead nowhere and, try as she might, the girl could not find the particular room that she sought. Many times, she tried to follow her husband, but soon lost sight of him and eventually found herself wandering in circles along interconnecting passageways, and peering into rooms which were manifestly empty and falling to rot. So she resorted to using all her feminine wiles on him, pleading with him, cajoling him, pestering him, all to see his secret magical workshop. At last, in exasperation, he gave in. 'I'll show you where I work and what I work upon, but it will only be upon one condition,' he told her. 'Name it,' she replied. 'That you make no sound,' he continued, 'no matter what you see.' His eyes narrowed menacingly. 'And you'll see horrors, I guarantee.' The girl swallowed, her heart nearly stopping within her, for she knew that this was no idle boast; but she had pestered her husband long and hard, so she agreed. 'Not a sound shall cross my lips, husband,' she assured him, and the earl seemed satisfied with the answer.

The next evening, Earl Desmond took his wife along a series of corridors that seemed somehow to double back upon themselves, and which were lit only by dripping candles. Here great mirrors, festooned with cobwebs, beguiled the senses, and false alcoves and doors betrayed the instincts. He led her up dark staircases which led to closed-up rooms with tightly fastened windows. Among these, at the farthest end of the castle, was the earl's workshop. It was a strange, old, high-vaulted room, set about with magical implements and great stoppered jars which seemed to bubble and hiss with mysterious contents. There were large casks, too, which appeared to contain the dust of human bodies, and glass bottles in which floated preserved anatomical parts, both human and animal. In a shadowy corner stood the great mirror in which visions of distant parts of the world came and went – now an endless desert, now a vast and violent sea. The whole place fairly seethed with ancient magic, and the girl was terribly frightened. She was very brave, however, and held her tongue. In the darkness of the chamber, bats fluttered and swooped, lightly brushing her cheeks with their passing, and eerie shadows flickered and mumbled in the far corners. The earl lit a candle which stood on a huge table in the very centre of the room, filling the place with a wan red light which made it appear even more inhospitable. Still the girl held her tongue and made no sound.

'Stand where you are!' commanded the earl, and he drew a chalk circle all around her. To this he added inexplicable glyphs and signs, so that, in the end, his wife stood in the middle of a curious pentagram. 'Now,' he said, 'as long as you stay where you are and make no sound, in spite of what you may see, nothing will harm you. But if you should move or utter even the smallest noise there will be dire consequences for us all. Not only for yourself but for me and mine as well. Do you understand?' The lady nodded, but made no spoken reply.

Turning away, the magician ignited a great brazier which stood nearby and threw some sort of herb upon it, making the flames start up and the shadows on the vaulted ceiling whirl and gambol in a madcap dance. Lifting a small phial from the table, the earl held it up to the light. 'Behold!' he cried, and drank its contents down. As he stood directly before his wife, his face seemed to contract, becoming lean and cavernous with a great hooked beak of a nose. Feathers sprouted from every part of his body and he took on the aspect of a huge and menacing vulture. A carrion smell filled the chamber as, on winnowing wings, the bird swept round and round the room, seemingly on the point of pouncing upon her with rending claws. Still the lady kept silent, although the perspiration was breaking upon her brow.

The bird alighted on the floor and immediately changed to a horrid, deformed, dwarfish hag with yellow, leprous skin and great bulging eyes, who shuffled towards the lady on a pair of wooden crutches. Mumbling to herself, she shambled around the outer edge of the pentagram, making frequent snatches at the girl with long and filthy talons. In the end, the hag roared at the terrified wife, stretching her open mouth impossibly wide and then began to roll on the ground in terrible convulsions, vomiting yellow and acidic bile. Still the lady kept quiet and made not the smallest sound, although she bit her lip so hard that the blood ran to the point of her chin.

Now the crone changed into a monstrous, scaled serpent which rippled around the outer edge of the circle, its tongue darting threateningly across the chalk. From time to time it reared up, towering above the girl and fixing her with its large, jewel-like eyes in a most menacing manner. Still the lady made no sound, even though she cowered away slightly from its awful threat. Suddenly, just as it appeared to dart at her, right across the chalk pentagram, it changed back into the form of her

husband. He looked extremely pale and, putting one finger on her lips, reminded her of her vow of silence. The lady nodded, though she had seen many evil things and her nerve was very close to breaking point. Still, she hoped that her test was finally over.

The earl laid himself on the floor of the chamber, just outside the outer rim of the chalk circle, and began to stretch. Longer and longer he grew, his face becoming more and more misshapen, until his vast head was almost touching one wall of the room and his heels reached the other. His arms and legs had stretched out of all recognition. An intense horror suddenly overcame the lady in the circle and, opening her mouth, she gave a very loud scream, which reverberated all through the castle. Outside, the sky darkened and lightning snapped crooked fingers between the massing clouds. A cold, fierce wind blew, and the waters of the lough heaved and rose in response. The tiny causeway, which ran between the castle and the shore, shattered and fell away as, in the blink of an eye, Earl Desmond's fortress crumbled away and sank beneath Lough Guir for ever. The instant that it was gone, the stormy clouds passed, leaving the lough as peaceful and untroubled as ever in brilliant sunshine. Neither the earl nor his wife was ever seen again.

Yet it is well known in the countryside round about that Earl Desmond continued to live under the lough and that, every seven years, at midnight on the anniversary of the sinking of his castle, both he and his retinue emerge from the deep and cross the waters in a shadowy cavalcade. At cockcrow, however, he is obliged to return to his underwater home for another seven years. He also has the power to take those whom he meets upon his travels back with him to the land below the lough, to live with him there for ever. This is a fact, for there are many accounts of people in the area having been unaccountably spirited away at a time when the earl was said to have been abroad.

As Earl Desmond had no descendants, his lands were given to the English who ruled over them as their own. By the late 1800s, the country around Lough Guir was in the hands of the Baily family and was the property of three old sisters, the eldest of whom was Miss Anne Baily. They were good people and their estate gave employment to many people who lived in the area. One of those who worked for them was a washerwoman named Moll Rail who cleaned their house and who washed Miss Anne's clothes for her. Now this was in the days long before washing machines, and in order to clean the clothes Moll had to take them down to the lough shore and beat them between two large stones, souse them in water and beat them again until they were thoroughly pounded and washed. It was backbreaking work and Moll Rail hated it. It was also a very lonely job, for she was out on the lough shore with nobody around her.

One morning, she was working away at the edge of the lough under the shadow of the Bailys' old house. It was between eight and nine in the morning and the sun was throwing strange shadows all across Lough Guir. A kind of gloomy fire lit everything, for it was not yet fully daylight. Looking up at the slope above her, Moll saw a grandly dressed gentleman walking down towards her. He had a great wig on his head and wore an old swallow-tailed coat, which was long out of fashion, with long knee-britches and buckled shoes that made no sound on the stones along the lake shore. He also wore a great red cravat around his neck, which seemed to make his face look very pale in the early light. However, Moll thought, he seemed extremely handsome and he had a good and stately bearing about him. She imagined that he might be some visiting gentleman – a guest of the Misses Baily – who had arrived the night before and about whom she knew nothing. He might, she fancied, be taking a stroll to enjoy the morning air before breakfast. As he drew closer, she noticed that he was smiling graciously, as though he recognized her, and was in the act of drawing a large golden ring from his finger. This was done with a kind of pleasant meaning as if he intended to give it to her as a present, for he raised it between his forefinger and thumb and placed it upon a large, flat stone beside her. She stepped back a little for she was unsure of his intentions, but he bowed low and spoke to her. 'You have earned your reward,' he said, in tones that were both soft and silky, 'so do not be afraid to take it.' He motioned to the ring, gleaming invitingly in the sunshine.

Moll was about to answer him, but she was a bit embarrassed to be standing in front of such a grand gentleman with her bare feet in the water and her skirts and petticoats hoisted up around her naked shins.

Shyly, she reached out for the ring but touched it awkwardly, making it fall into the water at her toes. Instantly, that lovely ring turned to a circle of blood which began to spread out across the waters of Lough Guir. Moll cried out, both in terror and alarm, using the Sacred Name, and when she lifted her eyes once more the courtly gentleman was gone. The blood ring, however, continued to spread out across the waters of the lough at the speed of light, and indeed the whole lake seemed to glow red, like a huge pool of blood. Nevertheless, this too was gone in an instant, and the lough was quiet and placid once again.

In later years, Moll Rail was certain that she had met with the Wizard Earl of Desmond in the first light of morning, and she often declared that, had it not been for the frightful transformation of the water, she might have spoken to him in the next minute and so would have fallen under his thrall. He might even have carried her away with him to his castle, far below the waters of Lough Guir. At least, in later years, that is what she thought might have happened, and there is no cause to doubt her for she was a very decent old woman. She had a lucky escape, sure enough.

Gerald Fitzgerald (also known as Gerald Oge or, more commonly 'The Great Earl') was betrayed and killed in 1581, believed to have been involved in a rebellious plot against the Elizabethan administration in Ireland. Many stories had already grown up around him, even in his own lifetime, most concerning darkest sorcery in which the earl was reputed to dabble frequently. He appears never to have bothered to deny these tales. There is no doubt, however, that he was interested in the sciences and that he may have been engaged in various experiments. The story concerning Moll Rail was so widely known in County Limerick that it surfaced in the general literature of the 19th century, notably in the works of the Irish writer, J. Sheridan Le Fanu, who knew Miss Anne Baily very well and who had stayed in the house at Lough Guir.

Even today the place still has a slightly sinister aspect to it, even on the sunniest of days when inexplicable clouds seem to mask an otherwise uninterrupted sun. Maybe the dark spirit of the Wizard Earl is lurking somewhere nearby.

# THE FAIRY WOMAN OF BODMIN

On the fringes of Celtic society there were those 'peripheral people' who were somehow apart from the general community. These were the odd, dreamy people who preferred their own company to that of their fellows and who 'kept themselves to themselves'. Some may even have been suffering from minor mental or personality disorders. Although few and far between in any community, they were still noticed and the Celts treated them with a mixture of fear and respect. There was a reason, it was argued, for the way they behaved – these were 'special persons' whose condition signalled that they were in contact with forces that were not readily available to others. They had been singled out by the gods or spirits as a channel between our own world and that mysterious Otherworld which lay just beyond normal perception. They heard voices which no one else heard and they sometimes glimpsed sights which were outside everyday human gaze. They had powers that were denied to others. They were 'touched' by forces beyond human comprehension.

The coming of Christianity made little difference, for these people were still regarded with a sense of awe and mystery. Now, however, certain Christian connections were made – they communed with angels, they spoke with saints (some of them were even considered to be saints themselves) – and their strange and eccentric behaviour was regarded as a sign of holiness. Some of them became hermits; some of these were associated with sacred places (many of which had formerly been Celtic sacred sites). Others were considered to possess a preternatural knowledge – healing, prophecy – which set them even further apart from conventional society. Stories about them passed into local legend, growing and becoming more fantastic with each retelling. Always, the tales involved their connections with the Otherworld, with unseen spirits or with the 'fairies'. Some of these individuals, their dreamy, anti-social ways sometimes compounded by physical deformities, were regarded as 'changelings' in certain communities. They were believed to be not altogether human, having been swapped when still children for spiritual or fairy beings. At the very least, they were in constant contact with the supernatural world, 'touched' by the mystical forces of the Otherworld, just as their Celtic forebears had been.

Until very recently, a curious set of human remains was on display at the famous Witchcraft Museum in Boscastle, north Cornwall. In earlier times, a skeleton hung in the front of a glass case and was marked as the last mortal remains of one Joan Wytt, the Fairy Woman of Bodmin Town, a person whose life is still somewhat shrouded in mystery. If indeed these few relics are all that are left of poor Joan, the skeleton would appear to be that of a very small woman, smaller than many women of the 18th century when Joan is supposed to have lived, its bones rather crudely linked together. Yet there is mystery surrounding these remains, just as there is mystery and superstition surrounding the life of Joan Wytt herself. Her story is incomplete, but certain facts are reasonably well known; the rest is simply folklore. What is known about her suggests that she was indeed one of those 'marginal people' around whom much legend was woven.

Joan Wytt was born in Bodmin, in around 1775, into a relatively poor household. Her family, as far as can be ascertained, worked as part of the so-called 'cottage industries' as weavers and twisters, employed by local businessmen at a low wage. They had a long tradition in the profession because the Bodmin town records show a John Wytt working as a weaver there as early as 1524. He seems to have been reasonably prosperous, but by the middle of the 18th century his descendants seem to have 'come down in the world' and were living in virtual penury. Food was probably short and so Joan (a common name in Bodmin at that time) was well below average weight and height, and grew up a small, stunted, sickly child. She probably had other deformities too, such as twisted or badly grown limbs. Such things were not uncommon for the period. Like the rest of her family, she went into the weaving business, twisting and winding the yarn. However, times were becoming increasingly bad for the weaving industry in the south of England and the Wytt family had to diversify.

They went into 'tawning' – making white leather – which was a more profitable trade as the weaving profession declined at the end of the 18th century. White leather was always in demand with both the London and rural gentry, and there was already an established and steady market in the commodity as Joan began her career in the trade. She was not a good worker, however. She was far too dreamy and distant in her ways. Her eyes were said to be frequently fixed on sights 'not of this world' and she often sat as though in a daydream, talking quietly to herself, or to others whom nobody else could see. Many of her neighbours said that there was something 'uncanny' about her.

Close to the back street where the Wytt family lived was a holy well, widely known as Scarlett's (or Scarlets) Well. Although it was widely regarded as 'holy', there is little doubt that this particular well had pagan connotations, stretching back into antiquity. Its waters were said to have curative properties, particularly for diseases of the stomach and for dropsy, but it might, if the time and conditions were right, also show the future. If lovelorn young maidens approached Scarlett's Well on Midsummer Night, left an offering and peered into its depths, they would see the face of their future husband looking back at them. Like some of the others in the leatherworking profession, Joan seemed to spend much of her time there. The well was what is known as a 'clootie well'. Those who sought healing from its waters would leave a piece of cloth (a 'clootie' or a 'jawn') tied to an ancient hawthorn tree which grew nearby and, as the cloth decayed, so the ailment was healed. At a time when none of the poorer classes had any access to formal medicine, such beliefs played an important part in their lives when illness struck (the waters of Scarlett's Well were later analysed by Sir Thomas Quiller-Couch, father of the famous writer 'Q', and were found to contain natural and health-giving fluorides and salts).

Perhaps Joan felt that, if she visited the well, leaving a 'clootie' behind, the spirits would heal her twisted limbs and make her grow tall. Maybe she even hoped that she might see a future spouse, just like the other girls. Scarlett's Well, though, also had a more sinister reputation – one which was more in keeping with its pagan past. It was said that, at certain times of the year, fairies and other unnatural beings gathered there to consider mischief against humankind and it was therefore a place to be avoided. Joan however, sat up by the well at all hours of the day, whispering, muttering and laughing to herself as if speaking to invisible people who clustered around her. Today, she would probably be regarded as a sad but harmless individual. However, in the 18th century, a more occult interpretation was often placed on her actions.

Her frequent visits to Scarlett's Well did not go unrecorded among her neighbours and, in the local mind, the pagan, prophetic nature of the waters was linked to her odd, dreamy, almost mystical nature, and she began to acquire a local reputation as something of a clairvoyant. Her long periods of 'idleness' were excused because she was deemed to be communing with a spirit world that only she could sense. Through these communications, it was said, she could predict certain future events, mostly of a local nature – a birth, a marriage, an illness, a coming death – and could sometimes also locate lost property. She was even said to be able to find stolen goods and name the thief. She was quickly becoming known as 'The Fairy Woman' – a woman who had contact with the fairy kind and who was able to persuade them to act on her behalf. Indeed, many thought that she was part fairy herself and that her physical abnormalities sprang out of the fact that she was a 'changeling' (a fairy left in place of a human child while the mortal infant was carried off into the fairy world). Undoubtedly her diminutive height and bearing added great weight to such a belief among those that knew her.

For much of her early life, Joan seemed to be a quiet and docile girl, more dreamy than forceful in her ways. When she turned 20, however, her temperament underwent a dramatic change. She became quarrelsome and ill-tempered, suspicious of her family and neighbours and ready to pick a fight with people whom she scarcely knew. Gone was the gentle, kindly girl of her earlier years and in her place was a ranting,

screaming harridan with malevolent ways and nature. Her 'clairvoyance' took on a dark and dangerous aspect, bordering on witchcraft, and it was said that, rather than speaking to the gentle spirits of the Otherworld during her 'dreamy' periods, she now conversed with demons and forces from the deeper, more ghastly planes. Rather than being an object of local affection and pity, she now began to be feared within her community. At times she would scream and shout to the empty air as though she were arguing with the Devil himself, and it was widely believed that she had been possessed by some sort of evil entity.

The truth was something far less dramatic and was certainly not supernatural. An examination of Joan's skull shows that she had developed an extremely serious case of tooth decay, which had made its way into her right wisdom tooth. Nowadays, we would visit a dentist to put the matter right, but in the 18th and early 19th centuries any form of dentistry was expensive and in extremely short supply. The wearing-down of the teeth on the left side of her mouth shows that Joan had learned to chew her food well away from the infected side, but gradually the decay began to form into a terrible abscess which poisoned her entire jaw and which must have been excruciatingly painful. Her small, frail body must have been racked with agony. Small wonder that her demeanour changed and she began to shout at her family and friends for the smallest reason.

Of course, in the early 1800s, no one suspected the true nature of Joan's affliction. In a gullible community, her odd behaviour was put down to supernatural causes – she had meddled in the affairs of the Otherworld for too long and it had rebounded on her. The stories concerning her began to take on a more sinister and menacing tone. Several neighbours claimed to have seen her in the lanes around Bodmin, shouting and screaming to herself in the most horrible manner and pulling herbs from the hedges, which she would, most probably, use in hideous potions. Others claimed that the air around her had been filled with dark and insubstantial shadows that weaved and flitted just outside of human eyesight. These were widely believed to be the evil fairies with which she now traded, and there was little doubt in the common mind that Joan Wytt was a witch. Joan herself did very little to counteract these rumours – it was true that she gathered herbs in the Bodmin lanes and it was also true that she brewed them into strange concoctions. Some of them may well have been in an attempt to relieve her own pain, but she also distilled them for other less healthy purposes – those associated with witchcraft.

In Cornwall, even in the 18th and early 19th centuries, the notion of witchcraft still had a grip on the popular mind, especially in primarily rural areas such as Bodmin. In such regions, the old spirit-based religion of the Celts had a strong hold and was difficult to shift. While most of the people were nominally Christian, many still clung to the tenets of the Old Faith which had existed in Cornwall, long before the Christians had come. The notion of wise-women, fairy women and witches was still foremost in many minds and the distinction between them was not always clear-cut. In her agony, Joan had crossed the line between being a simple country 'wise-woman' or a 'fey girl' and a dangerous witch. It was now whispered that she made obeisance to the Devil in remote areas, just beyond Bodmin Town, and that she called on his help against those whom she imagined to be her enemies. Others said that she had allowed a demon from the well to possess her and that there was no relief for her except the Office of Holy Exorcism.

If Joan had often visited Scarlett's Well in her early days, her pilgrimages to the place now became something of an obsession. For a time, she was to be found beside the well waters every day, attempting to rid herself of her terrible pain, but nothing worked. There was, however, one way in which she could relieve her agony – strong drink. As in other areas of the country, alcohol was readily available during the early 19th century – both homemade and smuggled. Woodcuts of the time show the wretched and poverty-stricken inhabitants of London, lying drunk in gutters outside the busy gin shops, and this sight was probably repeated in most major contemporary cities. In the more rural areas, especially, drink formed an integral part of daily life and was therefore easily obtained, particularly by the poor. In her agonized state, Joan took to alcohol with enthusiasm, spending part of her days drunk and the rest of her time quarrelling with her neighbours. The drink seemed to give her a hideous strength, well beyond her seemingly frail form, and her apparent fighting prowess only added to her supernatural reputation. Her nickname was amended to 'The Fighting Fairy Woman of Bodmin Town' in order to acknowledge her aggressive behaviour.

Joan was by now 'sailing close to the wind' as far as her public conduct was concerned. Even those who still consulted her for her predictions had come to fear her. For no apparent reason, she would suddenly fly into a rage and berate her client, and even show violence towards them, or go into terrifying trances during which she would shout at unseen entities or behave in a most alarming fashion. Sometimes she would reveal facts about her clients, shouting them out into the street through an open window or door – facts she would have no way of knowing and which the clients would far rather have kept out of public hearing. These attacks were probably brought about by a mixture of cheap alcohol and the poison that was coursing through her system from her diseased jaw. Her actions were now 'an accident waiting to happen' and soon spilled over into a public offence.

She cut herself a large, stout staff and hobbled around Bodmin Town, leaning upon it for support. At other times, she used it to great effect as a cudgel, especially when she got into a fight. One lamentable day, her ferocious temper spilled over and she became embroiled in an argument which ended in her belabouring a number of individuals with the staff and also, reportedly, lifting several of them (even though they were three or four times her weight and size), inflicting upon them such serious injuries that they were barely able to walk. Her behaviour was no doubt inflamed by the copious amounts of drink she is said to have taken before becoming embroiled in the dispute, but she is said to have beaten several of them within an inch of their lives. She was restrained and arrested and brought before the magistrates of Bodmin, where she was charged with grievous assault.

Her reputation preceded her, for by now she was both hated and feared by the majority of the townspeople, and the magistrates were well aware of her reputation and of her previous conduct and of the things which were said about her in the town. While a charge of witchcraft could not be brought, they had to give a decision which reflected the mood of the Bodmin people. Joan was found guilty of the assault but was also found to be 'of unsound mind' and therefore a public menace. Consequently, she was committed to Bodmin Gaol.

Conditions in most prisons of the time were neither comfortable nor hygienic, and in Bodmin they were frankly appalling. Prisoners were expected to pay for every little comfort which they were accorded, and those who could not pay were treated as little better than animals. Joan was kept in a stinking, draughty, cold, communal area along with several other prisoners whose wits had more or less gone. However, not being totally imbecilic, she was expected to work for whatever food she received and was made to labour each day on the prison treadmill. The effort of this and the conditions in which she was kept soon began to have an effect on her frail body, already weakened by pain and by excessive drinking. In all her time in prison, no attempt was made to examine her teeth or to treat the abscess, which was by now well advanced. The pain must have been almost unbearable. What food she was given consisted of a thin gruel and slops, all made to a consistency that was little thicker than water, in order to save any expense. Lack of proper nutrition only added to her condition. Owing to the fearsome reputation which she now enjoyed, the other prisoners gave her a wide berth, doubtless fearful of becoming victims of her alleged witchcraft. This probably suited Joan, who was by nature a solitary creature. Nevertheless, her argumentative disposition had not quietened and she was certainly involved in several fights and confrontations with her warders and with several figures of authority who came to see her in the gaol.

The dank conditions finally took their toll on her. In 1813, at the age of 38 (but reputedly looking much older), Joan finally succumbed to bronchial pneumonia. At the time of her death, her small body was little more than a withered husk. For well over a year, she had been living on a diet of stoneground flour and some water, made into a barely edible paste, her only comfort being a short clay pipe which she smoked ceaselessly. Her face had become thin and sharp with malnutrition, while her hands were now bird-like claws. Despite this undernourished appearance, rumours of her ferocious strength were widespread among the prison staff. In a newspaper interview regarding his job, the Bodmin governor, James Chappell stated: 'I admit that we have had a woman that we could not tame but never a man.' The woman to whom he referred was undoubtedly Joan Wytt.

After death, Joan's body was transferred to the prison mortuary where the surgeon, John Hamley, was fascinated by her reputation as a witch. Out of curiosity, he took a plaster cast of her head, which he then placed in the gaol's collection of death masks. Normally it was only the death masks of executed felons who were placed in such a grim museum, but Joan's reputation was such that Hamley deemed it appropriate that she should also be placed there. However, that reputation was already spreading further outside Bodmin and drew the attention of the Cornish-born anatomist, William Clift.

Clift himself had actually been born in Bodmin in the same year as Joan. His parents had lived at Berrycombe Hill, not far from the town, and shortly after William's birth his father, a miller, had suddenly died. Through the generosity of some wealthy friends, the Gilberts, he had obtained a good education and a position as an anatomical artist. One of the Gilberts' friends was the famous anatomical scientist, John Hunter, whose speciality was physical curiosities and deformities. (Hunter had long sought – and finally acquired – the skeleton of the famous Irish giant, Charles O'Brien.) Hunter was exceptionally famous for his large collection of anatomical specimens, which is now the Hunterian Museum at the Royal College of Surgeons in London. William Clift was promptly sent to London as an apprentice to Hunter and to oversee the fledgling Museum of physical oddities, and, on Hunter's death, he became its curator. On a visit home to Bodmin in 1813 (the year of the Fairy Woman's death), and while recovering from a minor nervous breakdown, Clift made the acquaintance of John Hamley, the surgeon at the gaol, and heard the tale of Joan Wytt and her phenomenal strength. He had already heard tales of the Fairy Woman but, unlike the local people of the area, he did not attribute her unnatural prowess to supernatural forces. He viewed the death mask which Hamley had made and then suggested that the body (which still lay intact in the prison mortuary) be sent to London where it could be dissected and properly studied.

Joan's corpse, however, never made it to the capital. Fired by Clift's enthusiasm and believing that Joan might be a medical phenomenon, Hamley kept the body himself and performed a rather crude dissection on it. If he learned anything from it, the records of his researches have been lost. The skeleton, when the experiments were finished, was unceremoniously dumped in a medical storeroom within the prison where it lay, forgotten, for a number of years. A new prison governor would add another curious strand to the history of Joan Wytt.

William Hicks, the new governor of Bodmin prison, was himself something of an eccentric character. A rotund and jocular man, he was well known as a wit and raconteur, and was even better known for his outrageous practical jokes. Hicks also had an unbounded interest in local history and particularly in bizarre and unusual aspects of it. He was greatly taken with the story of Joan Wytt, with tales of her independence and peculiar strength, and moreover with the legends of her alleged witchcraft that were still being recounted long after her death. Many people claimed to have seen her ghost along lonely lanes around Bodmin, always surrounded by dark and writhing shadows, which were taken to be the evil sprites to which she had allied herself. Hicks was fascinated by the notion that Joan's ghost might haunt the area and perhaps even the prison itself, where she had been incarcerated for so long.

One evening, the governor held a dinner party within the prison confines for a number of friends. After dinner, Hicks asked his guests to repair to an adjacent room where he had 'a little surprise' for them all. Dutifully, they trooped into a gloomy side-chamber in which something that looked like a coffin had been placed against a far wall. Eerily, Hicks told them that what they were faced with were the last remains of the Fairy Woman of Bodmin, which had been retrieved from the prison storehouse on his orders. Because Joan had been famed throughout Bodmin as a seeress, the governor planned to conduct a séance that would reveal the futures of many of his guests. Joan herself would act as a medium with the spirit world, and all questions would be answered by raps from inside the Fairy Woman's coffin. Hicks then produced the most grisly aspects of his 'experiment' – three bones which allegedly were taken from the poor woman's skeleton itself. One bone was placed on top of the coffin and the other two were handed to a couple of the guests. Through these bones, Joan would communicate – one would receive the 'yes's'; the other would receive the 'no's'. It would all be capital fun, he assured them.

The governor, however, had not placed all his faith in the spirit world. Off stage, he had an accomplice ready to play Joan's part by providing the requisite raps. The séance began. Hardly had the first question been asked when the lid of the coffin flew open with a roar of wind and the bones were torn out of the guest's hands. They swirled about the room with a terrible violence, sharply striking both Hicks and several of his friends. In fact, they began to rain blows on the head and shoulders of a number of the participants, just as Joan herself would have wielded her cudgel or stick when alive. Needless to say, the party broke up in terror and confusion and the uncanny whirlwind died down again.

Badly shaken, Hicks returned the bones to the prison storeroom where they remained until 1922, when a section of the prison was closed and they were removed to yet another repository within its walls. In 1927, however, Bodmin prison was completely shut and the skeleton was removed and given to a practising doctor living in north Cornwall. It was through his offices that Joan's remains came into the possession of the Witchcraft Museum at Boscastle. Here, at last in 1998, she was given a decent burial by the museum's owners and curators, Graham King and Liz Crow, her funeral paid for by the Friends of the Museum. Perhaps now she is finally at peace.

In both life and death, poor Joan Wytt was subjected to ignominy. The dreamy, lonely child was treated as 'fay' (of the fairies) and was regarded with suspicion and wonder by those around her. She was widely believed (even beyond Bodmin) to be a 'medium' through which the creatures of the Otherworld could communicate with the inhabitants of this one, and, in doing so, give warnings and reveal futures to those who would listen. In this youthful aspect of her life (which was perhaps her happiest), Joan was treated both as an oddity and an oracle. She was considered acceptable enough to consult about predictions of the future but not acceptable enough to befriend. In fact, it is highly probable that, even at this early stage, she was widely feared. This fear turned to terror as the affliction of her poisoned jaw took hold, turning her into a screaming and malignant harridan, as she is best remembered. In a community which was only slowly entering the Age of Enlightenment, her behaviour laid her open to charges of witchcraft and devilry. Many of her former clients forsook her, believing her to be dealing directly with the Evil One, or at least some dark fairy that had taken over Joan's frail body. The idea of witchcraft, of course, fitted well with Joan's adversarial temperament towards her neighbours.

There is also the question of her alleged supernatural strength. Accounts of this may well have been greatly exaggerated over the years and with each successive story. Her reputed prowess, however, may have also owed something to the intense and constant pain which she experienced as a result of her abscess.

In death she remained a figure of wonder and, in some cases, fun. While no longer considered to be a witch in the formal sense, she became a 'bogy creature' which still had the power to terrorize the Bodmin community, something which is not quite a ghost but is not quite human either. In this sense, Joan Wytt serves as an exemplar of the ancient power of the Otherworld reaching out to the present day. In fact the only way in which such an idea can be handled is through ridicule and ignominy. Yet, through the medium of folk and ghost tale, such power is preserved in all its intensity.

It is said that, even in death, Joan's powers were in no way diminished. Graham King, the curator of the Witchcraft Museum, points to persistent poltergeist activity within the building during the time that her bones were on display there. The medium, Cassandra Latham, the Witch of Buryan, was called in to see if the disturbed spirit could be contacted, and it was largely through her efforts that Joan's meagre remains were finally laid to rest. Yet many still state that her influence may linger on, for there are tales that her ghost may yet be seen in the gloomy country lanes around Bodmin. Perhaps the primal powers of the Otherworld have not quite dispersed and the Fairy Woman of Bodmin can still stretch across the years, even to the present day.

# THE DEMON IN THE CHURCH

In Celtic mythology and folklore, the line between priest and wizard has always been a thin one. The earliest form of Celtic holy men were the druids who may well have evolved out of the shamanistic figures who guided the worship of prehistoric societies and who performed various 'magics' on behalf of their peoples. The druids combined both the functions of religious leader and sorcerer – they determined appropriate times of sacrifice to the gods and also performed 'miracles' among their followers. The name 'druid' has been argued as deriving from the ancient Greek drus meaning 'oak', thus making them 'the men of the oak tree', and there is reputedly a strong connection between the druids and that tree. However, the eminent Irish folklorist, Dr Daithi O hOgain, in *An Encyclopaedia of The Irish Folk Tradition* (1990), points out that: 'The favourite tree of the Druids, however, was clearly the rowan and it was on the wattles of this tree that Irish practitioners slept in order to have prophetic visions. The hazel tree was also important as is evidenced by the Druidic name Mac Cuill, Son of the Hazel, and also by the lore concerning nine hazel trees at the source of the River Boyne, the nuts of which had a nucleus of wisdom.' Whatever the source of their name, it is clear that the druids exercised an important role in Celtic society in their functions both as sorcerers and religious leaders.

This dichotomy was carried on into the early days of the Celtic Christian Church. The arrival of Christianity only modified the powers of the druids, placing them within a more formal, devotional context.

Indeed, there is some evidence that some druids actually became early 'saints' within the Christian Church. This was sneeringly accentuated by the Roman Church who frequently accused its Celtic counterpart as simply being 'paganism by the back door'. There is no doubt, either, that many of these 'saints' did transfer their mystical powers from a pagan setting to a Christian one – while the Roman Church elevated the notions of teaching and dogma, the Celtic Church placed great emphasis on mysticism and miracles. The staff, made of rowan, which had come to symbolize druidical authority, now became the 'bachall' or 'rod' symbolizing the power of a Christian abbot (and later of a bishop, in the form of a crozier). Bishops and priests frequently boasted great supernatural powers within a community and were often the last defence against the Devil who ranged everywhere in the world, seeking out the souls of the innocent and the spiritually vulnerable. The Catholic Church, which had invested a great deal of power in its priests, had little trouble with such a concept. The belief also gave something of a sense of religious continuity, stretching back into the distant, pre-Christian past.

The Protestant church, however, found itself in something of a conflict. While it could not really deny the existence of evil spirits and the imminence of the Devil (since those were the foundations upon which it too based its authority), it did not afford its ministers the same supernatural powers as did its Catholic counterpart. Nevertheless, there seems little doubt that Protestant ministers, especially some Anglican ones, did exercise mystical powers and supernatural elements connected with their office. Powers such as the banishment of dark spirits, the laying of ghosts and foretelling the future all seem to have been the province of at least some of their number. Invariably tales of such mystical feats passed into the folklore of the area in which such ministers served.

Perhaps one of the most famous 'mystical clerics' was to be found in Cornwall. The Reverend Polkinghorn – an Anglican minister claimed by many Cornish parishes – is celebrated as 'facing down' the Devil himself with a huge rawhide whip. He is also said to have been the only man of God to have ridden across Dartmoor in the Devil's coach. In Highland Scotland, too, in the late 18th and early 19th centuries, the Reverend John Morrison was known throughout the parish of Petty, near Inverness, as the 'Petty Seer' and was credited as being able to foretell the deaths of his parishioners as well as forecasting national events. Clearly the religious calling of these men did not affect their mystical powers.

It was much the same in Wales where ministers of the cloth were often credited with miraculous feats which not only enhanced their own personal reputation but also provided an affirmation of their individual calling. Rather than receiving their powers from pagan deities, these men were blessed with special powers by God Himself. They had scripturally based abilities to cast out demons and sometimes to heal the sick. They waged a war against the forces of darkness, sometimes within the precincts of their own churches, as the following story demonstrates. The story is credited to a certain Mr Roberts of Llanfor, who heard it from his grandmother who was born in 1744.

From ancient times there was a spirit which had troubled the church at Llanfor. It was said that the holy place had been originally built upon a pagan burying-ground and that the spirit had risen from one of the ancient graves to make its abode within the church. The demon appeared in the likeness of a gentleman, very well dressed. It wore a long, old-fashioned dress coat of a plum colour, with dark knee-britches and white hose, and strange old shoes with curious buckles. In addition, it wore a great white wig on the top of which was an old, black, three-cornered hat. Moreover, it carried a heavy-looking cane with an ornamented top. The face of the spirit was indistinct, but seemed very long and afflicted with great weariness. It haunted the gallery in the upper part of the church, even during the hours of daylight, and was often seen during the morning services. When the minister entered the church to commence the service, it stood up, doffed its hat and made a courtly bow, then seemed to settle itself. However, when the service commenced, it would stand up again and shake its stick as if in anger. It also seemed to be speaking and uttering blasphemies within the house of God, although nobody could hear a word that it said.

Sometimes it appeared at night. When it did so, it moved in a glow of pale, rose-coloured light which lit up the entire gallery and was most disconcerting. Furthermore, when it moved, the staves between the railings of the gallery whirled about like so many spindles, although when checked they were always fast in their sockets. Although it appeared frequently, it was not reported as harming anyone, nor did it do any damage in the church. Even so, it caused great terror among the congregation, who were sure that it was some agent of the Devil or perhaps even the Evil One himself. In any case, it managed to put the minister off his sermon on several occasions.

Others saw the being walking along with its cane in hand, like a gentleman taking his ease, at the top of Moel-y-llan, a nearby hill. This caused further terror in the district and few would venture into Llanfor church alone. In fact, the church vestry, which usually met in the evening, had to adjourn to a certain nearby public house in order to conduct its business, so terrified of the spirit were its members. Nobody would go down to the church to collect the parish books. Seeing their terror, the landlady of the hostelry (a formidable woman) declared that she would go down to the place and collect the books. Taking a candle with her, she set off. No sooner had she crossed the church threshold, however, than the Evil Spirit blew the light out and left her in darkness. She relit the candle but the spirit blew it out once more, and the gloom about her seemed even more profound. Despite her growing terror, she went straight to the church coffer in the dark and brought the books down to her own house without any further molestation.

After this, however, the spirit became more unruly and troublesome. It began to make strange noises during sermons – sounds like the severe breaking of wind – and caused a number of things to fall and break within the church. As soon as the day ended and the light faded, peals of demonic laughter issued from the building – sounds so frightening that they seemed to issue from the Pit of Hell itself. Nobody in the surrounding countryside would even go past the place as soon as darkness had fallen. This could not go on, and in desperation the people of the area, together with their minister, turned to two professional gentlemen – Mr Evans and Mr Pugh (who was a minister and man of the cloth) – who were well skilled in the arts of divination and spirit-chasing to rid the being from their church. The two men agreed and said that they would drive the spirit into Llyn-y-Guelan-Goch, a certain very deep pool that was not far away. They entered the church and, keeping everyone else outside the building, apparently began to converse with the spirit. During the course of their conversation, the being became incredibly noisy, hurling things back and forth, and issuing sulphurous smells and hellish laughter, so that those around the building drew back even further. Eventually, both men came out, rather pale-looking but confident that they could remove the spirit. They announced that they would return at a certain hour that night and lay it to rest in the pool beyond. They were not, however, punctual, and arrived several hours after the appointed time to find the spirit extremely intractable and refusing to be moved. With many exorcisms and strange words, and with bells and Bibles, they at last managed to extricate it in the form of a black cockerel, which Mr Pugh carried to a nearby horse and set out for Llyn-y-Guelan-Goch.

Although the distance was only the width of two fields, the journey appears to have been a difficult one. The cockerel screamed with a human voice, uttering oaths and obscenities as it went, and Mr Pugh was pummelled about the head and upper body by unseen fists. It is said that the horse made the distance from the church to the pool in all of two leaps. On their arrival there, a fearful struggle ensued, for the fiend refused to succumb and tried to drag its captor into the water with it. More and more people gathered around the pool and many were beaten by invisible fists and badly kicked by unseen feet. Eventually, the spirit agreed that it would go into the water on condition that everyone would lie face down on the ground and would not look at it as it entered the pool. This was agreed, and the being apparently leapt into the water with a loud splash. Tradition further states that the horse which carried the demon to the pool left its hoofprint on a rock near its edge, although the informant, Mr Roberts, stated that he had looked for this stone but had not been able to find it.

The spirit only stayed in Llyn-y-Guelan-Goch for a little while and was soon back around the church, this time in the form of a black pig. Some legends said that it was imprisoned in the pool only until it was able to count the grains of sand which lay on the bottom – a task it seems to have accomplished in a surprisingly short time. The pig came snuffling around the church, and when hymns were begun commenced to squeal in a loud and most distressing manner. One night, a gentleman and his brother, driving past the church on a wagon, were pursued by the pig, which chased them as far as Llyn-y-Guelan-Goch and then disappeared into the water. This led to some dispute as to the spirit still being in the pool, and Mr Pugh was brought back to Llanfor to see if the being could be laid to rest again (in other versions of the tale, the name of a local wise man is given as the exorcist). He threw a large stone into the pool and, as it seemed to have no effect, solemnly pronounced that the spirit was no longer there. Local people, however, did not believe him and threw an even larger stone into the pool, which bubbled and foamed as though in great anger. At this, Mr Pugh immediately changed his story. 'Yes,' he announced. 'He is there and there he will remain for a long time.' Despite the clergyman's fine words, the spirit was not done with Llanfor village.

Although Mr Roberts' story ends here, it is taken up by an old woman named Ann Hughes, who lived in a little cottage by the roadside close to Llanfor Rectory. She states that the evil spirit was heard every night along a pathway leading between the church and Rhiwlas, making sounds like someone dragging chains or wheeling a wheelbarrow. These sounds went straight to the church where the spirit seemed to stay all night, making sounds as though engaged in manual labour. The noise was so great that nobody in the houses around could get a wink of sleep, and were kept from their beds by noises like someone digging or trundling heavy objects back and forth. There was a pathway, leading to several houses which stood close to the church yard, on its north side and the people who lived there were terrified to go out in the evening for fear that they would run into the spirit. In fact the whole village avoided this and every other path in the neighbourhood of the church as soon as the sun began to set. The spirit now appeared in its former guise as a gentleman in a plum-coloured coat, walking about the graveyard in the twilight and shaking its stick at all those who passed by. At last the disturbances became so great that the parson and another man (Mr

Pugh?) were determined to lay the malevolent spirit once more.

Following an ancient pre-Christian custom, they walked three times anti-clockwise around the church before going into it. Emerging once more from the building, they went straight across and into the public house which stood nearby, walking straight into the little parlour at the back of the inn. Both the parson and Mr Pugh had given strict instructions that nobody was to approach them, speak to them or even try to see them as they went, and so the area around the church had been well cleared of people, as had the inn. However, there was a man in the house who was determined to see what was going on, and he squinted through the keyhole. He distinctly saw three men sitting at the table in the parlour – the parson, Mr Pugh and another whose face he could not make out but who wore a reddish coat in a style long out of fashion. This worthy sat with his back to him, but turned his head frequently from side to side as though talking to the other two. No sooner had he done so, however, than the parson came out and said that if anyone looked through the keyhole again the plans under discussion would be frustrated. Notwithstanding, the man was determined to see if it was indeed the spirit, and he looked again when the parson had gone back into the room, but saw nothing. As he did so, the spirit struck him in the right eye, leaving him blind in it ever after. Eventually some agreement was reached between them all and the spirit departed from the church grounds. Ann Hughes could not tell what agreement had been reached, but it involved the spirit returning to Llyn-y-Guelan-Goch and remaining there until a lighted candle, hidden somewhere within Llanfor church, should go out of its own accord. Often Ann Hughes had searched for this miraculous taper but had been quite unable to find it. Presumably the light is still burning somewhere within the church precincts and the spirit is still confined to the pool.

However, there are further stories concerning the strange demon at Llanfor, though whether these are much later additions to the original story is open to question.

A terrible spirit had taken possession of the old church at Llanfor and had ejected most of the congregation, preventing them from completing their worship by use of fearful noises, horrid visions and abominable smells. Members of the congregation therefore decided to get rid of the spirit and consulted with a certain local wise man, a retired cleric, for that purpose. After much thought and prayer, he advised them to procure a white mare which they did. A man riding upon this mare then entered the church with his friend in an attempt to exorcize the spirit. This particular man had prayed and fasted for three days and had abstained from worldly pleasures in order to prepare himself for the undertaking. Absolute silence had to be observed throughout the whole proceedings. Before too long, the man emerged from the place, still seated on the horse, but with the demon seated behind him like a passenger and in the guise of a pig. An old woman who saw them pointed and cried out, very loudly, 'Duw anwyl! Mochyn yn yr Eglwys!' ('Good God! A pig in the church!'). Upon hearing this, the pig became exceptionally fierce as the silence had been broken and because the Holy Name had been used; it grew to a monstrous size and seized both the horse and its rider and threw both of them right over the church to the other side. It is said that an old gravestone in the churchyard bears the mark of a horse's hoof and this shows where the mare was thrown. The spirit's anger was all in vain, however, because a local parson, with prayers and exorcisms, drove it before him to the pool at Llyn-y-Guelan-Goch on the River Dee, eventually casting it into the water there. However, the effort was so great for the holy man that he lost most of his hair and was not able to sleep in the same bed for two consecutive nights for the rest of his life.

Llanfor was not the only Welsh church to be troubled in such a fashion. An old church at Llandysilio in Montgomeryshire was similarly infested. Here the spirit was said to have had the most disconcerting habit of announcing the name of the next person to die in the district while a service was in progress. Its disembodied voice could plainly be heard over the minister's sermon or the singing of any hymn, and it always seemed to make sure that the person concerned (or their relatives) were actually present as it called, much to everyone's alarm and distress. The journal Bygones (1886) relates a curious tale concerning this particular spirit which contains echoes of the events in Llanfor (the writer of the piece uses the fictitious name of Gypt).

The church was troubled by a spirit of the most fractious kind. Things had come to such an extreme that the local people resolved to send for an expert in such matters, who was said to be a former clergyman. The person involved came and went into the church in front of inhabitants of the whole district, telling all those that had gathered to make no sound until he came out again. This they did, and the ghost-layer came out several times for air and beer. His arms were bare and a sheen of perspiration covered his forehead as if he were exerting himself in a mighty struggle and there was a conflict of epic proportions going on within the church. His efforts proved successful, for eventually he emerged carrying a bottle in which was something that looked like a large fly. The thing, which was bigger than any normal housefly, appeared to be very fierce and threw itself repeatedly against the glass in an effort to escape. The bottle was taken to the River Verniew, where it was thrown into a deep pool, and it is said to remain there to this day. Gypt adds that as proof of the story he, personally, was taken to Llandysilio church and was shown a number of cracks and splinters in the wooden beams there which were damaged during the struggle with the demon and from the time when it troubled the church. It was thought that the demon was a very ancient being which had inhabited the spot since pagan times, before the church had been built.

The exact location of another Welsh church which was troubled by an evil spirit, and the name of the minister who ejected it, are now both lost to history, but there are some clues in an old folktale. The church, apparently, is referred to as Ffinant Trefglwys, and it stood by the site of a road which had reputedly been the site of a pagan enclosure. Close by was an old and almost derelict barn. This spot was frequently and almost completely filled with crows, giving it the name Crow-barn, a name which it held for many years. The discordant cawing of these birds often interrupted the sermons and hymn-singing which went on during the church service. It was widely thought that the crows were in fact evil spirits, and that they were under the control of some sinister person who wanted to disrupt the worship of God.

Suspicion fell on an old man who lived locally in a tumbledown house not far from the church and the barn. He had been a servant to one of the farmers in the area, but had to be dismissed because of his dark ways and dubious reputation. It was said that he had sold his soul to the Devil in return for unearthly powers, on the understanding that he would do all that he could to harm God's people. His name was Daffyd Hirradug, and at the time he was quite an elderly man. Nevertheless he could perform feats of stamina and strength which would have defeated many younger men. At night, strange music was heard coming from his hut – the sound of whistles, fiddles and drums – even though old Daffyd was there on his own. Many local people were afraid to pass the place after night began to fall, and there were stories of weird lights around his back door in the late evening. It was said that he had been seen down by the Crow-barn, that he sometimes spoke to the birds and that they answered him in a strange croaking tongue. The following Sabbath, they would make the loudest racket they could, drowning out the words of the minister as he spoke.

At last the local people could stand it no longer and, led by their preacher, went to confront the old man in his hut. Daffyd Hirradug came out and told them to go home, swearing at them and using foul oaths to which the man of God (who was with them) shut his ears. However, the mob who had gathered on the road began to abuse the old man and to pelt him with stones, driving him back indoors. They then threatened to set fire to his hut unless he came out and admitted his guilt. The minister assured him that if he did come out he would not be harmed. This the old man did, stating that he was indeed a servant of the Devil and that, on the orders of his Infernal Master, he had caused the crows in the barn to make an awful din while the holy service was in progress. On this admission, the minister surged forward, overwhelming the old man and driving him to the ground. As he lay there, the mob punched and kicked him. By the time they had finished, Daffyd Hirradug was dead.

The old man's last request was a curious one. He had left instructions that his liver and lights were to be taken out and thrown on the local dunghill, and that particular notice should be taken as to whether a raven or a dove swooped down to take possession of them. If it was a raven, then his body was to be taken from the foot of the bed rather than the side, and through the wall rather than the door. If it was a dove, then he was in the arms of the Lord. This strange request was carried out by whatever relatives the old man had and a watch was kept on the dunghill. Late in the evening, a great crow swooped down and carried the remains back to the Crow-barn. The second part of Daffyd's request was not carried out since no minister could be found to officiate at the burial. On the instructions of the preacher, he was buried not in the churchyard but under the church walls, outside the burying-ground. A piece of doggerel began to circulate in the countryside:

Daffyd Hirradug, badly bred,
False when living, false when dead.

Shortly after the old man's death, a great crow settled in the rafters of the church and began to interrupt the sermons with its loud cawing. From time to time, it flew down and settled on the hats and bonnets of the congregation, creating much confusion and alarm among them. No one doubted for a moment that this was the unquiet spirit of Daffyd Hirradug, come to take revenge upon those that had killed him, and everyone was frightened to approach the creature.

The bird became so troublesome – perching up in the rafters and fouling the seats beneath with its droppings (which were greater than that of any ordinary bird), cawing at inappropriate junctures in the worship and sailing around the interior of the church on dark wings, swooping at certain members of the congregation in a most threatening manner – that in the end no proper service could be held inside the place. The minister decided that he would have to go in and wrestle with the terrible spirit and drive it out. He prayed and sang holy psalms for seven days and seven nights before embarking upon the undertaking, and then went up to the church. As he approached the building, he saw that the air around it was black and thick with crows, all rising out of the Crow-barn as if in defence of the unclean spirit within. Reciting more prayers, the preacher went forward, and although several of the dark

crows plunged menacingly towards him none of them touched him. At last he reached the door of the church and went inside. The great crow was perched upon the end of a pew and seemed to be waiting for him, its bright eyes twinkling with evil intelligence. Walking timorously towards it, the minister mumbled further prayers, calling on the Divine Name for help, whereupon the bird rose up and flapped above him, well out of his reach. Its wings seemed to grow longer and longer, until they covered much of the church ceiling.

'Spirit of Daffyd Hirradug! I charge you to return to your grave beyond the church wall and to trouble God's children no further! I do so in the name of Jesus, the Risen Christ!' cried the holy man. At this, the spirit turned into a frightening shape, which was somewhere between a raven and a great pig, and sought to tear at him with a huge and powerful hooked beak. Its screaming filled the church. 'In the Name of Christ, return to the grave!' commanded the minister, but the being took little heed of his words. It wheeled and darted above him and threatened him as he shrank back from its talons. At last he fled from the church, leaving the demon in sole occupation.

After some consultation with an 'expert' in exorcism, however, he returned to the possessed building. This time he brought with him two long-horned oxen, which had been specially blessed for the purpose. These beasts were large and strong and he took them with him directly into the church. When it saw what it was up against, the demon shouted at them in ancient Welsh, fierce oaths and blasphemies which made the man of God blush. Nevertheless, he advanced on the nightmare creature, uttering prayers and singing hymns as he did so. The struggle in the church was certainly a titanic one, and the preacher emerged drenched in sweat. The oxen roared and trampled about inside and their noises were matched by that of the demonic beast itself. The preacher re-entered the church, this time carrying a long piece of extremely stout rope with which he once more confronted the demon.

'Unclean spirit of Daffyd Hirradug!' he proclaimed. 'Submit to me in the Name of the Risen Jesus Christ! This I command you in God's name.' In response to his command, a flock of rooks rose from the Crow-barn and proceeded to wheel around the church, making a most distressing noise. This did not deter the minister in the pursuance of his task. Once more he struggled with the demon, and this time he was victorious. He emerged from the ancient place with the demon, now completely in the shape of a great pig, being pulled by the oxen and secured by the strong rope. The oxen made their way to a nearby lake with the intention of confining the dark spirit beneath the waters. However, everyone was afraid to untie the demon to throw it in, and so the animals were driven into the lake itself, still pulling the spirit fastened by the rope, and both of them were drowned. The violent spirit of Daffyd Hirradug could not now get out of the lake, and is said to remain there until this day. It is said that it is still attempting to extricate itself from its underwater prison and that, consequently, people still tend to avoid the lake, which has a sinister reputation. No location is given for this mysterious stretch of water.

After the spirit had been removed from the church, the birds in the Crow-barn became more restive and began to make more and more noise. Once again they interrupted the services within the church, and it was thought that the ghost of Daffyd Hirradug was somehow exercising a control over them, even from his prison in the lake. It was decided to exorcize the old barn as well. After consulting with the 'expert' in exorcisms once again, the minister took a large iron cross and went up to the dilapidated structure. The crows rose up from it in a black swarm, filling the air with their raucous noise. The minister went up to the door of the falling barn and, pushing it a little way open, threw the cross inside.

'In the Name of God, be gone!' he cried in a loud voice. There was a sound somewhere nearby like a clap of thunder, and the crows exploded from the collapsing building and up into the air. The minister prayed loudly as the foul birds dived all around him, and then suddenly he was alone in the field. The birds were gone! Never more did they trouble the area, and the church remained tranquil ever after. After much research, it was found that the holy house, together with the Crow-barn, had actually been built on the site of a pagan graveyard – probably of Celtic origin – and that the unquiet spirits which manifested themselves in the form of crows probably had their origins in this. On the orders of the minister, after consultation with several 'experts', the

Crow-barn was completely pulled down so that no trace of it remained.

Throughout Wales (and other parts of the Celtic world besides) ancient churches often became the focus of eerie and unsavoury powers, and it was left to local ministers or 'experts' in exorcism to drive them out. Gradually, such beliefs died out, but it is still a brave person who will venture into derelict churches or long-abandoned graveyards even today. Perhaps a vestige of this ancient Celtic belief still lingers on, somewhere in the deepest recesses of all our minds.

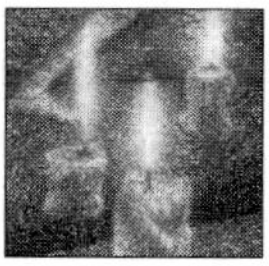

# WITCHFINDER

The ancient world of the Celts was one of checks and balances. For every evil, it was believed, there was a counter to be found somewhere in the world: for every sickness there was a naturally occurring cure; for every curse there was a blessing which would remove it; for every malignant force there was a protective presence. Wise-women throughout the Celtic countryside sought out herbs and growths to create the potions which would ward away the fevers which often gripped communities; local 'seers' searched their 'divining glasses' for lost or stolen objects; various protections were placed around the beds of the very young or very sick to keep away malign and unwelcome fairy influence. It was as well to raise one's hat or to curtsy to a stone in the neighbourhood to ensure that one would not fall victim to evil spirits and be haunted by unquiet ghosts. Thus while, say, the clothes of a promiscuous woman could draw phantoms and goblins to a house, the blood of a black cockerel sprinkled at the four corners of the building would certainly repel them. It was the ancient law of measure and counter measure.

This premise continued into the human world as well. For every evil that entered the world, someone was born who could stand against it. For every dark power that existed, there was somebody with equal powers to repel it. Sometimes those who possessed such powers were unaware that they had them until a supernatural evil threatened; others were aware of them from birth.

A tradition of 'white witches', 'spae-women' and 'cunning men' (also known as conjurers or conjuring men) existed across the Celtic world. These were people who had the power to lift curses, to negate spells and to offer advice to a community on occult matters. Normally, they appeared as ordinary members of the local society, although many had an 'uncanny' air about them. Their knowledge of the supernatural, however, was extensive: they were well versed not only in herbs and potions but also in the charms and incantations which could drive away fairies and demons. These were the people who were consulted when other community members felt they had been 'bewitched' in some way – when butter would not churn, when inexplicable misfortune continually befell them, or when children were strangely weak and sickly.

In some cases, too, these people also dealt with ghosts. In County Derry, in the North of Ireland, for example, a man named Joseph Black was called to deal with a phantom (curiously known in the locality as 'Stilty') who pelted passers-by with stones on a lonely mountain road. Several travellers had been extremely badly hurt by its activities. Black went to the spot and spoke to the apparition; he found it to be the ghost of a suicide who had killed himself in that very location many years before. This act had been long forgotten in the locality, but the unquiet spirit still remained to plague those who travelled on that particular stretch of road. Joseph Black confronted the spirit and spoke to it, discovering what had caused its suicide so many years before, although he never disclosed what it revealed to him. Whatever passed between them seemed to placate the ghost, as it never bothered travellers again. Joseph Black was later consulted by many other people to exorcize ghosts and restless spirits from other sites and buildings, which he did with great efficiency. In some versions of the stories about him, he is portrayed as a defrocked priest or clergyman, in other variants he is simply a 'working man' who happened to live in a locality which appears to have been plagued by ghosts.

Similar stories are told about Moll Anthony, who dwelt at the Hill of Grange in County Kildare. Not only was she alleged to be able to foretell the future and to cure many diseases in both humans and animals, but she could also drive away both fairies and ghosts with her occult powers. Such powers over the supernatural world were also attributed to Maurice Griffin, the celebrated 'fairy doctor' of County Kerry who drove troublesome fairies out of several raths in the county. In the famous 'witchcraft' case (see Burn Witch Burn) in Ballyvadlea near Clonmel, south Tipperary, in 1895, in which Bridget Cleary was suspected by her husband and her father of being a supernatural creature from a nearby fairy hill, local 'fairy doctors' or 'fairy men' John Dunne and Denis Ganey were consulted in order to verify the suspicion (which they did). The death of Bridget Cleary was the result of a belief that she had been 'changed' by occult forces, a belief which was urged on by the 'fairy men' or 'slieveens' (now a term of ridicule meaning 'rascal' or 'trickster') of the area.

In Scotland and Cornwall, too, 'spae-women' and 'conjurers' held sway in many local communities, chasing away evil spirits that caused illness or misfortune in that society, and dispensing occult wisdom as they saw fit. Such people had great hold on the public consciousness. In Wales, their grip on the social mind seems to have been slightly less strong (perhaps owing to the religious influence in the countryside), but in certain areas the role of the 'wise-woman' or 'cunning man' was significant. Such people dedicated much of their work to rooting out witches and evil-workers in their midst, and were continually sought by those who were afflicted by eerie powers or dark magics. Although the names of many of these people are now lost (as is the case in most rural areas across the Celtic countryside), one name still stands out – that of Huw Llwyd of Cynvael, near Betws-y-Coed, Llan Festiniog. Like many of those country 'conjurers' he remains a rather shadowy figure, and the tales told about him are conflicting. Some make him out to be a clergyman in Llan Festiniog, others a former soldier, and yet others a simple labouring man. None of the tales agree as to when he lived; some give his dates as 1533–1620, but others state that he lived in North Wales at some time during the 18th century. However, all are agreed that he was possessed of extraordinary powers and that he was an implacable hunter of witches and goblins in the Festiniog area. We owe much of what we know of him to the Reverend R. Jones, Rector of Llanycil in Bala, who collected many of the folk stories concerning this mysterious character.

On the side of an old road which ran between Cerrigydrudion and Betws-y-Coed, and which had been used since very ancient times, stood an inn. This was much used by travellers on their way to Ireland, as it was the only such establishment on the entire length of the road and the only place offering shelter to wayfarers. Nevertheless, it was a sinister place – old and dark, with a thatched roof which overhung its only doorway like a frowning brow. Its rooms were narrow and full of smoke from the fires which burnt there, and its passages were twisted and wound in on themselves, often misguiding the guests who lodged within its walls. Its windows were narrow, letting in little light, and the whole building seemed filled with shadows, which seemed to come and go of their own volition. It was a forbidding and frightening place.

The inn was owned by two elderly sisters, both of an unprepossessing appearance. The younger was a bearded crone, large and corpulent and with a heavy, florid countenance, while the elder was a raddled, pipe-smoking hag, seemingly frail and with a narrow, almost cruel face. Yet, despite their shadowy inn and their unwelcoming appearance, the sisters did a good trade. This was probably because there was nowhere else for a weary traveller to stay on that lonely road, and even an evil-looking place is most welcome when tiredness slows the limbs and weighs on the shoulders. Even so, there were stories about the place, none of them too savoury. Guests had been raised from sleep in their narrow beds by scurryings and whisperings, and many had lost both money and valuables as they dozed. Others had been disturbed by dreams in which shadows bent over them in a most alarming fashion, and it was even said that some wayfarers had met their end there, their bodies hidden in a spinney of trees that stood close by. Nobody could prove anything, though, and the sisters were hospitality itself.

The tales of dark goings-on, however, persisted all across the countryside. Property which had been taken into the sinister inn never came out again and, it was widely reported, neither did some of the travellers who stayed there. In the end, some of the people who had lost their valuables went to consult with the famous conjuring man, Huw Llwyd, who lived over by Cynvael. It was said that he could drive off witches and chase away ghosts through the mere power of one of his words. Huw Llwyd listened to what they had to say, puffing frequently on an old clay pipe. He told his enquirers that he was not sure exactly what was going on within the inn, but that he would do his best to find out. The people around Betws-y-Coed believed him for it was said that he had once been a soldier and that he feared nothing, neither of this world nor of the next.

So it was that Huw Llwyd turned up at the dark inn in disguise. He came disguised as a military man, recently home from foreign parts and with a great deal of money about him. His bearing and clothing (for he wore a long soldier's coat of bottle green) gave strength to his story, as did a large bandage about his right hand, which he said was the result of a serious wound in a faraway battle. The sisters received him well enough and seemed to have no cause to doubt him. They brought him into the best room and set him down before a good blaze, where he regaled them with stories of travel in foreign parts. They plied him with a good deal of strong drink which, when they were not looking, he emptied into a pot that stood by the fireside. He suspected that the drink might be drugged and he may well have been right. Finally, they set him down a great meal, which once more he suspected had been laced with some form of sleeping draught, and so he did not eat it but slid it into his knapsack which he kept by his feet. The two sisters were none the wiser.

At length Huw Llwyd said that he would like to retire to his bedroom for the night. Before he went up, he told them that it was his habit to have a number of candles burning in his room all through the hours of darkness. This was a custom, he stated, which he had acquired in the army (he feared that he might be killed under cover of darkness) and it had never left him. The sisters agreed and furnished him with a good number of candles for the night. Given his alleged military background, their suspicions were not aroused. Huw retired to his room and made preparations for a night-long vigil. He was well armed – beneath his pillow he placed a small pistol, and a sword lay unsheathed on the bed close to his bandaged right hand. He had tightly barred the door and now, as night drew on, he took off his clothes and laid down on the bed. As the hours passed, he was all attention, waiting and watching for something to happen. A profound silence descended on the inn. Shadows came and went in the jaundiced light of the candles, dancing and leaping across the walls. Huw Llwyd tried to rest but his nerves were on edge. Strangely one of the shadows – a silhouette which looked almost human and for which he could find no substance – appeared to crane over him, spreading out along the wall in a most alarming manner. It was joined by another which seemed to leap and weave in the candlelight as though it had a mind of its own. Even so, Huw Llwyd did not move but lay stock still, as though he were sleeping soundly.

The shadows drew themselves in upon each other and gradually coalesced into the forms of two great cats, one plump and bloated, the other skinny and feral-looking. Still Huw feigned sleep, but moved his hand closer to the hilt of his sword. The cats came down the partition between his room and the one beside it, and began to cross the floor towards him. They gambolled and frisked playfully in the candlelight, but he sensed that there was something altogether sinister about them. They chased each other around the room and romped and played, but Huw Llwyd continued to pretend to be in a very deep sleep as though he had been drugged. The cats frolicked over to the spot where he had laid out his clothes and began to play around them, turning over the sleeves of his jacket with their paws. They touched his belt, then a button, then a piece of braid. As he watched, one of them slid a paw into the pocket of his coat and drew out a purse. With a swift motion, Huw Llwyd leapt to his feet and struck out at the uncanny pair with his sword. The lean, feral cat drew back to the wall, arched itself and proceeded to hiss at him. In the candlelight of the room, it appeared to grow, to lose some of its shape and became a menacing shadow once more, which reached for Huw with long and taloned fingers.

The saintly man stretched out his right hand and, whipping off the bandage, revealed a small crucifix which had been strapped to the palm of his hand all the time. 'Avaunt thee, creatures of the night!' he cried loudly. The plump cat hissed and spat but came no closer, flowing and losing shape, as it too partly became a shadow-thing. Huw waved the crucifix in its direction and it shrank back. The other cat, meanwhile, had resolidified, only this time it was much bigger and seemed all the more fierce, like a wildcat. It came at him, striking out with its claw. Huw immediately swung his sword and cut the paw from the animal,

sending it scuttling back into the corner of the room with a savage yowl. He found himself covered with a black, sticky, tar-like substance, which was the creature's blood. Both animals disappeared like smoke, wafting up to the ceiling of the room. He had no more trouble from them that night. When he looked where the severed paw had fallen, he found that it was a human hand that lay there.

Next morning only one of the sisters – the plump and florid one – presented herself at the table to serve him his breakfast. When Huw Llwyd asked where her sister was, the stout beldame replied that she was indisposed and would not be down that day. Huw expressed his regret, but added, 'I must say goodbye to her before I go, for I so greatly enjoyed her company last night. It would be very churlish of me to leave without bidding her farewell.' Rather reluctantly, the stout sister took him up to a narrow bedroom at the back of the inn where her companion lay abed. As he went up, Huw noted the spots of blood along the walls and staircase as though someone or something had bled all the way into that section of the building. The room into which he was shown was small and dark and he could just make out the figure of the thin sister, propped up with pillows in the bed. He announced that he was about to take his leave and sympathized with her regarding her illness, and she wished him every speed. Huw then stuck out his hand to thank her for her companionship on the previous night. The old witch (for such he believed her and her sister to be) offered up her left hand to be shaken, but Huw Llywd, affecting great gallantry, said that he had never taken a left hand in his life and would not do so now. Very reluctantly, and evidently with great pain, the old harridan raised what appeared to be a bandaged stump and offered it to him as her hand.

Drawing his sword, Huw challenged them both: 'I am Huw Llwyd of Cynvael,' he announced, 'and I charge you both as witches!' Hereupon the two sisters went into a hideous wail, which reminded Huw of screaming cats. He raised the crucifix, which he still had about him, and drove them back, cowering into a corner of the room. 'I warn you,' he went on, 'that, by your witchcraft and by your evil robberies, you have incurred the wrath of the Living God.' He pointed to the lean and sharp-faced sister. 'You have lost your hand this night but I tell you now that, if you continue with your evil ways and use your dark powers any further, far worse will befall you. This I swear in the Name of the Risen Christ!' They fell back, mewling and groaning. 'Pray to whatever blighted spirit that you worship that I have no need to visit you again!' Turning on his heel, he walked from the room.

Huw Llywd returned to Cynvael and there were no more robberies at the inn. Furthermore, travellers who stayed there during the hours of darkness were no longer molested, either by shadows or by cats. Yet there was still an odd, gloomy air hanging over the place like an unpleasant smell. The sisters continued to dwell there and it was said that their evil, though somewhat subdued, continued to flourish in the countryside like a rank weed.

One Sunday morning, Huw Llwyd was just setting out from his house in Cynvael to go to the church at Llan Festiniog, where he was the minister, when he felt a sudden and unexpected chill in the air. It was unusual, he thought, for the morning was quite warm and only a gentle and temperate breeze was blowing. The feeling unsettled him greatly. Looking along the road, he saw two women approaching. Although they were still a little distance away, the hairs on his neck began to prickle for, even at that distance, he recognized the two sisters from Betws-y-Coed, and he knew that they had come all that way to bewitch him and take revenge for their humiliation. He could feel their rage and the powers fairly crackling in the air around him, and he was greatly afraid. All the same, he had enough occult knowledge to realize that he was in their power only if he turned his back towards them, whereas if he faced them full on they could do him no harm. To avoid their evil influence and to frustrate their designs, he faced them and began to walk backwards every step of the way from Cynvael to the Llan. The women spat at him and threatened him, the skinny one waving her stump of a hand in the air in a most menacing manner, but Huw Llwyd never faltered. He stepped out as surely as if he could see where he was going. He knew that, when he reached the Church porch, he would be beyond the witches' reach and that they could not harm him with their sinister powers. When he arrived there, he shook his fist at the two women. 'I defy you now', he shouted at them, 'and before I leave this Church I will make sure that you never witch any of God's people again!' He was as good as his word for, by his own skill in the secret arts, he deprived the two ladies of their evil powers before he stepped down from the Church porch. They now could no longer bewitch people and were forced to live out the rest of their days as ordinary women. Such was the occult influence of Huw Llwyd.

The witches at Betws-y-Coed were not the only such sorceresses that the saintly man had to face in the course of his long career. In the countryside around Cynvael and the Llan, there was great evil at one time – sickness and misfortune – all of which was laid at the door of an old woman and her two daughters. These three were disreputable people, given to begging and (some said) thievery. One evening, Huw Llwyd was on his way home past a certain hill near Cynvael. It was late evening, and as he walked he thought that he saw figures moving on the summit of the hill. Now this place had a bad reputation and was said to be a spot where witches gathered in order to perform their black arts. Huw walked a little way up the hill to see what was going on. There was the old woman and her two daughters dancing about to the strains of unearthly music which seemed to come from nowhere, although the very air was full of it. He knew that they were performing what was called 'a witch's dance' – drawing down evil upon their neighbours – but he felt powerless to intervene. He hurried home and considered the problem.

The next evening Huw Llwyd went back to the sinister hill for he knew that the old woman and her daughters would return there to work some more of their evil. However, before he went, he cut himself a large whitethorn stick which he marked with the sign of the Cross, using a large-bladed knife. As soon as he began to climb the hill, he could hear the first strains of the eerie, unearthly music once again, and he could see some movement near the hill's summit. He knew that the witches were there. They were still dancing an ancient reel and calling down great evil and sickness upon the surrounding district. Raising the marked stick, Huw Llwyd walked across to them but they steadfastly ignored him.

'Get you gone to your homes and cease these uncanny ways,' he commanded them. 'I am Huw Llwyd of Cynvael and it would be best for you if you heeded my words.' Still they paid him no heed. He struck the nearest daughter and she danced close to him. Normally the stick would not have hit the girl, protected as she was by the dark sciences, and would have bounced back and hit Huw himself; but, because it was marked with the holy symbol, it injured the girl, striking her hard on the upper arm. She gave a loud squawk, like a bird in pain, and stumbled to the earth. Almost at once, the unearthly music stopped and the mother and her other daughter stopped their dancing. They squared up to Huw Llwyd like cornered animals. Raising the stick even higher, he showed them the mark of the Cross upon it and they drew back, spitting and murmuring. The other girl climbed to her feet and the three of them made off down the hill as fast as they could go. Satisfied with his evening's work, Huw Llwyd made his way back home and began to read his Bible. However, the witches had certainly not forgotten about him, because, several days afterwards, he experienced a severe fall in which he broke his leg and could not walk for quite a time. People said that it was the witches' revenge upon him for interfering in their evil spells.

Another time, a neighbour of Huw Llwyd in the Llan believed that she was being tormented by a nearby witch. She went to Huw Llwyd and named the woman whom she thought was persecuting her, a woman to whom she had refused some kindness in the past. At night, she claimed, the neighbour woman would come to her house while she was asleep, and would go through her larder, eat her food, take whatever she could and then leave again. All the while, the house was locked up. Furthermore, the house seemed blighted and the woman had no success with her spinning or churning. After much thought and prayer, Huw confirmed that this was indeed the case, and that her neighbour was actually blighting her and taking all the luck from her house. He would come to the good woman's house and see what he could do. That night he came to the cottage and took up his bed in the kitchen, where the larder was and where the household utensils were kept. Laying himself down on a straw pallet, he pulled a number of old coats around him – covering himself up to the crown of his head – and prepared for sleep.

Under his pillow, however, he had placed a large hammer, and he slept with his right hand on its shaft.

Shortly after midnight, he was disturbed by the faintest of noises. Opening one eye, he saw that a strange creature, like a large stoat or ferret, had come in through the barely open window and was nosing about in the kitchen near him. He heard it patter about from here to there, as if it knew the layout of the kitchen well. As he watched through half-closed eyes, it pulled open the door of the larder with a dark paw and, leaping up on the shelf inside, began to eat and drink what was there. Huw Llwyd never moved, but kept a steady watch as the thing began to eat all of the poor woman's food, and drink what beer was in her larder. Nevertheless, his grip tightened on the shaft of the hammer beneath his head.

When it had eaten and drunk its fill, the creature jumped down to the floor once again and proceeded to prowl about, poking its sharp nose into the corners of the kitchen. All the while, Huw lay very still, never moving a muscle. He could see it better now as it crawled about in the moonlight which streamed in through the window. It had long, thick, shaggy, dark hair, a sharp little face with a long, pointed nose and bright, intelligent eyes – far too intelligent, he thought, for an animal. It came closer and closer to him, as if to check that he was truly asleep, its eyes twinkling in the half-light. Then, seemingly satisfied, it drew closer to see what it could steal from him. It reached out a paw and began to pull at his pockets, trying to see where he kept his money. Huw's hand was now firmly clasped around the handle of the hammer and, when the creature was close enough, he suddenly started up and lashed out with the implement. With his first blow, he struck the creature on the paw; with his second, he hit it on the upper part of the foreleg; and his final blow fell upon the thing's back leg. It howled with a human shriek and fled back towards the still partly opened window. Huw Llwyd jumped up and, still waving the hammer, pursued it as far as the back door of the cottage.

'I know you to be a witchy creature,' he called after it. 'Let you go back to your evil abode and never trouble this Christian house again. This is the command of the Living God through his servant Huw

Llwyd!' The creature darted away across the fields in the direction of the house of the neighbour who was suspected of being a witch. It was soon lost in the darkness and Huw Llwyd could see it no longer. Later, he went to the good woman of the house and told her that he believed that her troubles were over.

The next day, in his capacity as a Christian minister, Huw called upon the old lady whom he suspected of being a witch, and found her confined to bed, apparently very ill. She was not fit to rise to greet him because her body ached and was extremely sore. When she put out her hand to take his, he saw that it was covered in dark bruises, as though she had been struck several times, and he knew then that it had been she that had broken into her neighbour's house the previous night in the form of a stoat-thing. The bruises were certainly where he had struck her with the hammer.

'I know who you are and what you have been doing,' he told her sternly, 'and I vow that if you ever take on a supernatural form again it will be the worse for you. This I tell you as a Minister of God and in His Name.' At this point the old woman broke down and gave her word that she would no longer taken an inhuman form, nor would she torment her neighbours any more. Huw Llwyd returned to Cynvael and there was no further trouble. All the same, witches and wizards continued to practise their evil ways in the district and, indeed, all across Wales.

The name of Huw Llwyd was now well known all over the countryside as a finder and destroyer of witches, and his services were called upon by communities in many parts of the land which had been blighted by the foul stain of witchcraft. He was once called away to Caerwys, in the Vale of Clwyd, to deal with his most famous adversary, the witch Moll White. Moll was not Welsh but came from somewhere in England; however, she had once come to the great fair in Clwyd and had remained in Wales ever since, practising her witchy ways against the people there. Folk around Caerways were terrified of her, for her power was indeed awful. It was remarked that she went about the countryside, even in daylight hours, in the form of a great black greyhound, which snarled and snapped at everyone who came near it. Those whom it crossed never prospered. Everyone knew that it was Moll White in an animal form, but none dared say so. Finally, a few brave souls in the district could stand it no longer; they went to Cynvael to speak with Huw Llwyd to see if he could do anything to help them. The minister listened to what they had to say and thought very deeply. In the end, he agreed to come and see what he could do.

There are many variations of the tale – such as how he went to the shack where Moll White lived and confronted her, or how there was a battle of the dark sciences between them (for Huw was as well acquainted with the black arts as any witch) – but the most common version is as follows.

Huw Llwyd went first of all to an old graveyard near Caerwys where the black greyhound most frequently appeared. He knew that witches sometimes drew their uncanny powers from the dead, who hated the living to a frightening degree, and he suspected that Moll White was probably using the forces of long-dead phantoms in her evil work. The place was very gloomy, even on the brightest day, with a kind of dusky pallor hanging over it, suggestive of the ancient evil that permeated the tumbled grave-markers. Huw swallowed loudly (for, despite his holy offices, he was still very much afraid), but nevertheless opened the creaking gate and stepped inside. Under his arm, he carried a large Bible and in his pocket an iron knife, and, with these protections about him, he advanced into the Caerwys cemetery. The graveyard was derelict. Everywhere, long grasses, thorns and nettles pushed their way among fallen stones, and half-ruined mausoleums were weighed down with thick and clinging ivy. Dark clouds seemed to gather over the site and a chill wind blew across it. Then, between some of the weathered grave-stones, Huw saw the black greyhound, darting from one patch of shadow to the other. Huw watched it and he could tell by the way it moved that it was no ordinary dog. There was something too human about it, and he suspected that this was probably Moll White, doing her evil about the countryside. All the same, he hunkered down amid the grass and called out to it, in Welsh, 'Hei! Ci du' ('Hi! Black dog!'). The hound ignored him, so he gave another shout in its direction: 'Hei! Mam gu!' ('Hi! Grandmother dear!'). At this, the hound (taken by surprise) turned its head and looked at him, for it understood full well what he said. Huw held up the Bible and the dog appeared to flinch. Rising to his feet, he advanced on the animal, holding out the iron knife between it and himself. When it saw both the Bible and the knife, the greyhound gave a squeal, jumped over the churchyard wall and raced off in the direction of Moll White's cabin as hard as it could go.

Later, that evening, Huw Llwyd called at Moll White's rundown shack. He still had the iron knife about him (since this is a sure defence against witchcraft, even from pre-Christian times) and he kept the great Bible firmly under his arm. When he opened the door of the cabin, he found the old woman lying upon her bed, panting like a dog, as though she had just run a great race. Then Huw Llwyd knew that he had got the right witch.

'I forbid you to torment the Christian people of the Clwyd Vale any further!' he commanded her sternly. 'If you do, I shall return to Caerwys and it will be the worse for you and for those like you. Remember, it is Huw Llwyd of Cynvael, Minister of the Living God, who commands you. Now pay heed to my words!' Without any further word, he turned upon his heel and went back to Cynvael. From that day forth, some stories say, the people of the Vale of Clwyd were never troubled by Moll White any further. (Although some other tales say that she was back at her old tricks, still in the guise of a black greyhound, not long afterwards, and had to be dealt with by another Welsh conjurer or cunning man. She never crossed Huw Llwyd's path ever again.)

There are some people who will tell you that Huw was a witch himself and that he was extremely well skilled in the black arts. However, most Christian people will swear that he was the foremost hunter of witches that Wales has ever produced. The above stories are only some of the tales told about him, and there are many, many more. Some say that he was a minister of the Gospel, and some that he was a soldier and that he led the forces of light against the forces of darkness all across Wales. He took away the powers of witches certainly, but he also faced ghosts and other night-creatures and, in one case, even the Devil himself. No one really knows when he died or where he was finally buried, but all sources agree that he was a very saintly man and that Wales has never seen his like again.

Huw Llwyd corresponds with many of the Celtic 'conjuring men' or 'witch-hunters', tracking down and destroying those who would turn their powers against the community. Many of these 'witches' also corresponded to the widespread Celtic belief that they could turn themselves into animals of some kind – cats, hares, dogs and stoats. Indeed, in his *History and Topography of Ireland*, written in 1187, Gerald of Wales firmly avows that there are many old women in the Irish countryside who could take the guise of animals as and when they desired. There are also many tales of Celtic witches everywhere transforming themselves into animals – especially hares – to suck from the udders of cows as they grazed in the fields, thus leaving no milk for their owners. Such stories have continued in some country areas right up until the early 20th century. Undoubtedly there was much work (and perhaps still is to this day) for 'cunning people' like Huw Llwyd to do!

# CRUEL COPPINGER

Will you hear of the cruel Coppinger,
He came from the foreign kind,
He was brought to us by the salt water,
He was carried away by the wind.

Sometimes, in the Celtic world, ruthless tyrants and overlords have acquired an air of mystery and magic. This was sometimes used to explain their status in the community (namely that they achieved it by supernatural or diabolic means), or provided a reason for their dark and evil natures. Legends often grew up around their births or deaths, and significant actions which they performed were sometimes given extremely gruesome or mysterious embellishments. This tradition continued well into the 19th (and even the 20th) centuries when supernatural attributes were sometimes attached by tenants to bullying local landlords. In parts of Ireland, for example, where English landowners were sometimes cruel or indifferent to the needs of their tenants, certain landholders were credited with unusual powers which they obtained by bizarre or occult means – by selling their soul to the Devil, for example. The Ormsbys of County Roscommon, who were notorious rack-renting landlords and corrupt local magistrates, for example, were also widely believed to be sorcerers. When Robert Ormsby was buried at Fuerty churchyard, legend states that a hideous worm rose from the open grave and swallowed his coffin whole. This was believed to be the Devil reclaiming his dark soul. Robert Ormsby was, of course, a cruel and greedy man and his name (together with that of his 'dark family') has been deeply woven into the tapestry of local folklore.

Few local tyrants, however, can have gained such notoriety, yet have remained so mysterious, as the cruel Cornish landlord who signed himself 'D. Coppinger'. Indeed, although his name appears on several land deeds in Cornwall, it is not known for certain what the letter 'D' actually stood for. Some have argued that his name was David Coppinger; others have stated that he was called Daniel. Whatever the truth of the matter, all agree that he was not a Cornishman (it is generally thought that he was of Scandinavian birth, possibly Danish) and the manner of his coming to and departure from Cornwall was quite spectacular.

Coppinger seems to have arrived in Cornwall around the beginning of the 19th century. Late one evening, about 1801 or slightly before, a fierce storm lashed the north Cornish coast with massive waves smashing at the rocks and a banshee wind screaming in from the ocean. Local people said that they could never remember such a fury. In the midst of this tempest, a strange vessel with a foreign rig was struggling to make land through the waters of the Harty Race. She was either heavily laden or badly waterlogged, because she rolled dangerously with every swell of the ocean. Frightened crew lined her side, looking desperately for the coastline; their pale faces were becoming more and more visible as the vessel drew nearer to the landward rocks. Her sails hung in tatters and, although her rudder had been lashed for running ashore, the draw of the current and the strength of the wind seemed too strong for her and she appeared to have no chance at all of reaching Harty Pool.

Suddenly, among the terrified faces, appeared a giant of a man – obviously the vessel's captain – who berated the crew in a foreign tongue, his voice almost audible over the roar of the wind. Then, stripping off his clothes, he suddenly leapt from the bow of the doomed craft and into the surging ocean. For a second he was swept back against the bulwarks but then appeared to make some headway through the swell, swimming like some wild animal for safety. As the ship drifted on, to its seemingly inevitable doom with the loss of all aboard her, the captain survived the massive breakers and made land, scrambling through the surf and onto a little beach. There, a crowd had gathered to watch the probable wreck of the ship, and they drew back slightly as her only survivor came ashore. For a second he stood, dripping and naked on the sand, then rushed into the midst of the gathering and snatched a red Welsh cloak from the narrow shoulders of a terrified old woman. Wrapping it loosely about him, and without even catching his breath, he came striding up the beach leaving the crowd wondering behind him.

Just where the beach met the land another, smaller crowd had gathered, and among them was a young woman on horseback. Her name is frequently given as Dinah Hamlyn, and she was reputedly the daughter of a relatively wealthy local landowner (some versions of the tale give his holding as being at Welcombe, where he maintained a large house). She had come down to the beach on her father's horse to see the spectacle and it was towards her, as the only mounted person there, that the strange seaman strode. Grabbing the bridle, he shouted to her roughly in a foreign tongue, and suddenly swung himself up behind her on the startled animal. Unnerved by its double burden, the horse took off for home as fast as it could.

When she reached her father's door, Dinah felt the load lighten as the stranger jumped down. He struck the door with a huge fist and, in broken English, demanded to be admitted. Dinah was forced to bring him in with her and, in the presence of her astonished father, the stranger introduced himself by a memorable name: 'Coppinger – a Dane'. Without any apology, he demanded that the old man feed him and put him up for a time and he arrayed himself for dinner, without scruple, in the very best attire of his rather unwilling host. This consisted of a long-skirted coat of purple velveteen, which was thrown around his bare shoulders together with an embroidered waistcoat, worn over the naked skin and long riding pants. Nothing matched, but it apparently made no difference to the wild man. He came forward to the family table and placed himself near its head as though he was the most honoured and longstanding friend of the family. He ate with his hands like a ravening animal, throwing bones here and there on the floor; and, when he had done, he stretched himself out on the settle by the hearth and fell into a deep sleep from which he did not wake until noon the following day.

Next morning, several people went down to the seashore to view the wreck of the foreign vessel but, strange to say, no trace of her was to be found. It was almost as if she had never existed, and some of the watchers secretly averred that she seemed to have disappeared as soon as her master had left the deck. In any case, she was not seen again either on land or sea. Coppinger, however, continued to live at the house of the local gentry.

At first, he seemed to have subdued all the wilder elements of his nature and seemed genuinely grateful for his rescue. He appeared to be more cultivated than his initial impression. He was certainly very well read, because he was able to engage his host in profound philosophical discussion on various topics, displaying a breadth of knowledge of literature. He also wrote a number of letters to certain persons of high rank in Denmark, and these were duly answered. He received several remittances from friends in Norway, Denmark and even England, from which he gave Squire Hamlyn a portion towards his rent and upkeep. He further announced himself to be of wealthy parentage and holding high rank in his own country, stating that he had fled from Denmark to avoid an unfortunate marriage to a titled lady whom he did not love. In order to escape from her clutches, he had left his father's house and gone to sea, becoming one of the youngest shipmasters in the country. His story seemed so romantic and so plausible, and his manners were so charming, that he completely won Dinah over and dashing good looks settled the matter – Coppinger proposed marriage and Dinah accepted. Her father's sudden illness postponed the wedding for a while, but eventually the old man died and so was spared much of the evil which was to come.

After the funeral, with only Dinah and her mother to stand against him, Coppinger naturally assumed the management and control of the house and lands as though he had been born to it. Squire Hamlyn's widow, the lawful heiress, had only a small say in the domestic affairs, and soon her wishes were ignored altogether. Coppinger's evil nature, which he had suppressed for so long, now began to manifest itself once again. He was rough and brutal to his wife, keeping her locked in her room for hours and even days on end, while he 'attended to the estates' in his own particular way. He raised rents and treated the tenants abominably, evicting them without reason or recourse if he took even the slightest dislike to them. Worse was to come, however.

Almost from the time that Coppinger became virtual master at Welcombe, the great house received a number of rather unsavoury visitors. Strange ships, many with foreign flags, dropped anchor off Harty Pool, and their crews came ashore. They were men of the worst sort; locals suspected that most of them were either pirates or smugglers, and all of them seemed to be cronies of the new landlord. They had the run of the great house, which they began to use as a kind of headquarters, and soon the rooms and passages of the place were reputedly stacked high with contraband and looted valuables. There was great bawdiness and drunkenness among these rogues, with frequent fights and disputes which were terrible for the servants to hear. Over all this thievery and quarrelling, Coppinger sat like some pirate-lord, and a single word from him could quell even the fiercest dispute. It was also widely known that he took the lion's share of whatever booty was brought in.

Indeed, he began to take on all the trappings of a robber-chieftain, for he gathered about himself a band of the most lawless ruffians – desperados, smugglers, wreckers and pirates – over which 'Cruel Coppinger' was the undisputed captain. In those days, and in such a remote region of the country, the more law-abiding inhabitants were largely unprotected, and soon Coppinger and his rogues began to demand money from the surrounding gentry to 'ensure the safety of their estates'. It was an early form of protection racket. There was not a resident gentleman of property or weight in the entire district, nor a clergyman, who was safe from the attentions of these ruffians. No magistrate or revenue man west of the River Tamar could move against them, for Coppinger exercised total control of the area. One excise man who did try to capture the gang had his head chopped off and slung across the gunwale of a boat. The grand old house now became a robber's den where the 'Cruel' band continually drank and caroused, and all the while Coppinger's wife was locked in her room or in the cellars.

The number of unlawful ships in the area began to increase steadily. On dark nights, strange vessels would appear along the coast, and lights were flashed from the headlands round about to lead them into a safe creek or cove. If the sea was too rough for landing, boats would put out from the ship from which the illegal spoils were unloaded. One of these ships was a fully rigged schooner that began to appear along the Cornish coastline with increasing frequency. She was called the *Black Prince*, and belonged to Coppinger himself, having allegedly been built to his own specific orders at a dockyard in Denmark. With the arrival of this vessel, it began to be suspected that the Dane was, in fact, a pirate in his own country, and that he had simply transferred his operations to Cornwall. For a long while, both he and his dark craft were the terror of the Cornish Channel.

There seems little doubt from the legends that Coppinger was an extremely able seaman and that, as such, he was able to avoid capture by even the swiftest naval cutter. On one famous occasion, the stories say, he led an excise ship into a dangerous, intricate and rocky channel near the Gull Rock where, through skilful seamanship and a thorough knowledge of his bearings, he sailed the *Black Prince* to safety while the King's vessel perished, with the loss of all those aboard her.

All those who opposed or spoke out against his activities in the district around Welcombe (and even further afield) suddenly 'disappeared'. There were allegations that Coppinger was in league with the forces of darkness and that he was using supernatural means to carry off his enemies, but it is more probable that those who vanished were either killed or held prisoner by his gang. The Reverend Sabine Baring-Gould, the eccentric Cornish folklorist and historian, and author of the *Book of Cornwall*, claimed to have interviewed a 97-year-old man who, as a youth, had been abducted by the ruffians, and had to be ransomed by his relatives after two years' service on the *Black Prince*. He had been abducted because he had witnessed the 'execution' of a local farmer by one of Coppinger's men, and it was feared that the youth might talk. Local folktales also said that the lawless crew had to enrol themselves into the gang by using fearful and unGodly oaths – which pledged their souls to the Prince of Darkness – during which they swore absolute and undying loyalty to Coppinger himself in their own blood. The evil Dane was now taking on something of the aspect of a local warlock.

With large amounts of ill-gotten money passing through his hands,

Coppinger was now an extremely wealthy man. He began to enlarge the Hamlyn estate by buying up neighbouring farms and by instructing their owners to sell to him and quit. At one time, he chanced to buy a freehold farm bordering on the sea. On the day of the transfer, he appeared, weighted down with moneybags from which he spilled coins of various kinds – dollars, ducats, doubloons, pistoles, and the currency of every foreign country with a seaboard – before the eyes of the astonished lawyers. This money was undoubtedly the proceeds of piracy, and at first the lawyers demurred from handing over the papers for Coppinger to sign. However, a pistol, placed beside the ear of one of them, soon convinced them otherwise, and they even agreed to accept the currency by weight rather than value. It is from these traditions that much of the documentation emerges bearing the legend 'D. Coppinger', although none carry the buyer's actual Christian name. Once again, stories began to circulate that Coppinger had acquired all his vast and multinational wealth by sorcery, and that he and his evil crew had actually turned Welcombe House into a magician's den. Servants reported that they had heard strange and eerie voices, which could not have come from a human throat, echoing along the corridors of the house, and that they saw strange shadows (some bearing bags which were assumed to contain gold) coming and going about its grounds. However, these were merely tales used to embellish the reputation of the dark pirate captain. Coppinger now began to consolidate his empire with other forms of illegal activity.

His smuggling 'runs' increased. All around the Welcombe area, there are still tracks and bridle paths over which he is once said to have exercised absolute control. Although these were common 'rights of way' to be used at any time, he issued orders that nobody should use them after nightfall, and no one ever did. These paths came to be known as 'Coppinger's tracks', and they all appeared to converge on a headland known as Steeple Brink. Here, the cliff fell away down a 300-foot drop, with an almost perpendicular face of smooth rock, down to a gravelly beach, far below. The cliff itself was surrounded by natural arches and gullies; one of the most prominent of these led to a great cave, vaulted like a church – bigger, said some, than the church at Kirkhampton – and exceptionally gloomy and menacing. It was protected from view by a projecting crag and was inaccessible from the beach, but could be reached by a rope or ladder lowered from above and secured to the crag itself. The cavern, needless to say, was also piled high with kegs of brandy, chests of tea and great ironbound boxes of valuables, taken during raids at sea. No man ever attempted the perilous descent, except those from the 'Captain's' own troop, even though more than one ruffian fell to a terrible end on the beach.

Now that he had gained actual (if not legal) control of her estates, Coppinger turned once again to his wife in order to make her sign over a financial inheritance which she had received on the death of her father. The girl had obtained a considerable sum of money as part of her dowry, but wisely had not handed it over to her husband. Having tied Dinah to the pillar of a great oaken bedstead, Coppinger called her mother into the room and, producing a seaman's cat-o'-nine-tails, threatened to beat her daughter to death if she did not persuade her to sign the money over to him. The demand worked, for Dinah gave him all the money he wanted. In some versions of the tale, it is Dinah's mother who receives the inheritance and who hands it over to spare her daughter from the lash. Whatever the truth of the matter, Coppinger reduced both mother and daughter to abject poverty without much thought.

There are many other stories about him, too, regarding both his cruelty and savagery. He is said to have beaten a local parson with a riding whip to within an inch of his life, simply because he had mildly reproved him for evicting a tenant. It is reported that he dragged a tailor along behind his horse simply because the man had forgotten to sew a button on a coat which Coppinger had left him for repair. There were also stories of how he possessed a terrible black horse on which he would ride across the countryside at full gallop while storms crackled and roared overhead. The emphasis of these tales added greatly to his supernatural reputation throughout the countryside. He is said to have had only one son, but the child was an idiot, born deaf, dumb and half-witted. Nevertheless, he possessed the same cruel streak as his father, and seemed to delight in torturing animals; he was, at one time, arraigned for murder, having allegedly pushed a neighbour's child from the top of a cliff, but the charge was not proved owing to lack of evidence and the mental state of the defendant. Small wonder, however, that local people said that the child had no soul. Other stories reported that the master of Welcombe's monstrous offspring was shut away in a secret room in the manor house, very much like the legendary hideous creature at Glamis Castle in Scotland.

Coppinger's excesses increased. He was brought to court on a charge of smuggling, but openly threatened the judge and the case was dismissed. By now his reputation, both as an outlaw and a sorcerer, was so strong that he considered himself well above the law in any case. On another occasion, when one of his men appeared in court on some minor charge, Coppinger filled the court with his henchmen and threatened to burn the courthouse down and roast the judge in the ashes. Once again, the case was dismissed for lack of evidence. Nobody would now testify against the pirate or his gang and he ruled the region around Harty Pool with an iron fist. Rumours increased that he was none other than the Devil himself in human form.

So much for the legends, but how much of the above is true? There is little doubt from the anecdotal evidence that Coppinger was both a vicious man and a cruel landlord. According to another source, he was also extremely wealthy, and with part of his fortune bought a small estate in Roscoff in Brittany which he also used for his smuggling operations. This was the time of the Napoleonic Wars between England and France, and it is thought that the English authorities used Coppinger to carry despatches and military intelligence between Cornwall and the French coast. He may even have acted as a spy for them on occasion. In return, they turned a blind eye to both his smuggling and piracy activities. Perhaps this is how the Master of Welcombe acquired so much wealth and why he apparently outwitted the English revenue vessels for so long.

However, Coppinger's criminal 'empire' could not last indefinitely. Money was beginning to grow scarce (perhaps the English authorities now had little use for his dubious 'services') and the contraband in the cavern at Steeple Brink began to dwindle. More than once, a fully armed naval cutter was seen cruising off the headlands around the Harty Race as if keeping a wary eye on Coppinger's activities. Fewer and fewer lawless seamen began to show up at the great house and the number of strange vessels arriving offshore steadily declined. The stage seemed to be set for the Dane's death or disappearance.

When his departure did at last come, it was as spectacular as his arrival. It too was heralded by a fierce and persistent storm. A wrecker who had gone to the shore saw, just as the sun went down, a full-rigged ship standing just offshore near the Harty Race. At first he thought that it might be the *Black Prince*, so closely did it resemble Coppinger's own vessel, but then he saw that its rigging was slightly different and that it flew a flag which he had never seen before. As he watched, a rocket went up from Gull Rock, a small islet with a narrow creek running through it which had been the sign of many a run of smuggled cargo. The rocket was answered by the blast of a gun from the vessel. Again, signals were exchanged and, as the terrified wrecker watched further, a shadowy but unmistakable figure emerged on the highest point of the islet and waved to the anchored ship with a cutlass. It was Coppinger himself.

By this time, the sea was beginning to rise and the vessel's position was starting to look dangerous. Even so, she lowered a boat with a number of men pulling on every oar, straining against the fearful tide that runs through the Harty Race. They neared the rocks, coming daringly through the surf as though guided by some experienced coxwain, and landed on the Gull Rock. As the wind rose to a fury, Coppinger leapt into the boat and appeared to assume command, instructing them to 'haul away!' With every muscle straining, the men in the boat rowed back towards the sinister ship which still rode at anchor in the bay. Only once did one of the men falter at his oar and, with an oath and a merciless swipe of the cutlass, Coppinger beheaded him and threw his headless body into the surging tide.

The boat drew alongside the vessel and the men clambered on board, Coppinger among them. Bolts of lightning and crashes of thunder filled the sky as the ship set sail, and the sea appeared to rise and swallow her up in a shower of mist and hail. The craft simply appeared to sink into the boiling sea and disappear without trace, as if she had never been there in the first place. As she did so, the storm broke with all its pent-up fury, tearing up trees by their roots and ripping roofs from the coastal dwellings. Poor Dinah watched it pass from the rattling windows of her mansion, holding in her shuddering arms the idiot child who mewled and cried as if he instinctively knew that his father was gone. As she stood there, a large lump of meteoric rock – called a 'storm bolt' in that part of the country – whistled past her, shattering the window and embedding itself in the great, winged wooden chair in which Coppinger had always sat. It was taken as a sign, and as further confirmation that Coppinger was the Devil's spawn. The cruel landlord of Welcombe was never seen again in the locality.

That is not to say, of course, that he has gone away. Many Cornish legends tell how he still lives beneath the waters of Hartland Bay as some sort of wizard or devil-creature, creating storms out in the Channel and causing ships to founder on the north Cornish rocks. Many shipwrecks in the area have, over the years, been blamed upon his malign influence and power. Through legend, he has become more evil and more supernaturally powerful than he ever was in life.

The above tale is a distillation of a number of stories collected by the Reverend R.S. Hawker who, like Baring-Gould, collected much of the folklore, traditions and remembered histories of Cornwall. Undoubtedly, Hawker has added his own embellishments to the legends. There are, however, more historical hints at the identity of 'Cruel Coppinger' to be gleaned.

A Daniel Herbert Coppinger was the only survivor of a ship wrecked at Welcombe Mouth on 23 December 1792. He was taken in and sheltered by a William Arthur, a yeoman of Golden Park, Hartland. On 3 August 1793, he married Ann Hamlyn of Galsham Farm, also in Hartland – she was not therefore the daughter of his protector, but may have been a relation. Both Golden Park and Galsham Farm still exist today. It is not clear whether Daniel Coppinger gained any financial advancement from the marriage but, in 1802, he was declared bankrupt and a prisoner of the King's Bench. His wife died on 31 August 1833, but Coppinger himself seems to have disappeared from historical record. Quite simply, he vanished – perhaps back to wherever he had originally come from. Maybe he was the cruel landowner who was spirited away by the spectral ship.

Another Coppinger – perhaps also 'D.' (David?) – was a substantial merchant in Roscoff during the 1780s and early 1790s, and certainly traded with Cornwall. He was also involved in the smuggling trade and was widely suspected of being an English spy, carrying French secrets to London. He was of Irish descent but frequently claimed that his ancestors came from Denmark. He too, seems to have disappeared in mysterious circumstances, probably connected with his alleged spying activities. He did run despatches for the English military, and was allowed to continue his smuggling trade as a result. He may also have been the inspiration for the legendary Cornish tyrant.

It could also be, of course, that the character of 'Cruel Coppinger' was forged from an amalgamation of the two men. If so, then their individual exploits have been added to with each retelling across the course of the years, and a supernatural element has been incorporated into them. Songs and poems were composed from folk-memory, and these have also added to the dark and sinister reputation of the man. He was rapidly equated with the Devil in the popular mind – indeed there is a legion of stories concerning both Coppinger and the Evil One engaged in a game of dice in an upper room of the house at Welcombe.

As with many other tyrants, the air of mystery surrounding 'Cruel Coppinger' has deepened over the years. His 'wizardry' has become legendary and it has been stated that there was no other 'enchanter' like him in all of Cornwall. Tales of his arrival and departure have only added to this reputation. Storms were often associated with witches and wizards in the early Celtic mind (such enchanters usually had a firm mastery of the elements) and the rising of a strange ship from the ocean creates a link with reputed ancient Celtic realms far beneath the waves. The fact that Coppinger was said to have a house under the sea – a dwelling in which he is still said to live, using his dark powers to create more recent shipwrecks – only serves to strengthen such a linkage.

It may also be that the tales of Coppinger may have become confused with those concerning another dubious Cornish character, Tristram Davey. Like the Dane, Davey is s fairly nebulous character from a historical point of view, but it is known that he was the landlord of an inn on the coast and that he murdered several of his guests as they slept. He is also reputed to have kept French prisoners in his attic, at a time of Anglo-French discord, chained and treated like animals before he turned them over to the authorities in return for a substantial reward. Something similar appears in several of the tales about Coppinger. In this respect, the conduct of both men mirrored the crimes of the notorious American 'witch', Patty Canon, on the Maryland-Delaware border. Like Canon and Coppinger, Davey was believed to dabble in the occult arts, some of which were rumoured to involve human sacrifice. He too was a wrecker, luring ships with signal fires built on several dangerous headlands. Some of the worst elements of the obnoxious Davey, who entertained pirates and smugglers at his inn and who may have fronted a criminal gang, have undoubtedly transferred themselves to Coppinger. Maybe tales of other Cornish pirates and wreckers have also added to the mystery of his character.

Beneath the layers of legend, however, lies the notion of the supernatural tyrant, which has its roots in ancient Celtic belief. The more evil Coppinger became the more he acquired miraculous and magical powers – a common theme in Celtic folklore. As Christian elements were built into the motif, he almost became the embodiment of the Devil himself. Indeed, it is still said that he sometimes rises from the ocean and stalks through the country, snatching away souls to live with him in his undersea house, very much in the manner of the Fiend himself. This connected the Celtic mind with the antique forces of darkness which lay in the landscape around them.

There is no doubt that Cornwall's most notorious landlord is a complex character, but what is the real truth about him? Will it ever be known? Perhaps the answers lie at the bottom of Hartland Bay.

# THE BLACK SISTERS OF CHRISTIANSBURG

Although witchcraft was known in, and indeed central to, early Celtic society, Celtic witches were not the stereotyped figures in black conical hats and dark cloaks with which we are all so familiar today. This stereotype is a much more recent innovation and portrays the sorceress as an 'outsider' or alien figure, who is not really part of a more tightly bound society (the tall conical hat has been modelled on the headwear of medieval Jews who were accused of poisoning wells in Christian communities). By contrast, the Celtic witch or warlock was a member of his or her community and was an integral part of that society. The witch functioned on a number of social levels: as a physician or healer; as a detector of criminals; as a predictor of future events; and as a locator of lost or stolen property. In many respects, the Celtic witch was a part of the druidic tradition which had existed in the Celtic world from pre-Christian times.

This is not to say, however, that none of the Celtic witches were strange or antisocial. In fact, there were many who were. The fierce territorial perspective of the Celts often made any stranger a potential object of deep suspicion and mistrust. Many of the strangers and settlers who came into a community were regarded as sorcerers or witches. This was even more of an issue if the person concerned were somehow physically 'different' (deformed or ugly) or was 'strange' in his or her ways (that is, differed from the communal 'norm'). Other forms of behaviour or unfamiliar practices were often invariably viewed as indications of malign arts by the community as a whole. The Celts certainly regarded difference as something sinister and hostile; 'those who are not with us are against us' might have been their maxim. Physical peculiarities or differences also created an adverse attitude. The 17th-century Kentish Squire, Reginald Scot, spoke scathingly of 'the gobber tooth, the squint eye' in order to illustrate this very point (Scot's book *The Discoverie of Witchcraft* was designed to show the gullibility of many witchcraft judges and the foolishness of some of the charges that were brought to court). It is no coincidence, therefore, that the common representation of witches is one of ugliness and even disfigurement. It is also no coincidence that their behaviour lies outside the accepted social norm. Such perceptions may well have their roots in the Celtic psyche. There is little doubt, however, that many of these ideas were carried to the New World where they formed the basis of the colonial stereotypes which became ingrained among the early American settlers as they had been in Europe. In the New World, people were more dependent upon each other; societies were often even more tightly structured and cultural perspectives even more deeply entrenched, so that differences (whether they were differences in culture or in religion) were viewed with an even greater hostility and resentment. The idea of ugliness, age and eccentricity played a central role in colonial witch-perceptions. M.V.B. Perley in *A Short History of the Salem Village Witch Trials* (1911) cites the following description of an early American witch:

> An old woman of attenuated form, somewhat bent; clothed in lively colours and ample skirts; having a darting and piercing eye, a head sporting dishevelled hair and crowned with a sugar-loaf hat, a carlin's cheek, a falcated chin bent to meet an aquiline nose, by both of which was formed a Neopolitan bay; her mouth in the background resembling Vesuvius in eruption; and riding an enchanted broomstick with a black cat as her guide.

Such a figure must have seemed bizarre and outlandish to the early Puritan settlers and may well have gradually become emblazoned upon their minds as the personification of evil and malign forces.

On a grassy plateau overlooking Gloucester, Rockport and Ipswich Bay in Massachusetts, a collection of disparate individuals formed a loose colony in around 1661 which would later become known as

Dogtown (because of the number of feral dogs that wandered around it) and which lasted until 1830. Its inhabitants were mainly the widows of Gloucester fishermen and of soldiers who had been lost at sea, and they were primarily old crones with ugly faces and sharp and evil tongues. Many of them were either Irish or Scottish. They are described in contemporary accounts as sitting on the patch of grass which constituted the Dogtown Green, cackling and muttering among themselves. Local people branded this community as a 'witch village' and categorically stated that black arts were worked there under public gaze. It may have been that some of these old beldames told fortunes for the sailor-folk in the area, or they may have issued curses against their neighbours, and this was equated with the dark sciences within the locality. The majority of the inhabitants were named 'crones' (evil-looking women) and were to be strenuously avoided. In her book *Reminiscences of A Nonagrarian* (1897), Newbury's Sarah Anna Emory gives at least some indication of the eerieness of the place. 'Dogtown was two miles distant from Craneneck', she wrote. 'After passing Dale's Pond, the road ran through thick woods. This on some dark and stormy nights was rather bug-a-booish.'

Dogtown, she goes on, was a place that most people avoided even during daylight hours, for fear of the raddled hags who dwelt there. In his *History of Dogtown* (1896), Charles Mann makes mention of several of them: Judy Rhines (Ryan), a fortune-teller who met with the Devil in the surrounding woods (she had a queerly deformed mouth – 'teeth like a dog' – and went about muttering to herself); Cornelius Finson or 'Black Neil' (who had long teeth protruding from his upper lip) and Tammy Younger (with a beard like a man and 'a very choice vocabulary'). Dogtown, Mann continues, was 'a resort of buccaneers and low men' who only added to its queer and supernatural reputation. It was America's first 'witch-colony' and its inhabitants were 'peripheral people', those feared and shunned by the more established societies because of their grotesque appearance and unsociable ways. They were the links with the demonic powers that dwelt in the swamps and forests around; and, for those early highly religious settlers, America was certainly a place filled with evil. All around their settlements were deep, dark woodlands in which unimaginable horrors dwelt – strange, wild creatures and pagan savages who worshipped abominable and demonic gods, ready to destroy the immortal souls of those who believed in Christ. It is not surprising, therefore, that people such as the bizarre and antisocial inhabitants of Dogtown became the actual embodiment of this abiding and superstitious fear among early Americans. This fear had its roots in Celtic notions of 'strangeness' – fear of new places outside their own territories, fear of anything strange and unusual, fear of eccentric people. This terror largely contributed to the ideal of the American witch.

The number three also played a significant part in Celtic mythology, folklore and superstition. The number was widely regarded as an extremely mystical one and, as such, played a central role in Celtic life and magic. The structure of Celtic society was classified in three ways – priests, warriors, agriculturists – while, in Ireland and Wales, traditional teaching was carried out using 'concept clusters', each containing three truths. Irish legend abounds with the mystical number: there were three sons of Uisnech (although only one – Naoise, the lover of Deirdre – has any real identity); three sons of Tureen; three Great Sorrows of Irish Storytelling; Cu Chulainn also had his hair tied in triple braids and is recorded as killing his enemies in groups of three. Even in vernacular folklore, the number crops up time and time again – three sisters, three tasks, three wishes. The number, either individually or in multiples of itself, was considered to be especially lucky – after two failures, the third attempt at any task was sure to succeed; and three (or nine) items carried on a journey would ensure that the traveller arrived safely. Its power probably derived from the notion of the Celtic Triple-Goddess, who appears in many tales and was the patron deity of the Celtic lands and groupings. She was alternately the goddess of fertility, war and slaughter – depicted in Irish lore as Macha, Badb and Morrigain (Morrigu). Numerous other Celtic spirits and deities also possessed triple manifestations and their images have been found at various locations scattered across the ancient world. Among these were the Genii Cucullati ('hooded spirits') who were fertility deities to be found mainly in Roman Gaul (France) who were usually depicted wearing long, black, hooded capes. Hidden beneath these hoods were three faces, each representing a different aspect of the spirit. During the early Celtic Christian period, these localized deities became strongly associated with the missionary monks who came to Ireland and Scotland from the great centres in Gaul, and were still being worshipped long after Christianity had taken root in the Celtic lands of the West. Quite possibly, memories of these hooded spirits – now perhaps regarded as malefic – had been handed down across the generations and may well have been absorbed into the overall folklore that the first settlers took with them to America. Once established in the New World, these beliefs took on even deeper roots and perhaps passed into American witchlore, influencing the common image of the American witch. Certainly, the number three was passed down over the years – indeed it is still associated with luck and magic. It has even found its way into classical literature. It is no coincidence that Shakespeare places three witches at the very centre of what is, for many, his greatest play – *Macbeth*.

If there was a combination of all these disparate elements – the triple aspect and people of queer and eccentric behaviour (and perhaps not very appealing to look at) who affected strange and unusual dress and manners – then such persons must surely be considered to be witches. Such a combination occurred at the start of the 20th century in Christiansburg in southwest Virginia. Even worse, the incident and the persons involved in it were associated with a school.

The story of Christiansburg's celebrated 'Black Sisters' is strongly connected with the Montgomery Female Academy, one of the leading academic centres in the town's early history. The school was opened in 1852, just after Christiansburg was incorporated as the country seat of Montgomery County, Virginia. The town itself had been named after the rather obscure figure of William Christian, about whom little is known, but whom no less a person than Theodore Roosevelt described as 'a noted Indian fighter'. The Female Academy, a privately owned institution licensed by the Montgomery Presbytery (the same organization, incidentally, which had licensed a male equivalent in 1849), was initially set up in the basement of the Presbyterian church with the local minister, the Reverend Nicholas Chavalier, as its first principal. Under his able guidance, the school grew both in size and reputation until in 1859 it moved into new premises, valued at $12,000, which were custom-built for the purpose and now form the basis of present-day Christiansburg Middle School.

Throughout its successful expansion, the ownership of the school changed hands a couple of times. By the late 1800s, it was owned by a Mrs O.S. Polluck, an elderly lady who was not in good health and who had no children. When she died, around the end of the 19th century, she bequeathed the school to her sister, Mrs Martha Wardlaw, and, in turn, to Mrs Wardlaw's daughters – Mrs Mary W. Snead, Mrs Caroline Martin (both of whom were widows) and Miss Virginia Wardlaw. Martha Wardlaw did not enjoy the bequest for very long and soon died, leaving it to pass on to her daughters. It is here that something further needs to be said about the three sisters.

The three Wardlaw sisters were all members of a prominent Georgia family. Their father, John Baptist Wardlaw, had been one of the foremost Methodist ministers of his time and the three sisters were given an excellent if religious education, and all three eventually became highly respected teachers. Caroline, the oldest, was born in 1845, Mary in 1848 and Virginia in 1852 and, as sisters, they remained extremely close for most of their lives. Caroline taught in private and public schools, as did Mary, while Virginia taught in the Price School in Nashville, Tennessee, where she 'established a glowing reputation for her progressive methods of instruction'.

In 1892, Virginia was offered a job as President of Soule Female College in Murfreesboro, Tennessee. Soule, which had been founded in 1851, was considered to be one of the finest educational establishments in the South. Five years later, Mary Snead, who had recently become a widow, joined her sister on the faculty at Soule. Both women were reasonably well liked, although they were considered somewhat eccentric by students and other members of staff because of their rather bizarre dress code – they always insisted on wearing black. Southern author Norman Zierold stated: 'In the South, where strange legends abound and original behaviour amuses and fascinates, the wearing of black added to the occultness of the pair.'

After nine years, during which affairs at the College ran smoothly, the two sisters were joined by Caroline Martin, now also a widow. Almost immediately and imperceptibly, the nature and conditions of the College began to change and to deteriorate. Caroline was clearly the most dominant of the trio and became an authoritative figure within the College. Although sometimes (though not often) 'entertaining and persuasive', she ruled 'with a rod of iron, harsh and abrupt', her ideas and opinions taking precedence over Mary and Virginia (who was, after all, President of the College). Her behaviour was even weirder than that of her sisters, and rumours concerning her perceived eccentricity circulated everywhere. These were fuelled in part by Caroline's maid, who noted that:

> . . . she was powerful queer about her clothes and would wear a nightgown all day except when she was going out. Then she would put on an old black skirt and a waist without anything under them. Sometimes she would go without stockings and sometimes with only one and she would go for three or four weeks without a change of clothing. She would stay in bed for weeks at a time, her hair down, wild and loose. She never washed. I don't ever remember her using a bathtub and she wouldn't even let me change the bedclothes whenever she went away. Her room was the nastiest thing I ever saw for she never let me clean it in the two years that I was there. All over the floor was food and coal and ashes. She would never let me take any food away from her room after I'd brought it in and it would stay there until it rotted. She kept a big box of money in the room and she would scatter five and ten dollar bills about the floor, just for the pleasure of throwing the money around her. Mrs Martin kept a big double-barrelled shotgun, right at the head of her bed. One night I saw her sitting on the cot laughing with the gun between her knees. She'd just shot a hole in the ceiling.

The sisters' growing eccentricity was also having an effect on the college itself. Bills went unpaid and the growing rumour-machine made sure that the reputation of the Institution went into decline. The sisters took no interest in the lessons but were frequently seen wandering about empty classrooms or down corridors and hallways at all hours of the day and night. Always they were dressed in black. Often students walking in the grounds would look up to see Caroline glaring down at them from a high window with a ferocious expression on her gaunt face. One student claimed that she woke in the middle of the night to see the three sisters gathered around the stove in her room 'mumbling and chanting' to themselves. No one was allowed into the section of the college where the sisters lived, and the blinds there were continually down. Only at night did the three of them venture out – always dressed in black as if mourning somebody who was dead (or was about to die). A year after Caroline arrived at Soule, the sisters were joined by another family member. This was little Ocey Martin (although her name was later given as Ocey Snead), the ten-year-old daughter of either Mrs Martin or Mrs Snead – many people, however, noticed that she bore a remarkable resemblance to Virginia, and suggested that she might really be her daughter, but that Caroline claimed her 'because of Virginia's maiden status'. Whatever the truth of it, Ocey was kept well away from the other students and was taught privately, virtually a prisoner in the sisters' apartments. There was a story going round that Mrs Martin had placed an insurance policy of $15,000 on the little girl and that they were keeping her apart so that they could eventually kill her.

As the sisters' bizarre and malignant reputation grew, girls started leaving Soule College in droves. The situation got so bad that finally the school governors ousted the sisters from their positions and terminated their contracts of employment. All three sisters disappeared in the middle of the night. It was just about this time that Mrs Polluck died in Christiansburg and the Wardlaws suddenly found themselves another appointment. They swiftly caught the train to West Virginia. Whether or not they took Ocey with them, or sent her elsewhere, is not recorded.

Once in Christiansburg, the sisters resumed their old ways. They were not well liked, and the people around the town were more hostile towards them than the citizens of Murfreesboro had ever been. Once again rumours started to circulate. It was persistently claimed, for example, that there was something unusual about the death of Mrs Martin's husband and that she herself might have had a hand in it. However, nothing could be proved. If the good people of Christiansburg harboured suspicions that at least one of the sisters was a murderess, they kept it to themselves. If the rumours had reached the ears of the three women, they gave no indication that they were worried but continued to dress in black, to keep themselves to themselves and to roam the streets of the town after dark, pretty much as they had done in Murfreesboro. Shopkeepers were knocked out of their beds at odd hours of the night to find the sisters at their doors, 'veiled, sombre and austere', as though it were the middle of the day. Indeed, many citizens were afraid to venture into the town streets after dark for fear of running into the 'Black Sisters', which some invariably did. It was also claimed that chanting was heard coming from the Montgomery Female Academy at all hours of the day and night and that the sisters were involved in some bizarre Satanic worship. The aura of murder and witchcraft was steadily growing around the bizarre trio.

Mrs Mary Snead had a 28-year-old son, John, who lived with his wife in Lynville, Tennessee. He was an exceptionally bright lad who had received a good education. On inheriting the academy, the sisters thought that he would make a fine addition to the academic staff, and Caroline was despatched to visit her nephew in Lynville and bring him back with her to Christiansburg. John might have obeyed his aunt's imperious commands but his wife steadfastly refused to move. She had no great affection for her witch-like aunt-in-law; neither did she wish to move to Christiansburg or live anywhere near the Black Sisters. Caroline, of course, was insistent and, while her nephew dithered regarding the move, she and her niece-in-law exchanged hot and heavy words. In the end, John's wife called the law-enforcers, and Caroline was forcibly evicted from the home. In a short time she was back again, and this time she persuaded John to leave his wife and come back with her to take up a position in the academy. He returned with her on the next train, albeit reluctantly.

No sooner had he taken up his position than John became the victim of a series of mysterious 'accidents'. During the trip to Christiansburg, he fell from the train and was badly injured. Although the incident was reported as a formal 'accident', the train's brakeman who had witnessed the event said that John appeared to have thrown himself from the moving train as if in a desperate attempt to commit suicide. Perhaps, it has been suggested, he was being taken to Christiansburg largely against his will. Shortly afterwards, as a teacher at the school, John was rescued from a deep cistern by Sonny Correll, the academy caretaker. No explanation of how he had come to fall into the cistern was ever given, but had Correll been a moment later John would certainly have drowned. Correll said that the young man looked 'almost possessed' and this description only added to the suspicions and allegations of witchcraft which were already growing around the Black Sisters. Three weeks afterwards, John Sneed was discovered in what appeared to be a 'state of intoxication' (although he was not a drinker), lying in a burning bed. It was subsequently discovered that the mattress had been soaked with kerosene and set ablaze. John was so badly burned that he died soon afterwards.

It soon transpired that, as a member of the academy staff, John Sneed had been heavily insured by his aunts and that, during the course of his residence in Christiansburg, the beneficiary of the policy had been changed from his wife to Miss Virginia Wardlaw. When the insurance company, suspecting murder and fraud, refused to pay out, the sisters threatened legal action, producing affidavits signed by many townspeople that the death was accidental. It was said that the majority of these affidavits had been obtained by 'dubious means', which included witchcraft. Despite the sworn statements, the story was widely circulated that John's death was 'no accident'. (Faced with the prospect of a protracted court battle, the insurance company eventually made an agreed and undisclosed settlement with the sisters.)

The Black Sisters now approached John's brother Fletcher with an invitation to become a teacher at the academy. Not as academically bright as his brother, Fletcher nevertheless did not need as much persuasion to take up the offer. He swiftly divorced his wife and moved to Christiansburg. There he married his first cousin, Ocey Martin, who had suddenly reappeared. There was much speculation regarding the marriage and there was a suggestion (no more) that Fletcher might have married his own sister, or a half-sister at least, on the orders of his aunts. Again, nothing could be proved. Ocey's name was officially given as

'Martin' and all documentation appeared to be in order, but whispers and rumours continued to fly.

By now, speculation regarding the Black Sisters was reaching fever pitch in the town. Much of the rumour concerning them was inspired by Sonny Correll, the academy caretaker, and Lewis Hand, a local wagoneer. Correll said that, on the occasions he had visited the sisters (he was always interviewed by the three women together) in their library, he had noticed some of the books on the shelves there. These were terrible tomes indeed – books of witchcraft, devilry and black magic. There was no doubt in Correll's mind that the three of them were practising arcane arts at the college. This notion was reinforced by Hand's testimony. On a number of occasions, the wagoneer had been summoned to drive the sisters out to the local cemetery, where he allegedly witnessed a terrifying spectacle. When the three women had entered the graveyard, on one occasion, Hand had followed them. To his absolute horror, he saw them gathered about a freshly turned grave with their arms outstretched and muttering eerie-sounding incantations. Although he subsequently promised himself never to take them out to the place again, Lewis Hand found that each time they summoned him to come for them he could not refuse. There was witchcraft afoot all right!

In spite of their reputed wealth and the seeming success of their academy, the sisters began to run up large debts all over Christiansburg, just as they had in Murfreesboro. Daily, a steady stream of creditors and process-servers made their way to the academy door. Many of them were turned away without ever seeing the Black Sisters, and threats of legal action followed. Nevertheless, many of the citizens of Christiansburg were terrified to take on the sisters for fear of the dreadful magic that they might invoke. Eventually, though, matters ran their full course: in 1908, a court order was obtained against them and the bailiffs were called in.

When the bailiffs arrived at the sisters' dwelling, they found something strange. The place was deserted, and had been for some days. The sisters had gone, although nobody had noted their departure – quite an achievement in a small rural town like Christiansburg. It was also noted that Fletcher and Ocey had disappeared at around the same time. This seemed to close the final chapter concerning the Black Sisters, but there was still more to come.

In 1909, a New York newspaper carried the story of an alleged murder in the rundown suburb of East Orange in New Jersey. The body of a fairly young woman had been found in a bathtub in a tenement house, and foul play was suspected. The woman in question was Ocey Snead. Apparently, Fletcher and Ocey had moved to New Jersey and had taken out rooms in the squalid block. The janitor said that they had appeared happy at first – that is, he added, until two women, completely dressed in black, had come to live with them. Fletcher had become nervous and edgy and frequently talked about leaving New Jersey and 'heading west'. He and Ocey had a series of blistering rows, which the janitor was in no doubt had something to do with the women in black. Shortly after their arrival, Fletcher simply disappeared. He left Ocey pregnant and, for some unknown reason, she remained with the women who now revealed themselves to be Fletcher's aunts. Her decision to stay was a puzzling one, for she was quite clearly terrified of the two dark women, but, as she said herself, they were 'the only kin she had in New Jersey'. Five months after Fletcher's disappearance, Ocey gave birth to a baby boy.

While in hospital for the birth, she pleaded with doctors not to send her home again and claimed that she was being starved and was near to death. Her weakened condition seemed to confirm this, but before they could do anything the doctors were confronted by the Black Sisters and were told that Ocey had withdrawn her allegations and would have nothing further to say. Ocey discharged herself from the hospital (accompanied by the sisters) and was denied any further medical care. Shortly afterwards the baby died – a victim of a fever that was going around New Jersey.

One morning, several weeks afterwards, police were summoned to the tenement house by a woman who identified herself as Virginia Wardlaw. In the bathroom, they found the body of a woman, half-immersed in water and with her head resting under the bath taps. A crudely written note had been left nearby, which stated that Ocey had committed suicide because of the death of 'loved ones'. Miss Wardlaw

said that the girl had been in a severe state of depression for several days and that her suicide was not entirely unexpected. The police were suspicious – the note seemed forged or, at the very least, the crude handwriting suggested that Ocey had been forced to write it. Miss Wardlaw immediately changed the emphasis of her story in order to suggest that Ocey's husband, Fletcher, might have had a hand in her death. This made the authorities even more suspicious. They knew that Fletcher had disappeared at least five months before Ocey's death and that he was, in all probability, not in New Jersey at all. A will was now produced which left all of Ocey's estate to Virginia Wardlaw. The police were now convinced that the sisters were somehow involved in the death.

The two women now took over the house in East Orange, under the watchful eye of the New Jersey police force. They were joined by Mrs Caroline Martin who had mysteriously arrived in New Jersey, and the diabolical trio were now together once more. For a year, the East Orange authorities tried to bring the sisters to trial and to connect them with the murder of Ocey Snead, but the evidence against them was too circumstantial; there was really nothing that could be taken to court that would assuredly convict them. Sometimes witnesses would come forward, only to retract their testimony in mysterious circumstances before the case came to trial. The sisters were often seen late at night in old cemeteries in and around New Jersey and it seemed that they were establishing the same reputation as they had enjoyed in Christiansburg. However, they were dealing with a relatively sophisticated police force and one which was determined to bring them to justice. By 1910, enough evidence had been gathered, and the sisters were arrested and brought to trial on 9 January 1911.

During the course of the trial, the cold and austere reserve that had always characterized the Black Sisters deserted at least one of them. Mary Snead pleaded guilty to manslaughter. Because of her advanced age, she was released into the custody of another son and moved to Colorado, where she died soon afterwards. Fate was not so kind to the other two sisters.

Virginia Wardlaw never saw the inside of the courthouse. She refused to eat, protesting her innocence to the end. She died a day before the trial commenced. Caroline Martin was found guilty of complicity in Ocey Snead's murder and was sentenced to a long stretch in the New Jersey State Prison. During the trial, her mind showed signs that it was about to give way, and when she was transferred to prison she became so wild and uncontrollable that she was immediately sent to the State Hospital for the Insane where she died soon afterwards. Some accounts report that she took her own life in a fit of insane fury.

Another actor in the mysterious drama was found shortly afterwards. Fletcher Snead was discovered working as a cook in a Canadian logging camp. Using an assumed name, he had gone to great lengths to disguise his true identity and was clearly terrified of being found. He showed little apparent anxiety at the death of his wife and son, but seemed more frightened that he would be discovered by his aunts. The authorities decided that he was not involved in Ocey's death and no criminal charges were brought against him. He was allowed to disappear into the Canadian wilderness, never to be heard of again. Had he tried to escape his murderous relatives by hiding in the wild? Even when told of the deaths of the Black Sisters, he flatly refused to return to Christiansburg. Did he fear their supposedly occult powers, even from beyond the grave? We will never know the answer to that, since Fletcher Snead must now be long dead.

The body of Virginia Wardlaw, seriously emaciated by her weeks of starvation, was however returned to Christiansburg for burial. On the way back, the train carrying the corpse broke down several times before actually reaching the town. Was this one final manifestation of the sisters' power? On arrival at Christiansburg, the cadaver was quickly removed and was taken to the town's Sunset Cemetery where it was interred with as little ceremony as possible. The horror of the town's Black Sisters was finally over. Or was it?

Although the Female Academy which the sisters owned has been replaced by the Montgomery County Middle School, their influence does not appear to have completely gone away. It is said that, on certain nights of the year, lights blaze from one of the storeys of the building and that shadows come and go behind the windows – shadows which are very dark as if they were the outlines of women dressed wholly in black.

It is also said that the ghosts of the three sisters still prowl the streets of Christiansburg after nightfall. People who pass by the town's cemetery sometimes speak of having glimpsed dark figures by the side of a newly turned grave and of hearing strange voices mouthing unintelligible chants, just as Lewis Hand did all those years before. Do the Black Sisters still exert some kind of malign influence within the community, almost 100 years after their deaths?

In many ways, the legend of the Black Sisters of Christiansburg conforms to the common traditions concerning Celtic vernacular witches; there were three of them (reminiscent of the Celtic triad), they were highly respected members of the community, and were not 'outsiders' in the accepted sense – despite this, their ways and dress were extremely strange and non-conformist. They shunned much of local company and would not pay their bills to local traders on time. There seems little doubt that they were murderers and fraudsters, but did they really invoke supernatural powers in order to carry out their malignant will, as they are credited with doing? The stories of their gathering in the local churchyard, of the arcane and evil books in their library and of their travelling abroad only upon dark nights are probably nothing more than folklore additions to the central tale, added presumably to increase the sisters' already fearsome reputation. Witchcraft served as an explanation for the whole situation and offered a context for the undoubted evils which the three women carried out (including a mother, Mary Snead, being centrally involved in the death of her own son, John). Such beliefs and tales turned naturally malignant and scheming women into monstrous and supernormal hags who were, in all probability, plotting the destruction of the entire community. In the end, however, these may be little more than folkloric additions. Yet can we be entirely sure? Might there not be at least an element of truth in these wild fancies and stories? Such additions (if additions they are) have certainly achieved their objective, for Christiansburg's Black Sisters are still commemorated in legend, story and poem throughout southwest Virginia. Even though the Sisters are long dead, their shadow still stretches into modern times.

# THE VAMPIRE LADY OF RHODE ISLAND

In a remote and overgrown cemetery in Coventry in rural Rhode Island, there once stood a headstone bearing the rather singular inscription 'I am waiting and watching for you'. Although Nelly Vaughn's grave marker is now long gone (it was removed in around 1991 because of excessive vandalism in the surrounding churchyard), no explanation has ever been given regarding her curious epitaph. Little is known about Nelly's brief life (she died in 1889 at the age of 19) and it is possible, indeed probable, that the words may have some wholly innocent connotation – they may have been addressed to a lover who had gone away from the immediate area for a time, or they may have been a message to a close and loving family. However, in the climate of the Rhode Island countryside, they have acquired a particular and sinister resonance, because America's smallest state is arguably the 'vampire capital' of the entire continent. The roll-call of the state's 'vampire ladies' (there seem to have been fewer instances of male vampirism in Rhode Island) is extensive – Sarah Tillinghast, Nancy Young, Juliet Rose, and a number of others. The fact that no vegetation appeared to be able to grow on Nelly's grave (and on the graves of many other alleged vampires) only added to the suggestion that there was something unnatural about the body that lay there.

The notion of the vampire, or the 'undead', arguably has its roots in Celtic lore and, although parallels are to be found in Slavonic folktales, may have very little to do with Transylvania (or even eastern Europe) at all. The notion of the returning dead was central to the 'death cults' of the fragmented world of ancient Celtic religion. The important festival of the Failte na Marbh (the Feast of the Dead, held on 31 October – Hallowe'en) welcomed these spirits and corpses who traversed between the Otherworld and the mortal realm. This was a time in the Celtic world when the dead were allowed to come back to the places that they had known when alive, to see their descendants, to sit at their own firesides once again and perhaps to issue prophesies for the coming year. In later, Christian, times, this period became the Feast of Souls, when the dead were remembered in prayer and offerings were given for the repose of their souls. Over the years, both Christian and pagan aspects of the Feast merged, and it began to adopt a slightly more sinister tone. While the returning dead of the Failte na Marbh had been largely harmless, even pleasant, and protective towards their descendants, the Church now taught that such beings were generally hostile, particularly if their families had forgotten to offer up prayers for them throughout the years – prayers which, of course, added greatly to the Church coffers. The unquiet dead now returned in order to chastise and to take vengeance upon the living. They could do this in a number of ways: they could torment them during the hours of darkness and disturb their sleep with continual clamour; they could devour the contents of their pantries, leaving them with little or no food; and they could even physically attack the living as they slept. Thus the concept of the malignant corpse (the prototype of the vampire) was created, and it was largely of Celtic origin.

Indeed, cultural historians such as Peter Beresford Ellis have strongly argued that the vampire motif itself does not initially come from areas such as Transylvania at all (although there are vampire legends to be found there too) but may be partly rooted in Irish tradition. It is no coincidence, such historians note, that the two greatest writers in vampire literature (Bram Stoker, author of *Dracula*, and Sheridan Le Fanu, author of *Carmilla*) were both Irishmen. The oldest example of the vampire tale, 'The Legend of Abhartach', is to be found in Seathrun Ceitinn's Foras Feasa ar Eireann ('A General History of Ireland') written between 1629 and 1631. Mention is also made in Irish literature of the *Dreach-fhoula* (literally 'bad or tainted blood' and pronounced 'droc-ula') and this, argue some folklorists, serves as an indication that Dracula – probably the greatest of all literary vampires – may have both cultural and linguistic connections with Celtic tradition.

The great County Kerry folklorist and Archivist for the Irish Folklore Commission, Sean O'Suilleabhain, mentioned, during a lecture given in Dublin in 1961, a place in the Magillicuddy Reeks Mountains which he named as Dun Dreach-fhoula ('the Castle of the Blood Visage'), a fortress which guarded a lonely pass along a mountain road. It was said to be inhabited by blood-drinking fairies who continually preyed on travellers passing through that area. Similar stories come from Kintail in Scotland where terrible goat-footed women are also sometimes said to have attacked upland shepherds in their lonely shielings (shelters) at night. These beliefs persisted well into the 20th century, as is witnessed by the collection of stories concerning blood-drinking and flesh-eating ghouls, gathered in the parish of Sneem in County Kerry at the behest of the Irish Folklore Commission by Tadgh O'Murchiu (Tim Murphy) during the mid- to late 1930s.

These traditions and beliefs were almost certainly transported, in one way or another, across the Atlantic to take root among the settlers of the developing New World. The Celtic belief-strand proved a significant factor in the meld of traditions from many parts of the world which was to form the basis of the American supernatural psyche. Such beliefs were further shaped and modified by other constituent traditions – Dutch, American Indian, French, German and so on – but the belief in the unquiet, returning dead which had characterized both the pagan and Christian aspects of the Celtic imagination was the dark and sinister foundation for the American vampire legend.

The notion of vampirism in America is more widespread than is commonly supposed. From as early as the late 17th century we find references to so-called 'vampire attacks' upon members of the American community. The Reverend Deodat Lawson, minister at Salem Village from 1684 to 1688, and author of the first printed account of the Salem Witch Trials, records one such attack. He was staying at the house of Nathaniel Ingersoll when Mary Walcott, one of the 'affected girls' (those who had allegedly been subject to witchcraft) came to see him.

While standing near to the door, she suddenly felt a bite on her wrist, as if to draw blood, and by the light of a candle the minister saw teeth marks upon her flesh. There is no mention of any blood loss; however, the demonologist Montague Summers, when commenting on the case, states that the energy was drained from the girl.

During the late 1890s, a great deal of vampire speculation centred on a house in Green Street, in Schenectady, New York. This concerned a human silhouette, made out of mould, which had appeared upon the cellar floor. In spite of constant sweeping and scrubbing, it could not be removed, and the mouldy outline (which appeared to be that of a reclining man) would always return. It was later discovered that the house had been built over an old burial ground, dating back to the time of the Dutch occupation of the city. One interpretation of the phenomenon was that it was the form of a vampire trying to leave its grave. This explanation was accepted largely because many of the people who had dwelt in the house frequently felt unaccountably weak, as if their vital energies were being slowly drained away. It was prevented from adopting full demonic shape, said the legend, because of a 'virtuous spell' which had been placed upon the ground. The motif of a recurring shadow-form on the cellar floor appears in H.P. Lovecraft's *The Shunned House*, and this is almost certainly based on the New York occurrence.

It was in Rhode Island, however, that the belief in vampires seemed to take its most persistent root. Writing in an edition of the *American Anthropologist* (1896), George Stetson expressed his astonishment that such a 'barbarous superstition' had such a strong hold on the minds of the people of the state, stronger than in any other part of the country. He was particularly struck by the fact that, compared with other areas of America, Rhode Island enjoyed relatively high educational advantages and a much higher level of literacy and culture. There may, however, have been at least some reason for this belief.

Epidemics among the settlers, such as the great consumption (tuberculosis) outbreaks of the mid- to late 1800s in Connecticut, Massachusetts, Vermont and Rhode Island, cause once-healthy individuals to waste away inexplicably. This was coupled with some of the more peculiar religious practices of fundamentalist sects within these states (groups such as Shadrack Ireland's 'Brethren of the New Light' whose uncoffined dead lay in sealed underground tombs, ready to walk out on the Day of Judgement). Factors such as these may have resurrected the ancient beliefs about the hostile, returning dead, which had been buried deep within the colonial mind and which served to contribute to the overall patterns of supernatural belief.

Disease hit some states particularly hard, as the tombstones of many rural New England cemeteries will testify. Here too there is a connection with the Celtic world. Tuberculosis had occurred sporadically across the centuries in places like County Clare in Ireland (in the Burren region of the county in particular) and, in the absence of any real medical diagnosis, the gradual wasting away of the body was attributed to the malignant involvement of fairies. These sprites, it was claimed, carried away fit and healthy individuals and left pale and wizened representations in their place. It was but a small step in some rural regions of America to transfer that belief to the intervention of the hostile dead. Thus, vampires not only lurk in the remote districts of the Carpathian Mountains but they are also to be found at the heart of the New England farming countryside.

While it would take far too long to detail each instance of the undead in a vampire-plagued state such as Rhode Island, it is possible to give an account of the reputed unholy career of one of America's (and Rhode Island's) most famous vampire-daughters – Mercy Brown.

In the year 1883, George Brown and his family were struggling hard to make a living in the countryside of Rhode Island, a little way from the small settlement of Exeter. George Brown was a solid working man, the father of six children, who made his living as a farmer. He expected little more from life than good crops and kindly weather. He also hoped for strong and healthy children to farm the land when he could not, and he depended fervently upon the goodwill of his neighbours. The years 1882 and 1883, however, were not good for him. His wife, Mary, normally a healthy woman and well used to the hardships of rural American life, suffered a series of minor illnesses; but then, as the winter of 1883 approached, she began to sicken seriously. The cause was consumption (tuberculosis) which was raging through Rhode Island at the time. George and his daughters tried to nurse her back to health, but they were fighting a losing battle. On 8 December 1883, Mary Brown closed her eyes and finally succumbed to the illness. George did not have much time to grieve, and had to reorganize his shattered family almost immediately. They came together slowly after their mother's death, and gradually resumed their lives again, but even more difficulties lay ahead for them. The consumption had not gone away. In fact, it was still as virulent as ever and would claim further lives from the Brown family.

In the spring of 1884, Mary Olive, George's oldest daughter, contracted the disease and was already fading away. During her illness, the girl complained of terrible dreams and, most significantly, of a crushing weight lying across her as she slept. It was as though somebody or something had climbed on the bed and was trying to strangle her. It was difficult to breathe, she told her alarmed family. She grew pale and gaunt and refused to eat and it seemed to all who saw her that the very life was slowly being drawn out of her. Formerly, she had been a bright, intelligent and lively girl, but she was now a shadow of her former self, mooning listlessly about the house and sleeping most of the time, as though to conserve her fading strength. Finally, on 6 June 1884, she joined her mother. Devastated by the loss, George Brown was forced to pull his deeply shocked and stricken family together once more.

For a while, no further deaths occurred. Several years after the demise of his mother and sister, Edwin Brown, the only son of the family, married and bought a small farm near Wickford, close to his own home. All seemed to be going well at last. Yet, in 1889, almost five years after his sister's death, Edwin Brown also began to sicken and fade away. Once again, it seems to have been consumption which threatened his life, and he too spoke of strange dreams, of a great weight settling itself on his chest and of his difficulty in breathing. Given that tuberculosis attacks the lungs and generally causes a shortness of breath, this was not strange in itself, but in the charged climate of the Brown household Edwin's experiences took on a rather sinister slant. Each morning, he rose complaining that he felt inexplicably weak, as if all the blood had been drained from his body during the night. He was also ghastly pale (another symptom of the consumption) and this only seemed to add weight to such a perception. He passed from a healthy and robust young man into a ghostly, shambling figure upon whom clothes hung as on a scarecrow. He was advised to go to Colorado Springs, in the hope that the health-giving spa waters there would restore him. Taking this advice, he headed West. In Colorado Springs, he seemed to rally a little and appeared to be convalescing back towards full health.

At the end of January 1892, however, the awful curse which seemed to haunt the Brown family struck again. Still in Colorado Springs, Edwin received word that his youngest sister, Mercy Lena, was stricken with exactly the same illness as himself, and he rushed back to Rhode Island to be with her. He was too late. By the time he arrived, his sister was already dead. The news brought on another attack of the consumption, and Edwin was forced to spend some time at the home of his father-in-law Willis Himes, to rest and recuperate. The dreadful dreams and the crushing weight on his chest, which had all but disappeared in Colorado Springs, now returned with a vengeance, and his father-in-law advised him to stay at his residence for as long as was necessary. While he was there, he received several visitors who expressed an old theory that there was something supernatural at work in the Brown family. They recalled stories from their youth which spoke of the vengeful dead who subsisted upon the flesh and blood of the living – tales of Sarah Tillinghast in 1796, of Nancy Young in 1827 and (within living memory) of Juliet Rose in 1874 – and they suggested that an ancient evil had come back to haunt the state. The women of the Brown household had succumbed to the awful scourge of vampirism – the latest being young Mercy.

At first Edwin rejected all their theories, dismissing them as foolish superstition, but, as his own torments increased, he began to wonder. In several of his nightmares, he saw Mercy's face as the weight on his chest grew heavier, and at times he thought he heard her voice, especially when the sun was beginning to set. Maybe there was something in those old legends after all! There was another reason, too, why there might be some truth in the superstition. Because she had died during the winter months when the Rhode Island ground was rock-hard and frozen, Mercy's body had not been buried. Instead it lay, coffined and on a cart, in a stone crypt on the edge of the Chestnut Hill cemetery – Exeter's burying-ground. There it awaited the coming of spring when the ground could again be opened to receive it. With all these thoughts and suspicions on his mind, Edwin sought the advice of Harold Metcalf, the Wickford doctor and surgeon. Metcalf, himself not untouched by the weird superstitions of the area, suggested an exhumation of Edwin's mother and elder sister, Mary Olive. With Edwin's consent, the exhumation was made, but nothing was found. The skeletons of Mary Brown and her daughter were so decomposed that no firm analysis could be made. Metcalf then turned his attention to Mercy, now dead for some nine weeks, whose body still rested within the tiny crypt. Early in the morning (around 5.30am) on 18 March 1892, a sombre group of men, all carrying lanterns against the morning's darkness, made their way to the Exeter burying-ground. Once there, they congregated outside the stone crypt in which Mercy Brown's body lay. A rusty key was produced from somewhere, and it turned stiffly in the frozen lock. The door creaked open with a metallic groan, which was greatly amplified by the stillness of the morning.

The coffin still lay on the cart where Mercy's father had left her. The men entered the place warily, for they remembered the eerie tale of Sarah Tillinghast's mother – Honour – who had reputedly confronted her own daughter in her tomb (it was later suggested that this was nothing more than a dream, but the Exeter elders were not so sure). Might not Mercy also rise up and attack them with her bloodstained mouth? The sound of iron-capped boots echoed in that lonely crypt as the men approached the cart with its macabre load, and their long shadows, thrown by the light of their lanterns, flickered eerily against the stone walls and the low rounded ceiling of that chilly place. Metcalf pushed his way to the front of the throng, his youngish face looking slightly gaunt and pallid in the lamplight and paused to inspect the coffin. He had grave doubts about the whole activity – after all, nothing had been found with regard to the other two bodies – but he was also fearful of what his neighbours might do, and was therefore determined to see that reason prevailed in the rank atmosphere of vampire terror.

With a shaking voice, he instructed the caretaker to open the coffin, and from his pocket the old man produced a pair of pliers which he used to pull the nails from the casket lid. There was an ear-splitting shriek as each nail tore itself free of the woodwork. Soon the casket lid was lifted clear and those gathered round the coffin gazed down on the body of the young girl inside it. Even though it should now have been in a state of decomposition, many of those present remarked that she looked extremely fresh for a person who had been dead for nine weeks. Once again, Metcalf strode forward, this time holding up his doctor's bag from which he took a small scalpel. Bending over the open coffin, almost like a frenzied ghoul himself, the doctor made an incision; reaching into the cavity which he had created, he took out Mercy's heart and liver. A small quantity of blood fell from the organs, splashing on the stone flags of the crypt, and the older men in the crowd drew back with startled cries. Although it was probably no more than what might have been expected from another cadaver in the same state of deterioration, many of those gathered within the vault took it as highly significant and an incontrovertible evidence of vampirism. Mercy, they were to say later, had been lying in her casket 'gorged with blood'. There was only one thing to do now – the time-honoured New England way of laying a vampire to rest. At a secret ceremony in a remote corner of the cemetery, the heart and liver of Mercy Brown were burnt and the ashes scattered to the four winds. Boiling water, mixed with vinegar, was emptied into the coffin and over the remains of what lay there. With this, it was hoped, the scourge of vampirism which had beset the Brown family was finally ended.

The eerie events of that freezing morning proved too much for the now-frail constitution of Edwin Brown. Shortly afterwards he too died, a victim of the consumption that had taken away the other members of his family. It seems strange that nobody in the community expressed the view that he might also rise again as a vampire, and so his grave was left untouched. Perhaps it was believed that the vampire plague had now passed. The story of his mother and of his sisters, particularly Mercy, however, made interesting reading, and was recorded in the pages of the

*Providence Journal*, one of the leading New England periodicals of the time. Indeed, the issue dated 19 March 1892 carries a long piece (which would probably today be labelled an 'exclusive') which detailed many of the proceedings that occurred at the crypt (it is thought that a reporter might have been among those who gathered there), together with an explanation of vampirism in eastern Europe. 'How the tradition got to Rhode Island and planted itself firmly there cannot be said,' the journal informed its readers. 'It was in Connecticut and Maine 50 and 100 years ago and the people of South County say that they got it from their ancestors, as far back in some cases as the beginning of the eighteenth century. The idea never seems to have been accepted in the northern part of the state, but, every five or ten years, it has cropped out in Coventry, West Greenwich, Exeter, Hopkinton, Richmond and neighbouring towns.'

The theme also was widely developed and extended by other papers and journals. In 1896, the *New York World* ran the following headline: 'Vampires in New England – Dead Bodies dug up and their hearts burned to prevent disease. Strange superstition of long ago'. It gave details of what it referred to as 'a frightful superstition' concerning bodies being dug up at Newport, Rhode Island, 'for the purposes of burning their hearts'. The article was reprinted in a number of English and Irish journals, and doubtless influenced writers of vampire literature in both London and Dublin. Certainly, the writer and creator of the classic *Dracula*, Abraham (Bram) Stoker, was familiar with these tales. After his death, American newspaper clippings concerning the case of Mercy Brown were found among his files.

There seems little doubt that Stoker's creation had its origins in much wider folklore than simply that of Romanian fable. They may lie in the older Irish ghost stories that his mother and the County Kerry nannies and serving maids told him as they tucked him into bed at night; they may lie in the brutal slayings in Whitechapel and other areas of London of which he had heard in his younger days; or they may contain elements culled from rural American folklore. Certainly the harrowing scene in Mercy Brown's crypt has definite echoes of Van Helsing's confrontation

with Lucy Westerna in Stoker's novel. In the character of Quincy Morris, one of the vampire-hunters, the author has also given a 'tip of the hat' to the American connection. However, the roots of the American belief may lie deeper in the psyche of the United States than perhaps even Stoker was prepared to admit. Such beliefs contain strands which stretch all the way back to the Celtic era.

In the case of Sarah Tillinghast, for example, dreams and imaginings played a significant part. In fact, in a high number of allegedly true American vampire tales, nightmares have proved a central feature; and, throughout recorded case histories, visions and glimpses of the Otherworld have been prominent. In the Tillinghast case, Sarah's father, Stukely Tillinghast, believed himself to be in a diseased orchard (he was an apple farmer), where all the trees were either dead or dying, and where the voice of his deceased daughter called to him incessantly. In the case of Nancy Young, it was her sister Almira who dreamt that Nancy came to her each night, and who glimpsed, through the open bedroom window, another dead, frozen world from which the vampire had supposedly come. Records of such visitations and of these half-seen realms contain resonances of the Otherworld and are arguably part of the ancient Celtic tradition. As has already been noted, the revenants that returned to their families did so on the night of the Failte na Marbh, often demanding to be fed and sustained after spending a year in the cold, hard earth. It was then up to the families to support these *marbh bheo* (nightwalking dead) as best they could, even perhaps with their own blood. Sometimes, perhaps in what may have been drunken (or in the cases of the earlier Celts, drug-induced) visions or dreams, mortals were permitted to catch a fleeting glimpse of the Otherworld from which the deceased had come. Most descriptions of this sphere allude to a 'dead kingdom' filled with rotting trees and lank grasses, exactly the same landscape as was seen in many of the Rhode Island nightmares. Similar 'dreams' occurred in the case of Horace Ray in Jewett City in nearby Connecticut in 1852 and in the earlier Corwin case in Woodstock, Vermont, in 1834. Although, within the folklore of many countries (including Romania), the vampire will attack its family first and only then range out into the wider community, it is with the Celtic peoples with their close kinship ties that this particular belief is most widely and inflexibly held. This is a chilling characteristic of all the American vampire cases as, in a number of New England states, family member after family member followed each other to the grave.

It may also be that the vampiric scourge travelled far beyond the Rhode Island State Line. In the second decade of the 20th century, a female skeleton was unearthed in Bradley County, East Tennessee, which was found to have a large stake driven through its heart. The stake was found to be the carved leg of a distinctive and stylish form of chair. Were these the remains of a Southern vampire? Who knows? However, it is a sure signal that a belief in the 'undead' is not all that far away from everyday life, even in America. If United States folklore is to be taken seriously, then they may be still lurking just underneath the surface of American society. In the mysterious words written on Nelly Vaughn's now vanished gravestone, 'I am waiting and watching for you'!

# 'BURN, WITCH, BURN!'

For many of the Celtic peoples, spirits and supernatural beings were always very close and were liable to intervene in mortal affairs on the slightest whim. If not paid proper respect they could bring about misfortune or sometimes even death for an individual, or they might even spirit the individual away to live with them for a time. In the latter case, they sometimes left a representation of the person in his or her stead. This representation was in some cases called a 'stock' and in others a 'changeling' (one who had been exchanged). Sometimes the beings left were elderly spirit-beings; at other times they were things created out of clay or bits of old wood. In all cases they were extremely bad-tempered and their intelligence appeared (on the surface at least) to have been very limited. They were wizened and frail and, generally speaking, did not live long after they had been 'changed'. Some were even partly paralysed and had little or no mobility.

Small children were particularly at risk from the 'fairies', since these innocents were exceptionally vulnerable until they had been formally baptized by a clergyman. This, of course, explained why a previously healthy infant suddenly became weak or sickly, would not feed and was continually crying. It also served to explain why some children from a normally healthy family were born paralysed or deformed. Nowadays, we would attribute this to infant illnesses, but with a lack of medical understanding our ancestors attributed such changes to malign influences. Such beliefs gave a measure of comfort, too. When, for instance, a wizened and sickly child died, the grieving parents could console themselves that it was not actually their child who had gone but some 'changeling'. Their own infant was still alive, albeit with the spirits and fairies. Fairies were not human but they looked like humans, and their world operated along parallel lines to that of mortals, so while a child would be removed from its parents it was cared for in a place which was not unlike its own. Adults, too, were liable to be carried away, with some form of representation left behind. Women and those who indulged in antisocial behaviour were particularly at risk. In the tight-knit, family-orientated Celtic society, good neighbourliness and social conformity were highly valued, and those who did not follow the unwritten social rules left themselves exposed to occult influences. This helped to explain changes in mood or behaviour, and even certain mental conditions such as chronic depression. As Christianity moved across the land, it adapted the old folk beliefs for its own purposes. Those who did not regularly attend Mass, for example, were liable to be whisked away and to be replaced by a 'stock'.

Those who were close to priests and clergy were sometimes carried off by unseen forces. Lady Gregory, for example, in her *Visions and Beliefs in the West of Ireland*, notes that the sister of a priest in Kilcloud, County Sligo, who also acted as his housekeeper, was carried off and lived with the fairies for about seven years. During that time, a representation of herself lived in the Parochial House, but did no work. She sat on a mat in the corner of one of the rooms with a piece of cloth over her face, and when anyone came near her, even to feed her, she would moan piteously like an animal. It was deemed that she had been 'taken' because she was a priest's sister. In seven years she appeared to come to herself again and returned to her duties about the Parochial House. This was taken as confirmation, if confirmation were needed, that she had been 'with the fairies' but had been restored through prayer.

Arguably nowhere was the belief in changelings so strong as in Ireland, particularly in the west of the country. In the Burren country of County Clare, the belief in changelings explained a fearful tuberculosis epidemic which swept the region in the mid-1800s. Robust babies became scrawny, wheezing creatures almost overnight. Areas like County Galway also suffered the same phenomenon. The explanation many gave was that such 'changes' were due to an increased activity by the fairy kind. This belief was used not just in the southwest but all over Ireland.

There were, of course, many ways of driving a changeling out of a house and restoring the child or person who had been 'taken'. Most of these remedies were extreme and there is little evidence that they actually worked. A mixture of foxglove (a poison) and milk fed to the changeling every day for a week was said to get rid of it. After being fed consistent doses of poison, the already frail infant usually died. Another remedy was to try to get the changeling (if it was an infant) to talk and perhaps reveal its true age. This stratagem forms the basis of several Irish changeling legends and is the most 'gentle' of the methods employed. There were, however, more ferocious methods of driving out the changeling. One could place the person (usually an infant) in water, holding the head under until the supernatural creature fled. Another exorcism (frequently used in the cases of babies) was to put the infant on a red-hot shovel and hold it over a fire so that the imp would flee up the chimney. Although these may seem barbaric to us now, they were part of the repertoire of the 'fairy doctor' (a local person who was familiar with fairy ways) and were considered infallible.

Many of these 'remedies' were carried out at various times all across rural Ireland, mainly directed at those who were too weak or too confused to offer any resistance. In County Kerry, for example, the *Morning Post* reported the following account from Tralee Assizes in July 1826:

> Ann Roche, an old woman of very advanced age, was indicted for the murder of Michael Leahy, a young child, by drowning him in the [River] Flesk. This case turned out to be a homicide committed under the delusion of the grossest superstition. The child, though four years old, could neither stand, walk, [n]or speak – it was thought to be fairy struck…
>
> Upon cross-examination, the witness said that it was not done with intent to kill the child, but to cure it – to put the fairy out of it.
>
> Verdict: Not guilty.

This astonishing account was recorded by the Irish folklorist Thomas Crofton Croker in 1829. It was not, however, the only such incident of its kind. On 19 May 1884, the *Daily Telegraph* reported another case from County Tipperary which had disturbing similarities to the one in Kerry:

> SUPERSTITION IN IRELAND
>
> Ellen Cushion and Anastasia Rourke were arrested at Clonmel on Saturday charged with illtreating a child three years old, named Philip Dillon. The prisoners were taken before the mayor, when evidence was given that the boy, who had not the use of his limbs, was a changeling left by the fairies in exchange for their original child. While the mother was absent the prisoners entered her house and placed the lad naked on a hot shovel under the impression that this would break the charm. The poor little thing was severely burned and is in a precarious condition. The prisoners, on being remanded, were hooted by an indignant crowd ... But we must regard it rather as a protest against the prisoners' inhumanity than against their superstition.

The above account, quoted from Edwin Sidney Harland's *Science of Fairy Tales*, serves to demonstrate how deeply the notion of the changeling ran in Irish and indeed Celtic society. There are similar and equally disturbing tales from rural Scotland and Wales of invalid children being placed in hot ovens or suspended on meat-hooks over glowing coals in order 'to drive the fairy from them'. In certain circumstances, a changeling might also even be dismembered as a way of sending it back to the supernatural realm. On 30 January 1888, for instance, a Joanna Doyle appeared at Assizes near Killarney in County Kerry on a charge of child murder. At the time, she was 45 years of age, could not write and was scarcely able to speak any English intelligibly. She was charged with butchering her mentally retarded son Patsy with a hatchet, and in this she had been aided by her husband and three other children. She insisted that 13-year-old Patsy was not her child at all but a 'bad fairy and a devil'. Another of her children, her 12-year-old son Denis, was also described as 'an imbecile' and was considered to be under threat. She was placed in Killarney Asylum where she had to be restrained from tearing her clothes. Her 18-year-old daughter Mary stated that she was not surprised to hear that her mother had killed Patsy – 'I heard people say that he was a fairy and I believed them'.

There were allegedly similar incidents in Roscrea, North Tipperary, and in County Armagh.

The most famous case involving an alleged changeling, however, did not concern a child at all but an adult woman. The murder of Bridget Cleary in Ballyvadlea, South Tipperary, in 1895 made headlines well beyond Irish shores and drew the interest of several thinkers and writers in England. The most famous of these, the celebrated writer E.F. Benson (author of the 'Mapp and Lucia' books), wrote a lengthy article on it in the highly respected and influential journal *The Nineteenth Century* in June 1895. Although the article is rather priggish and supercilious in tone, partly reflecting 19th-century views, it also demonstrates a genuinely humane attempt to understand the events in the context of rural belief and superstition. 'That such a superstition should still be so deeply ingrained in the minds of these peasants as to lead in practice to so horrible a deed seems surprising enough on first sight,' he writes, 'and become doubly surprising when we consider to how primitive a stratum of belief it belongs.'

In this, Benson acknowledged the long tradition of the changeling which stretched back into early Celtic times. The notion of supernatural creatures taking the place of (and assuming the guise of) living mortals must have run very deep in the Celtic consciousness; but who was Bridget Cleary and why was she burnt as a witch or a changeling in a remote area of Tipperary just over 100 years ago?

Bridget Cleary died near the place where she was born, in Ballyvadlea, near Clonmel, South Tipperary. When she died in 1895, she was 26 years old. By all accounts, including those published in the *Cork Examiner*, she was a pretty woman of medium height and with a strong personality. As the young Bridget Boland (her maiden name), she was well known in her home area, both by labourers and gentry alike. Indeed, one of the local landowners, on his way to hunt with the Tipperary Hounds, had been so struck by her attractiveness as she passed him on the road that the memory of her had stayed with him into old age. Both her mother and father, Patrick and Bridget Boland, were local people and were of what was then described as 'the labouring classes'. They were staunchly Roman Catholic and deeply superstitious.

Their superstition was not out of place in the community, for the land round about was rich in folklore and tradition. From the road which ran through the area, travellers could see the fairy-haunted Slievenamon, the legendary mountain stronghold of the Fenian Knights and allegedly the abode of all sorts of supernatural creatures. Between its lower slopes and Fethard town, many 'slieveens' lived. These were 'fairy doctors' and 'cunning men' who specialized in the ways of the fairies (although the term now means a 'rascal' or 'trickster') – men like Denis Ganey, who lived 'in a thatched cabin' at Kyleatlea on the mountain's lower slopes, and John (Jack) Dunne, a limping, toothless man who tramped the streets of Clonmel and Fethard, relating terrifying stories of fairies and ghosts. As well as this, there were a number of mysterious sites scattered throughout the region, not least Slievenamon itself, reputed to be frequented by witches and fairies from all over Ireland. Near the Bolands' house there also rose the brooding bulk of Kylenagranagh Hill, topped with a fairy fort or rath – reputedly a place of dread where the Sidhe or Fairy Host held court. Local people mostly avoided going near the place.

Bridget grew up in this rural area and felt little need to move away. As her father stated at his trial for her murder, she earned her living as a milliner or dressmaker, and was one of the very first people in Ballyvadlea to have a new Singer sewing machine in her bedroom. (The Singer Manufacturing Company opened a depot in Mitchell Street in Clonmel under the management of Jeremiah Carey in 1893.) As such, she was a relatively prosperous young lady. Bridget Boland was much sought after by the young men from nearby Cloneen and Mullinahone, and it was said that she could have had her pick of any of them. It came as some surprise then when she chose the sullen and dour Michael Cleary to be her husband.

Bridget and Michael met in Clonmel. She was working as a dressmaker's apprentice, he as a cooper. It was an odd match; she was a lively young girl, and he was a dark, sullen man – morose and incredibly superstitious. They were married in August 1887 when Michael was 27 and Bridget was 18. For Bridget, it was an unusually young age at which to wed. Most Irish women of the time married at around 26, although the age was going up. Many did not marry at all, as there was a surplus of women in rural Ireland to the proportion of marriageable men. The marriage, too, was an unusual one. Michael Cleary continued to live and work in Clonmel while Bridget moved back to live at her parents' cabin near Ballyvadlea Bridge. To be fair, the reason for this may have been that her mother was ill (Bridget senior died sometime before 1895) and she may have gone home to nurse her. Nevertheless, the unusual arrangements caused much gossip in the community. Michael came to see his wife at weekends and stayed over, but to all intents and purposes as a married couple they lived apart. There were no children and, once again, tongues wagged.

Some time after the Clearys' marriage, the Cashel Poor Law Guardians erected a labourer's cottage in the district under the 1883 Labourer's (Ireland) Act. The dwelling was built about half a mile up the hill from Ballyvadlea Bridge beside the hill at Tullowcussaun and with a direct view of Slievenamon. It had a high-pitched, slated roof and a chimney at each gable, and was considered to be grander than the other, more crude buildings in the area. It had one disadvantage, however, in that it was built on the site of a fairy rath (or fort). There were many of these raths – ancient earthworks now referred to by archaeologists as 'ring forts' – dotted around the countryside, and they were always considered to be places of great mystery and evil. The majority of them appear to have been enclosures for early dwellings, but they were often (and still are in certain areas) regarded as 'fairy places' where the Good Folk dwelt, and, as such, they assumed a supernatural air all of their own. They were usually left well alone and most were overgrown with vegetation. Farmers were wary of pulling them down, for to do so was said to invite bad luck. However, this had not prevented the Poor Law Guardians from destroying the old rath to build the cottage at Ballyvadlea, although it might have prevented one or two souls from applying for its tenancy.

In the late 1880s, Bridget and Michael Cleary, together with Bridget's parents, applied to the Guardians for tenancy of the new cottage, but were unsuccessful. The cottage was given to another labourer, but shortly afterwards certain problems arose. What those problems were have never been fully specified, but it was said that the fairies took exception to the new tenant and disturbed him at night with their unearthly cries. In the end, he fled from the locality. The Clearys reapplied for possession and this time were granted it, although there is no record of when they actually became tenants. What is known is that they soon fell into rent arrears. While arrears of rent were not uncommon, it was strange that a couple like the Clearys, who were relatively well off, should do so. It seems also that they were badly in arrears, as the Guardians forbade any repair work to be carried out on the cottage until the back rent was cleared.

The cottage was comfortable and well appointed, and the Clearys were surrounded by friends and relations; Patrick Boland's widowed sister, Mary Kennedy, for example, lived a short distance away at Ballyvadlea Bridge. Her sons Patrick, James and William, all labourers, lived with her, together with an 11-year-old granddaughter, Katie Burke, who was her daughter Johanna's eldest child. Johanna and her husband, Michael Burke, also a labourer, lived close by with several other children. When Johanna had been married in August 1884, her bridesmaid had been her cousin, Bridget Boland, soon to become Bridget Cleary. The two girls were reasonably close, despite Johanna being much the older of the two (at the time of Bridget's death she was about 34). To Bridget and to many others in the district, Johanna Burke was simply known as 'Han' or 'Hannie', a pet name which demonstrated her relative popularity among her neighbours.

By all accounts, Bridget Cleary was happy enough in the new cottage in Ballyvadlea. While she still did some dressmaking, she had a new source of income – she kept hens. Hens were an important source of income to any household and Bridget made quite a tidy sum for herself by selling eggs to neighbouring people. She sold 'on tick', collecting the money that was due around the start of each month. As with many other women in rural Ireland at the time, it provided her with a measure of financial independence from her husband and 'allowed her to stand on her own feet' in a (superficially at least) male-dominated community. It could have its problems, however, too – not everybody was willing to pay for their eggs when the money was due.

The winter of 1894/95 was a particularly severe one in South Tipperary. Farm work was seriously delayed and many labourers were threatened with hardship and even destitution. It was not until mid- to late March 1895 that the weather picked up again and general conditions improved. Even so, money was still in short supply. On Monday 4 March 1895, Bridget Cleary walked from her house across Ballyvadlea Bridge and up to a squalid cabin near Kylenagranagh Hill where Jack Dunne lived with his wife Kate, to collect money for eggs. It was a dry and sunny morning, but very cold. It had been snowing the night before and the peak of distant Slievenamon was white. Dunne's house was a narrow, rough cabin near the side of the road and it seemed empty. Jack and Kate Dunne had no children and were sometimes in the pubs at Clonmel or Fethard, leaving their cabin empty for long periods of time. Bridget knocked but received no answer. She waited a little while, feeling the cold penetrating her bones, then walked home again and entered her own house shivering. She tried to warm herself at the open fire but, according to her cousin 'Han' Burke, it did not relieve her because she was so cold.

The next day, the shivering fit still had not left her and she now complained of a violent headache. Great attention was paid in the locality to where she had been and to whom she had been visiting in order to ask for money. Jack Dunne lived near the mysterious Kylenagranagh Hill and was widely regarded as a shanachie – the traditional teller of tales (particularly ghost stories) and custodian of ancient lore. He was also said to be a 'fairy man' who was in contact with the Good People. He frequently told wild stories about how the fairies danced and played hurling close to his back door; he complained of a pain in his back which he said had occurred when the fairies lifted him bodily out of bed one night and threw him into the yard; and he had been chased into his own house by a man in black and a woman in white. All the same, he claimed to know a great deal about the fairies, especially those from Kylenagranagh Hill near to his own house, and he certainly played on that knowledge. To demand money from such a man might be to invite danger.

Bridget Cleary was put to bed with what her parents thought was no more than a morning chill which she had received at Jack Dunne's door. Several days passed and she showed no signs of improvement. It is possible that she may have caught pneumonia, but doctors were few and far between in the Irish countryside, and were very expensive in any case. Although still feverish, she was able to sit at the fire and walk a little bit around the house for short periods. Even so, she was certainly not her usual sprightly, attractive, well turned-out self, and there was clearly something wrong. Hearing of her illness, Jack Dunne himself called to see her as she sat up in bed one afternoon. The room was dark and the ageing man's sight was not good. Peering at the woman in the bed, he made a dramatic pronouncement. 'That is not Bridget Boland,' he announced. Placed in a wider medical context, the remark may have lent itself to another interpretation such as 'She's not herself today' or 'She's badly faded away', but coming from the lips of a 'fairy man' they were taken literally. In any case, Jack Dunne was only echoing what others had already suspected. Bridget had a number of enemies around Ballyvadlea – those who were envious of her, suitors she had snubbed, people who thought she was a bit too 'high and mighty' – and some of them had been remarking upon her sudden deterioration from a lively woman to an invalid who could not even go out of the house. The general consensus was that there might be some fairy involvement in the sickness, especially as she appeared cursed to be childless. Following Dunne's pronouncement, he was asked to look at her more closely and immediately stated that the woman in the bed was indeed a fairy – one leg was longer than the other (a condition which was close to Dunne's own). While he measured Bridget, Michael Cleary arrived at the house. A moody and superstitious man, he listened carefully to Jack Dunne's opinion and took it to heart. 'She is not my wife at all but a fairy-thing from Kylenagranagh Hill,' he muttered. Even so, he did nothing.

By Saturday 9 March, Bridget Cleary's condition had grown worse. Johanna Burke believed that she had caught a fresh cold or 'founder'. Whatever Jack Dunne said about fairies, the family were determined to put their faith in a trained medical doctor. Patrick Boland walked the four miles to Fethard to ask Dr William Crean to call at the house. On his way there he stopped at the house of one of the Poor Law Guardians for a 'red ticket' which entitled him to a medical examination under the Poor Law Scheme. Then he walked to Fethard Dispensary, presented it and asked Crean to visit his daughter. The doctor did not. The weekend was wet and dull and there was a strong wind blowing. The road into Ballyvadlea was muddy and covered with 'natural refuse' (blown-down branches, leaves and so on) and perhaps Crean did not fancy venturing into that remote area; perhaps he was busy elsewhere. There were also stories that the doctor was a little too 'fond of the bottle' (strong drink) and only attended to his medical duties in a rather haphazard fashion. On Sunday night and Monday morning, it rained heavily and the rain persisted until midday on Monday; but by 2pm it had passed. There was still no sign of Dr Crean. All the while, Bridget's condition worsened. Johanna Burke suspected that she had a fever and said that a doctor must be brought. Michael Cleary walked to Fethard to fetch William Crean. Still the doctor did not come, nor did he come on the Tuesday. On the morning of Wednesday 13 March, Michael Cleary once again walked to Fethard to fetch the doctor and sent also a messenger to Drangen Church to fetch Father Cornelius Ryan to attend his wife who was dying. It did the trick, for on Wednesday afternoon Dr Crean called at the Cleary home. After examining Bridget, he diagnosed 'nervous excitement and a slight bronchitis', prescribed a medicine and went back to Fethard. He did not know if the Clearys had obtained the medicine, nor was he able to determine the cause of the 'excitement'. Later, in court, he would reveal that Bridget Cleary had been attending him in Fethard for 'about six to eight months', but he did not say why. Popular belief said that she was suffering from tuberculosis and that she had even been seen attending the TB clinic in Clonmel.

Desperate to lift the spirits of his sick daughter and also of his son-in-law (who seemed to be growing more depressed by the day), Patrick Boland visited his sister, Mary Kennedy, and asked her to call with Bridget. Mary said she would come but she would also bring Johanna Burke who lived at Rathkenny, a mile to the west of the Cleary household. When Johanna arrived, both she and Bridget got into extremely earnest conversation. Johanna was of the opinion that there was (and had been) some sort of marital difficulty between Bridget and her husband. 'He's making a fairy of me,' the sick woman told her cousin. In local parlance this meant that Michael Cleary was distancing himself from his wife for some reason. However, in the charged atmosphere created by Jack Dunne it might also mean that he suspected her of being one of the fairy kind and was keeping a safe distance from her. The term means to 'isolate or repudiate with disdain' and suggests that Bridget and her husband were drifting further and further apart. There might also have been a certain animosity between Michael Cleary and his mother-in-law who, as Bridget Keating (her maiden name) had been considered to be a 'fairy woman' in the style of Jack Dunne, widely credited with a knowledge of fairies and herbs. There is little doubt that, at this time, Bridget's mother was dead, and it might have been thought that she had passed on her arcane knowledge to her daughter, making the superstitious Michael Cleary nervous of his wife.

Standing by his front door and looking towards Slievenamon, Michael Cleary considered what he should do about Bridget. Three times, they had tried to bring Dr Crean and even when the doctor had come his diagnosis had been less than satisfactory. Jack Dunne had suggested that the Clearys now consult with Denis Ganey, the 'fairy doctor' who lived at Kyleatlea on the lower slopes of the fairy mountain. Still, Cleary was wary of consorting with the slieveen as no good might come of it. Nevertheless, on 14 March, he set out for Kyleatlea to speak to Denis Ganey.

Denis Ganey was middle-aged, tall and with a full beard, greying but streaked with yellow. Like Jack Dunne, he walked with a limp and was reputed to have one leg shorter than the other (a sure sign of a 'fairy man'). According to Michael Cleary, Ganey listened to the problem and then gave the distraught husband something with 'nine cures in it' which would drive the fairy influence out of his wife. Cleary returned home to Ballyvadlea in a rather confused and excited state. By the following day, he was already starting to show signs of strain. The 'cure' that he had obtained from 'Ganey over the mountain' probably contained lusmore (foxglove) which was supposed to 'burn the entrails out of any unearthly creature' including fairies. It had to be mixed with the 'beestings', the first milk drawn from a cow directly after calving into a bucket into which a silver coin had been placed. If the 'cure' did contain a substantial amount of foxglove then it was poisonous, and if anything would only have worsened Bridget's condition. Nevertheless Michael Cleary was determined that she should have it – he had now become convinced that his wife was a 'changeling' and that the real Bridget had been captured by the fairies as she stood at Jack Dunne's door and taken to Kylenagranagh Hill where she was now held prisoner by them. What had come home to Ballyvadlea was a supernatural being.

Later that same evening, a crowd of neighbours – the Burkes, the Simpsons – all made their way to the Cleary house to see if Bridget's condition had improved. As they approached the building, they became aware of a man's voice shouting from somewhere inside: 'Take that, you rap!' Some of them looked in at the window but the wooden shutters were drawn and they could see nothing. They knocked on the door but Michael Cleary's voice replied from inside that nobody could come in yet. For about five minutes, the neighbours outside waited while the voices from the house continued, shouting snatches like 'Take it, you old bitch!' or perhaps 'Take it you witch!' Then the door suddenly flew open. From somewhere inside came a man's voice shouting 'Away she go! Away she go!' Michael Cleary came to the door and invited his neighbours inside. He explained that the house had been full of fairies.

According to Johanna Burke, inside the cottage they saw a scene of brutal horror. Patrick Boland was sitting in the kitchen by the light of a large oil lamp, but everyone else was in the bedroom. Bridget Cleary was lying in bed with Jack Dunne (who was not a strong man) sitting beside her and forcibly holding her head down by the ears. Her cousin, Patrick Kennedy, was on the far side of the bed, gripping her right arm while his brother James held her left. The youngest brother William lay across her legs to prevent her moving them and trying to get up. They were forcing her to take something on a spoon from a small saucepan which Jack Dunne called 'a pint'. Later, when covering Cleary's trial, the *Irish Times* reported:

> Cleary was giving her medicine – some herbs on a spoon. Bridget Cleary was trying not to take it. She said it was too bitter. When Cleary put the milk into the mouth he put his hand on her mouth to prevent the medicine coming up. He said if it went on the ground that she could not be brought back from the fairies. Cleary asked her was she Bridget Cleary or Bridget Boland, wife of Michael Cleary, in the Name of God. He asked her more than once. She answered three times before he was satisfied.

Michael Cleary finally succeeded in forcing some of the herbal mixture down his wife's throat. He managed three doses when his neighbours were there and had made her swallow three doses before they had arrived. When this was done, all the men shouted, 'Away with you! Come home Bridget Boland in the Name of God!' They clapped their hands and slapped her. One of the neighbours who had just come in noticed that she had a great burn mark across her forehead, and they discovered later that she had been threatened with a red-hot poker held close to her face to make her take the herbs. At the sound of their voices, Bridget screamed loudly. Then Cleary asked his wife again, 'Are you Bridget Boland, wife of Michael Cleary in the Name of God?' Bridget gave no answer, or else her reply was so faint that nobody in the room could hear it. Turning to him, Jack Dunne said, 'Make a good fire and we will make her answer.'

The fire was burning steadily in the fireplace although no fuel had been added to it. The men lifted Bridget bodily from the bed, 'winding' her in the bedclothes, and carried her to the grate. Jack Dunne took her head and James Kennedy her feet, with Michael Cleary following with the spoon and saucepan. She was apparently conscious and seemed well aware of what was going on. Holding her over the grate, just above the lapping flames, Patrick Boland asked his daughter, 'Are you the daughter of Patrick Boland, the wife of Michael Cleary?' Bridget, clearly terrified, answered loudly, 'I am, Dada!' The men continued to hold her over the flames for at least ten minutes before carrying her back to bed.

Rumours were now widely circulating about the Clearys all across Ballyvadlea. It was said, for example, that Bridget had a lover in the locality – William Simpson, a Protestant who lived at Garrangyle, the next townland to Ballyvadlea with his wife Mary and two children and who described himself as an 'emergencyman' (land steward). It was also rumoured that Michael Cleary himself had 'another woman' in Clonmel, which was why he only came home at weekends. Speculation was rife in the district about what was really wrong with Bridget Cleary.

At 7am on 15 March, Father Ryan was summoned from Drangan to visit Bridget. The priest had actually called on Bridget two days before, as requested, and had given her the Last Rites of the Church, but had refused to come when asked again on Thursday. Now Michael Cleary turned up at his door once more and asked him to come again. Reluctantly Father Ryan did so. He said Mass in her bedroom and gave her Holy Communion. Bridget, however, was reported not to have swallowed the Sacred Host but surreptitiously removed it from her mouth with her fingers – something expressly forbidden by Catholic teaching. Whether this was communicated to Michael Cleary is unknown, but it would certainly have strengthened his belief that Bridget was one of the fairies. He might also have thought that she might be using it to make a pishogue (a charm or spell) to use against other members of the house. (It was believed in the countryside that witches and evil-doers sometimes used the Holy Wafer in the preparation of their dark charms.) On the doorstep of the house, Father Ryan asked Cleary if he was still giving his wife the doctor's medicine and the man replied that he had no faith in it. Father Ryan seemed to concur as he spoke of Dr Crean as being 'always drunk'.

Later that evening, two neighbours, Tom Smith and David Hogan, called to see how Bridget was, and Johanna Burke joined them. She made some stirabout (coarse porridge) for them. During the evening, an argument developed between Mrs Burke and Michael Cleary regarding some new milk which she had sold to Bridget. As if to settle the dispute, and because tea was being made, Cleary got his wife out of bed, had her dressed and brought to the kitchen where everyone else was sitting. Tom Smith asked her how she was and she replied that she was 'middling' but that her husband was 'making a fairy of her'. She made to answer some questions about the milk but her husband told her to 'hold her tongue'. More neighbours joined them in the house. As Bridget was being handed a cup of tea, Cleary suddenly asked, 'Are you Bridget Cleary, my wife, in the Name of God?' He asked her three times and she answered him twice. She was eating a piece of bread and jam and, when she did not answer the third time, he rose and forced the bread down her throat, shouting, 'Swallow it. Is it down? Is it down?' He then struck her across the face, flinging her to the earthen floor of the cottage. She called on her cousin to intervene – 'Oh Han! Han!' – but Mrs Burke did nothing. In a fit of rage, Cleary then tore off most of his wife's clothing, leaving her lying in her chemise. Taking a piece of burning wood from the grate, he brandished it in her face, trying to shove it down her throat. Michael Cleary was said to be a silent, moody man, but he was now clearly beside himself with anger. Taking the house-key, he turned it in the front door, effectively locking everyone in the cottage. Mrs Burke withdrew into the bedroom. By this time most of the house had cleared of neighbours, although a few still lingered, and she intended to stay over to see if she could help Bridget. She would not, however, interfere between husband and wife and was slightly resentful that Bridget had made her the centre of a marital dispute about the milk. A few of the others who had come – Mary Kennedy, for instance – had gone into the bedroom to have a bit of a doze. As she went into the adjoining room she heard Bridget Cleary shout, 'Give me a chance!' She heard Bridget's head strike the floor and then heard her scream. The kitchen must have been in pandemonium. Cleary was now apparently standing over his wife, gesturing threateningly with the still burning stick. He thrust it close to her body. It only took a moment for the calico chemise to catch fire.

Mary Kennedy was hardly more than dozing when her son William cried out from the kitchen, 'Mother! Mother! Bridgie is burned!' Both she and Johanna Burke started up shouting, 'What ails ye?' At the door, they were met by Michael Cleary who turned to Mrs Burke and said, 'Hannah, I believe she is dead!' Walking over to the window, he took down a lamp and emptied the paraffin from it over the body. Clearly now out of control, he attempted to set fire to the body but was stopped by Mrs Kennedy whom he pushed away. 'What are you doing with the creature?' cried Mrs Kennedy. 'Is it roasting her you are?' Bridget appeared to stir. Cleary asked if she was his wife Bridget in the Name of

God and she seemed to reply that she was. In an instant Michael Cleary had set fire to her, her paraffin-soaked body easily catching light. It was a risky, panicky thing to do – Cleary could have burned the entire cottage down – but Cleary seems to have taken leave of his senses.

'For the love of God, Michael,' James Kennedy who had been sleeping in Patrick Boland's room now witnessed the horror. 'Don't burn your wife!' Cleary looked at him. 'She's not my wife,' he replied in a low voice. 'She's an old deceiver sent in place of my wife. She's after deceiving me for the last seven or eight days and deceived the priest today too, but she won't deceive me any more. As I beginned with her, I will finish it with her. You'll soon see her go up the chimney!' By this, he was referring to the traditional escape route for a changeling. William Kennedy, who had come down with his mother, asked him for the house-key so that they could go, but Cleary only drew a knife and told him that the door would not be opened until his wife was returned to him from Kylenagranagh Hill. He threatened to 'run the knife though him', and poor William fainted away. As his mother Mary laid him on the bed in Patrick Boland's room, Cleary warned them, 'If you come out any more, I'll roast you as well as her!' Everyone withdrew from the kitchen, leaving Cleary alone with his burning wife. He threw lamp-oil on her three times before sitting down in a chair to watch her burn. As some of the others came to the bedroom door he shouted, 'You're a dirty set! You will rather have her with the fairies in Kylenagranagh than have her here with me!' Patrick Boland then came out and said that if there was anything he could do to save his daughter he would do it. Cleary answered and said that he would bury her with her mother. The following Sunday, he would go to Kylenagranagh Fort where the real Bridget would come to him riding on a white horse. If he could cut the straps which bound her to the animal, she would be free. This, he said, was what Denis Ganey had told him, although later he would declare that Bridget herself had told him that. All the while, said Johanna Burke, Bridget's body crackled on the hearth and 'the house was full of smoke'. The body was later removed and buried at a spot near the Cleary cottage in Ballyvadlea. At Cleary's insistence, Patrick Boland and Johanna Burke knelt down and swore on the Holy Name not to tell what had happened.

He gave out that Bridget had simply 'gone away'.

Jack Dunne, however, was 'badly agitated'. On Saturday 16 March, he accompanied Michael Cleary and Michael Kennedy to Drangan village to attend confession. That evening, it was being heard by the curate, Father McGrath, although Father Ryan, the parish priest, was also present. Jack Dunne went in first and spoke to the curate who told him to send Michael Cleary (who was in the chapel yard and in a very distressed state) in to speak with him. Cleary came in and, weeping, spoke to the priest, but Father McGrath claimed that he was 'in no fit state' to receive absolution. He went to speak to Father Ryan, and the two of them talked for a long time; then, as Michael Kennedy watched, the parish priest turned and walked across the road and into Drangan police barracks.

Although no one knows what was said, either by Jack Dunne to Father McGrath or by Father Ryan to Acting Sergeant Patrick Egan in the police station, it was enough to arouse police interest. Egan had probably heard the weird stories already circulating in Ballyvadlea concerning Bridget's disappearance, but he could not move without evidence or without a formal complaint. He and another policeman followed Cleary along the Fethard road. As they reached Mary Kennedy's cottage, Egan approached Michael Cleary and asked him about his wife. Cleary said that she had left 'about twelve o'clock last night'. He had not seen her going, he added, as he had been in bed (adding that he had not slept for about eight nights previously). Egan walked home with him and repeated his questions there. Cleary repeated that Bridget was gone, but as he left the house Patrick Egan heard Patrick Boland shouting in the house, 'My daughter will come back to me'. The old man would insist right up until the trial that his daughter was alive and well and living 'elsewhere' (with the fairies).

Egan was suspicious and a few more police from Clonmel were drafted into the area, ostensibly to look for Bridget. Now there was a formal complaint, too. The name of the complainant has never been disclosed, but it is likely to have been William Simpson, long suspected of being Bridget Cleary's lover. Simpson was to claim that Michael Cleary had approached him for the loan of a revolver (which Simpson was known to keep) so that he could go up to Kylenagranagh Hill and 'bring back his wife'. Simpson did not lend him the gun but later saw Cleary going up to the hill with a large table knife. He had waited there for Bridget to appear on a white horse, but had seen nothing.

Patrick Egan had now informed the authorities of Bridget's disappearance and of the complaint. Inspector Joseph Wansborough, based at Carrick-on-Suir, ordered a full-scale search of the area by police from Drangan, Clooneen and Mullinahone. He visited the house in Ballyvadlea himself and took notes.

On Monday 18 March, William Simpson formally swore an 'information' before W. Walker Tennant, a Justice of the Peace, that Bridget Cleary had been ill-treated and that something had transpired in her house the previous Thursday night. He also named the people whom he considered 'responsible'. Police now swarmed all through the area and many of those present on the night were questioned. Later Johanna Burke would also swear a further 'information' in front of Justice Tennant who then called on Inspector Wansborough to come and state whether he would prefer charges against anyone. Ironically, the first person whom Wansborough charged was the slieveen Denis Ganey, 'with causing Bridget Cleary to be ill-treated and great actual bodily harm done to her'. Ganey had probably never met Bridget Cleary, but his influence had been profound. The police net was beginning to tighten around Michael Cleary.

On 22 March 1895, officers of the Royal Irish Constabulary, guided by William Simpson, searched an area of boggy land in the area of Tullowcrossaun. In the corner of a field, about a quarter of a mile from the Cleary's house, Sergeant Patrick Rogers of the Mullinahone Constabulary noticed some badly broken down bushes and some freshly turned earth. Constables Somers and O'Callaghan helped him to dig and soon had completed a hole about 18 inches deep. There they found a dirty sheet, wrapped around a woman's body. The corpse itself was pulled up into a crouching position with its knees almost against its chin, and was very badly burnt. It was naked, apart from some bits of ragged clothing which had been burnt into the skin, and a pair of black stockings. The head was covered in a sack and was largely untouched; there was a gold ear-ring in the left ear. Looking at the face, Rogers had no doubt regarding the body's identity. They had found Bridget Cleary.

Following the discovery of the body and the arrest of several people in the Ballyvadlea area, including Michael Cleary, world interest focused on that remote area of County Tipperary. The case became known as the 'Clonmel Witch Burning' or the 'Tipperary Witch Burning'. Michael Cleary, Patrick Boland, Jack Dunne, Mary Kennedy and several others were arraigned at the summer assizes in Clonmel and were brought to trial on Thursday 4 July 1895. Michael Cleary was found guilty of manslaughter and was sentenced to 20 years' penal servitude. The judge, Mr Justice O'Brien, was unmoved by all the talk of 'fairies' and 'witchcraft' or by the state of Cleary's mind at the time. Jack Dunne and the Kennedy brothers (who had assisted in forcing Ganey's potion into Bridget) were found guilty of 'wounding' – Patrick Kennedy was sentenced to five years' imprisonment, Jack Dunne to three and the other two to one year each. Patrick Boland and Michael Kennedy received six months each, but Mary Kennedy was set free by order of the court.

The prisoners were taken to Mountjoy Prison to begin their sentence. Jack Dunne was later released on licence and returned home to Ballyvadlea, to find that his wife Kate had died. He finished his days, by all accounts, as a labouring man, still living in the area. The Kennedys, too, returned to the district on release, mainly as labourers. Michael Cleary spent part of his sentence shuttling between Mountjoy and Maryborough prisons (Maryborough is now Port Laios prison) and learned to work as a tailor. He was released on licence from Maryborough on 28 April 1910. On 30 June that same year, he boarded a ship bound via Liverpool for Montreal and vanished from the pages of history.

The horrors of the Ballyvadlea case highlight the strength of folk belief which underpinned a rural Irish community even at the turn of the 20th century. It also serves to demonstrate how such beliefs served as a ready explanation when community tensions and problems bubbled to the surface. For the people of 19th-century Ballyvadlea, fairies and witches were not the charming imps of children's fairy stories but neighbouring demons, ready to do mortals harm if they could. That superstition forced its way into the 'rational' world in a terrifying way.

There are still descendants of many of the participants living in the area, and some vestiges of the Cleary home still remain (although the original house itself has been long converted into another dwelling). Kylenagranagh Hill is still there, although much of the fort has been cleared from its summit, but it is said that fairies still congregate there. Local schoolchildren still sing an odd rhyme as they play their skipping games:

> Are you a witch or are you a fairy?
> Are you the wife of Michael Cleary?

The dark superstition of those former times is not quite dead.

# BEAUTIFUL NELL

In the ancient Celtic world, even reality was not all that it seemed. Beyond what the eye could see or the hand could touch lay another world, unseen and unexperienced by the majority of people. This realm they called the Otherworld – an area which lay outside the human senses but which could impinge on human existence. It was the abode of the dead, of supernatural beings or quite simply 'another country', cut off from this world by a veil which, for most of the year, served as a barrier. At certain times, however, this veil was thinner, and thus creatures from the Otherworld could cross into the natural sphere while individuals from the natural world could sometimes be carried away into that 'other realm'.

Legends concerning those who were 'carried away', usually by fairies, abound in Irish, Scottish and Welsh folklore and mythology. In a classical tale, the great Irish hero-poet Oisin was taken into the Otherworld by a fairy queen who had fallen in love with him. He returned briefly to visit the natural realm only to find that 100 years had passed and that, by setting foot on the soil of our own world, he had become a very old man. The same theme is taken up in vernacular folklore, drawing attention to the belief that time passed at a completely different rate in the Otherworld to that in our own. Country people 'passed a night' dancing or sporting with the fairies in the great banqueting halls and castles of the 'other realm' only to find that, on their return, seven years or more had passed.

Where did the notion of another world come from? Its roots clearly lie in Celtic belief, in Celtic perceptions and perhaps in Celtic history as well. The Celts were originally a nomadic people. Although their point of origin is unclear, it is possible that they came from beyond the Alps, and may even have come together on the Great Steppes of Russia. They became more 'settled' in the valley of the River Po in northern Italy, but their culture and customs (it is widely believed that they were a polygamous people) meant that their continually expanding population was always on the move, looking for new lands. They wrote nothing down and their tradition was a purely oral one, made up of songs, stories and memories. Some of these orally transmitted tales probably concerned the lands which they had travelled through; lands which were now little more than a race-memory. With a little imagination, these rather ordinary landscapes became fantastic and magical countries which existed within the memory of the people, just beyond reality.

Central to Celtic culture was a relationship with the natural world around them. For the Celts, unseen spirits and forces dwelt in rivers, mountains and trees, and these natural aspects had to be both placated and venerated. The very landscape was the manifestation of their awesome powers. Even looking up at the sky, the individual could see great banks of clouds, which often took on strange and striking shapes – shapes that resembled castles, animals, vessels and so on. It was but a small step of perception to imagine these formations as the actual fortresses, strongholds and towns of another country which appeared to exist elsewhere. This belief may have been reinforced by mirages – optical illusions which occurred on hot days and which usually beguiled the senses into thinking that they represented some sort of other reality. With climatic changes at the end of the great Ice Age, such phenomena may have been more common in Europe than they are today, and these illusions may well have been part of the Celtic experience. Distantly glimpsed lakes, for example, may well have disappeared as soon as the traveller approached them, faraway towns and cities may have vanished in the wink of an eye, and offshore islands may have faded away to nothing when boats tried to reach them. Indeed, evidence from relatively modern times supports this latter theory. On 7 July 1878, the inhabitants of the Irish seaside town of Ballycotton, County Cork, were both excited and alarmed by the sudden appearance of a reasonably large island, out in the ocean where none had existed before. Observers could see this new land quite clearly from the shore – with a rugged shoreline, deep woodlands and seemingly fertile valleys. As boats approached it, the whole illusion melted away, leaving no trace behind.

The combination of mirages, illusions and cloud formations stirred the Celtic mind to imagine them as the dwelling places of other races, of strange creatures and even spirits and gods. The 'other country' became the place where the dead went immediately upon their demise, or from where the insubstantial spirits that governed the Celtic world issued their demands and decrees. The Otherworld was a real place – and a place of formidable supernatural power. Not for nothing did the Irish King of the World, Brasail, live away on a mysterious island in the west which could be glimpsed just above the horizon only at sunset. So persistent was this belief that when Spanish sailors landed in an area of South America they believed that they had arrived in the Otherworld and named it after the mythical king. They called the country Brazil.

If the distant and alien world was a place of awe and terror for the Celts, then so was the expectation of being carried away into it. One might expect never to see one's friends or family again, given that time passed in a different way upon 'that fatal shore'. There was worse, however – the rigours of the other existence might prove too much for the human frame; the denizens of that other place might well be malignant and cause the human great harm; he or she might never be allowed to return. Thus the Otherworld assumed a monstrous aspect in the Celtic mind, an aspect which was to continue down across the generations. The sheer unfamiliarity of the environment in which the Celts found themselves gave depth to this belief.

The same alien terrain, probably coupled with a deep sense of isolation, met the earliest American settlers when they landed in the New World, and doubtless stirred up the ancient Otherworld memories which they had brought with them from Celtic lands. Here was a place of awesome mountains and endless plains, lakes and bogs, coupled with deep and impenetrable forests filled with bizarre and exotic animals, the likes of which they had never seen before. There were also wild savages who might well be men but just as likely might be demons from another plane. The villages of the colonists huddled tightly together, forming (in their minds) a bastion of reality and sanity against the threatening alien landscape all around them. It is hardly surprising that the notions of the 'real world' and the supernatural Otherworld resurfaced in colonial perceptions once more. Beyond the end of each village lay the uncharted woods or the mysterious prairies in which a man could be lost or upon which fantastic creatures waited. The American Indians who dwelt there gradually assumed the status of dark, supernatural beings who made obeisance to strange gods, and became part of the mysterious and threatening landscape itself.

Consistent with the early Celtic legends and folktales, colonists also started to disappear. Probably there was some rational explanation for such disappearances – they may have become lost and died in the wilderness, they may have been attacked by wild animals or savage American Indians, or they may have blundered into bogs, lakes or rivers and their bodies completely lost. Legends, however, began to surround these disappearances, which were consistent with the earlier Celtic beliefs. Individuals had been spirited away, said the legends, by supernatural creatures living in the Otherworld which lay just beyond rational vision, in the unfamiliar landscape which surrounded them. Sometimes, entire settlements themselves vanished, such as that on Roanoke Island, North Carolina, in 1591. While there seems little doubt that the colonists were massacred and/or carried into slavery by confederations of local American Indians, the legend that the 'Lost Colony' still exists in some kind of unseen Otherworld is certainly still persistent within the surrounding state. In North Carolina, once again, certain individuals have also mysteriously vanished, leaving behind no trace. The famous Reverend W.T. Hawkins, a 73-year-old retired Methodist minister widely known as the 'Shepherd of the Hills', disappeared in the beautiful Sapphire County region in the western part of the state in March 1930 (reputedly near a natural landmark known ominously as the 'Devil's Courthouse', which was said to mark the gateway to another world). Not so much as a bone or belt-buckle was ever found to mark his passing on a trail which he had frequented for many years. Local wisdom suggested that he might have been carried away into some other reality by beings who were said to hover around the Devil's Courthouse. Some of those who had vanished returned, days, months or even years later with absolutely no memory of where they had been. John Byrne, for example, returned home in 1902 after searching for a calf in a chain of valleys near Lake Lure on the Little Tennessee River. He thought he had been gone for most of one day – in fact, he had been gone for 21 years.

Sometimes, however, those who vanished were returned dead, unmarked by disease, beast or savage American Indian. The most abiding story in North Carolina – an area which was extensively settled by the Scots-Irish and which is still famous for its mysterious disappearances – is that of Nell Cropsey in 1901. This was a case which involved local law-enforcement agencies, right up to the State Legislature, and serves to show just how closely the Otherworld can impinge on our own and how easily individuals can cross from one realm to the next.

The Pasquotank River lies in the east of North Carolina. It is a big, sprawling, muddy stream which broadens out in the vicinity of Elizabeth City to form flat and swampy low country, bordered by reeds and nodding cypress-trees. It is great fishing country, but it can be dark and mysterious territory as well. Cattle and hogs were said to vanish there without trace and there were legends that American Indians had disappeared there too, probably, said the sceptics, into the boglands all about. It was to this beautiful but sometimes rather brooding environment that W.H. Cropsey came with his family from New York State in the summer of 1898. He was a buyer of potatoes and grain for a New York commission merchant, and the family had previously lived in Brooklyn. Although a Yankee, Cropsey had only a little amount of prejudice to face (the region had been largely Confederate) and soon settled into the community well enough. He established his family (the two parents and a number of daughters) in a large house on the banks of the Pasquotank, and they lived happily enough.

All his daughters were exceptionally pretty, though at the time the family arrived in Elizabeth City only two were of marriageable age. Ollie, aged 18, and her sister Nellie, a year and a half younger, certainly turned heads among the young men of the district. Although Ollie was certainly attractive, Nellie outshone her. Indeed, so pretty was she that the nickname 'Beautiful Nell' was attached to her and stayed with her until her disappearance in 1901. The description was well deserved, for a coloured miniature depicting her head and shoulders existed until fairly recently. It showed ringlets of chestnut-brown hair, a delicately formed mouth and nose, and blue, intelligent eyes, which were also brimming with mischief and fun. The whole effect was one of a highly dignified young lady.

Although she had many suitors, Nell had her heart set on only one – James Wilcox. He was 25 years of age and the eldest son of Thomas P. Wilcox, a former sheriff of Pasquotank County. He was a good-looking young man and an extremely dapper dresser. The two of them were often seen walking out together soon after the Cropseys arrived in Elizabeth City and were courting for almost three years. Jim Wilcox worked in a local lumber mill but was trying to better himself by taking a correspondence law course. He often came calling at the house to pay court to Nell and there was some talk of an engagement. However, as Nell grew increasingly impatient on the matter, Jim appeared more and more reticent. He really was not ready to settle down.

Things went from bad to worse in the relationship. Tired and irritated by Jim's slowness to marry, Nell began flirting with other local boys. Being so attractive, she could have her pick of the neighbourhood swains, but this was only to make Jim jealous and to spur him into a proposal of marriage. It had the opposite effect, however, for Jim sulked and stayed away from the Cropsey household for several evenings. In retaliation, Nell began to flirt openly with Lucas Vance, a young labourer who was working for her father. The boy was a drifter and it was a calculated insult to her former beau. Jim sulked even more and then, a couple of days later, Vance suddenly disappeared without drawing his wages. There were those who said that he had simply moved on – he was a strange, wandering sort of fellow anyway – but others who suspected foul play. Nobody dared voice their suspicions, however.

On the night of Wednesday 20 November 1901, Jim Wilcox began calling at the Cropsey homestead again. Nellie was sure that he had come to propose, but the evening steadily developed into a quarrel. For most of the evening, Jim was sullen and silent, hardly saying a word to the family. Besides Jim and Nellie, there were a number of young people there that evening: Ollie Cropsey, Roy Crawford, a young bank clerk who had been paying attention to her, and the girls' cousin Carrie Cropsey from New York. As if to reflect the sombre mood of the evening, their talk gradually turned to what had happened to Lucas Vance. While Ollie was certain that he had run off, Roy suggested that he might have accidentally drowned in the marshlands along the edges of the Pasquotank. Following this line, the conversation morbidly drifted to various preferred methods of dying.

'If I could choose the way that I was to die,' Jim announced, 'I'd die by drowning.' 'Oh well, I'd freeze to death,' countered Nellie lightly, 'preferably in the snow. Why, I'd just go to sleep and never wake up – just like in bed.'

Jim, however, kept watching the clock, Ollie later recalled, as if he wished he were somewhere else. Finally, around 11pm, he rose and said that he was going home. When he had left, the talk began to flag. It was then that something strange happened.

Nellie had been sitting near a screen door which led out into the front porch and, about 15 minutes after Jim Wilcox had left, this door opened a fraction, though not enough for the others to see who had opened it. Through the narrow opening came a voice which Ollie said sounded like Jim, 'only more low and wheezy'. It asked Nell to step outside, as he wanted to speak to her urgently. Ollie said that her sister assented with a nod. She got up and stepped out onto her own front porch in order to speak with her sweetheart, and was never seen again. It was as though she had simply walked out of her own world and into a strange Otherworld. Ollie was to say that, a moment after her sister walked out into the night, there was a faint sound like a thump as though someone had fallen or bumped against the screen door. She seemed to remember this, but she could not altogether be sure of the time.

A neighbour named Caleb Parker happened to be driving past the Cropsey place around 11.20pm, and he reported that he saw somebody who looked extremely like Nell standing by the yard gate in the moonlight. Her head was bowed, Parker said, as though she were crying.

Standing in the shadow of the gatepost was another figure with its arm around Nell's shoulders as if trying to comfort her. Parker thought that it looked like Jim Wilcox (he assumed that it was), but he would not swear to it. In a moment, Caleb Parker's wagon was gone past the gate and both figures disappeared behind him into the gloom.

Back in the Cropsey house, the young people had moved down to the parlour. Cousin Carrie went upstairs to bed and, shortly afterwards, Roy Crawford took his leave. It was now around 11.45pm. Roy saw nobody on the front porch as he swung off and into the street, and he wondered exactly where Jim and Nell might have gone. Still, it was none of his business. Nell had not come back into the house, as far as anybody knew, and Ollie went to the front door and found it standing wide open. The screen door through which she had thought she had heard Jim's voice had been pushed back so far that a hinge had been broken. Stepping out into the night, Ollie called to her sister but received no answer. Puzzled, she went back into the house and off to bed. Perhaps Nell had already come in and gone to her room very quietly so as not to disturb anyone else. She slept in the same room as her sister and, in the darkness, she felt along the bed. It was empty. Through the window, Ollie would later recall, the moon shone in – a strange, bright light, totally unlike any moonlight she had experienced before. It was as if the moon were shining from some other world, right through her window. Getting into bed herself, she waited for Nell to come in. Downstairs, the clock struck midnight and Ollie dozed lightly, still alert for any sound of her sister.

About 12.30am, she was jerked back to full consciousness by a commotion in the back yard. The dogs were barking and the pigs were squealing. From somewhere nearby a voice called. Later, W.H. Cropsey would claim that it was the voice of a neighbour (although he could not really say which one of the neighbours it was), but Ollie was sure that it sounded like the thin, wheezy tones that had spoken to Nell through the crack in the screen door. There was an odd, inhuman quality about it, she thought. 'Cropsey! Cropsey! Get up! Someone's stealing your pigs! Get your gun!' it shouted, and then fell silent. Ollie first of all ran to the window and looked out into the yard. The moonlight still held that same strange brilliance which she had noticed before, and, as she looked down, she saw her sister standing below the window, looking up at her. Ollie was sure that somebody was also standing close by, but she could not be sure because the line of the house blocked out any other figure.

Hearing her father stirring and coming out of his bedroom (presumably with his gun), she rushed out into the hallway calling on him not to shoot as 'Nell and Jim are outside somewhere'. Cropsey was in the act of pulling on his pants over his nightshirt and, sticking his feet into a pair of shoes, he grumbled 'What's that girl thinking of? Wandering about at this hour and disturbing the dogs and the pigs!' Still grumbling, he marched out to find his daughter. Although he searched all around the yard, he found nobody and the dogs and pigs soon fell quiet. He then came back in to see if Nell had come back in without her sister's knowledge. Again they found nothing, and the family's uneasiness increased.

Assuming that she had gone to the Wilcox home, Nell's father dressed and walked for ten minutes through the night to fetch his daughter back. He pounded on their front door, bringing a drowsy ex-sheriff from his bed. Cropsey explained his mission and thundered his displeasure at Jim's behaviour. 'But Jim's been home since midnight,' Tom Wilcox answered. 'I seen him come in myself. He's in bed, sound asleep.' Jim was called and appeared in his nightshirt, apparently just roused out of a deep slumber. 'What have you done with my daughter?' Cropsey demanded. Jim Wilcox looked at him blankly. 'Nellie? But she's home, isn't she? I left her with the others around 11pm. That's the last I saw of her.' A cold sweat broke out on Cropsey's forehead and, almost involuntarily, he felt his hands begin to tremble. Where was his daughter?

Together with both Wilcoxes, W.H. Cropsey made his way to the home of local police chief, Henry Dawson, to report Nell's disappearance. They then returned to the Cropsey home and thoroughly searched the house and grounds. They searched a boathouse and landing down by the river's edge; they searched neighbours' yards; they searched the woods which ran along the banks of the Pasquotank. They found nothing. Under Dawson's questioning, Jim Wilcox gave a detailed account of the evening's events.

He had decided, he said, to finish with Nell Cropsey. She had been putting too much pressure on him to get married, and Jim was not ready to settle down. Around 8pm he had gone to the Cropsey house to tell her his decision and to return two items which belonged to her – an umbrella she had lent him and a miniature of herself that she had given him two years earlier. He had not intended to stay – just say his piece and go. However, Ollie had answered the door and he had to go into the house and wait for Nell to come downstairs. The evening wore on and at last he decided to go. He did not want to embarrass Nell by splitting with her in front of her sister and friends, so he decided to come back another day. Before he left, however, he had put the umbrella and the miniature in the hallway of the Cropsey house, just behind the hall rack. Chief Dawson later discovered the umbrella exactly where Jim had said, but the picture could not be found. Then Jim had gone to Barnes bar, where he had a glass of beer with Len Owens before returning home and going straight to bed. He had, however, been troubled by dreams during which he had continually heard Nellie's voice saying, repeatedly, 'Well! Go then!', but he had put these down to his own guilty conscience. He denied going back and speaking through the screen door and asking Nell to step out with him. Whatever voice Ollie had heard, it was not that of Jim Wilcox! Whose was it, then? Dawson decided to detain the young man until the case was either cleared up or Nell reappeared, and by 21 November the young man was behind bars in Pasquotank County jail. The sheriff now began a full-scale investigation, aided by Deputy Sheriff Charles Reid.

The next day still brought no trace of the girl. She had vanished so completely that she might just as well never have existed. The case grew slightly more complicated. Bloodhounds followed her trail from the front porch to the boathouse at the edge of the Pasquotank River but there was no other sign that she had even been there. The river itself was dragged in more than a dozen places and over 100 houses were searched in the town and in the adjoining neighbourhood. There was still no sign of Nell. The river was dragged again, over a wider area, but no trace of the girl's body was found. All the while, local feeling was growing against Jim Wilcox, who was still in the jailhouse, now formally charged with abduction.

Weeks went by and Nell still had not been found. The river was dragged time and time again without result. During that period Jim was questioned again and again. His story only changed in minor details. However, certain other facts were emerging. It seemed that he did not reach home until 1am (a neighbour had seen him going into his own house). The boy, however, insisted that he had assumed he had come home at midnight as he had left Len Owens at 11.50pm and it was only a short walk from Barnes bar to his own front door. If an extra hour had been added on, he could not even remember it, much less account for it. It also emerged that Jim Wilcox had recently bought a blackjack (a type of truncheon) which he had showed to one or two friends (including Owens on the fateful night), but once again Wilcox insisted that there was nothing to this. Nevertheless, public opinion was now gradually beginning to turn against him.

The Cropsey family now received letters from all over the state, saying that 'Beautiful Nell' had been seen here and there – in Asheville, Thomasville and so on. Ollie recalled that, several nights before her disappearance, Nell had experienced a terrible dream in which she was being pursued by something monstrous but ill-defined, something which was intent on capturing her. The recollection added to the family anxiety. Then two letters arrived which also added to the mystery.

The first was an anonymous message postmarked Atlanta, Georgia, which simply said that Nell had been carried away by evil spirits and was now languishing in some unseen other world. It was filled with Biblical quotations and was dismissed by Dawson and Reid as a 'crank' letter. The second was signed and bore an address in Utica, New York State, and purposed to be from Lucas Vance, the boy with whom Nell had flirted prior to her disappearance. The letter told a strange story. It said that Jim Wilcox and Nell Cropsey had met on the front porch of the Cropsey home and that Jim had left Nell crying. She had been there for quite some time (the writer did not say why Roy Crawford had not seen her when he left). When the Cropsey dogs had barked, Nell had come off the front porch to investigate the commotion and had confronted a man from Elizabeth City who had been intent on stealing her father's pigs. She recognized him and had threatened to tell her father. At this, the letter went on, the man (who was not named) had stunned Nell with a stick, carried her body to the river and dumped it in the water. He then rowed away, leaving her for dead. The writer went on to state that Nell's body would be found at a certain spot on the river, which was marked on an attached diagram. Cropsey turned the letter over to Henry Dawson who had the area dragged – but nothing was found.

The mystery deepened when Charles Reid began to investigate further. He discovered that, several days after quitting the Cropsey house, Lucas Vance had been accidentally and fatally stabbed in a fight in the South Carolina Low Country. His body had been buried in South Carolina and a man had already been charged with his murder. There was no way that he could have written the letter, and the address in Utica simply did not exist (and never had). No further action was taken by the police. By now, however, events had taken another peculiar twist.

Various people began to hear Beautiful Nell's voice, calling from along the banks of the Pasquotank. The first person to hear them was Nell's mother, who had distractedly gone down to a certain place where the river formed a little bay, to see if she could find any trace of her daughter. While there, she had heard Nell distinctly calling 'Mamma! Come and fetch me!' This was simply put down to the poor woman's grief at the loss of her child, but then others began to hear the cry as well. Sometimes, it was a distinct call for help; at other times no words could actually be heard, but the voice sounded like Nell. One evening, just on the edge of twilight, Mrs Cropsey thought that she saw 'something white' floating on the surface of the river near the little cove. Even as she spotted it, she heard her daughter's voice say quite distinctly, close to her side, 'Mamma! I'm coming back!' Three days later, Nell Cropsey's body was found, just a little way from the cove near the Cropsey home. A fisherman rowed out and brought it ashore to the grieving family. There was now no doubt that Nell was dead, but where had her body been? That particular stretch of the river had been dragged several times and nothing had been found. There were theories that the body had lodged in weeds along the river bottom, but this seemed rather unlikely.

Feelings were now running high in Elizabeth City, following the discovery of the body, and Jim Wilcox was in danger of his life. A lynching party was quickly formed, but the young man was saved from death by the intervention of the Cropseys themselves. While the mob approached the jailhouse door with a length of rope with which to hang Jim, Mr and Mrs Cropsey stood by and urged them not to be so rash. The mob eventually broke up, but the threats of a lynching hung over Elizabeth City for days. Finally, Federal Marshal Grandy wired the State Governor, Charles B. Aycock, for the assistance of 'naval reserves' – a part of the State Guard. The arrival of the military – a reserve group which had been on standby – quelled the mob and gradually talk of lynching subsided.

By now, other 'unrelated' pieces of evidence were pointing an accusing finger at Wilcox. Ollie Cropsey recalled that, a few weeks before Nell's disappearance, Jim had tried to persuade both of them to go sailing with him along the Pasquotank. They had not gone on the adventure, much to Jim's irritation. When some of the other sisters, together with Carrie Cropsey, had agreed to go with him, he had not brought them back until well after 6pm when it was getting dark. Jim had also played a trick on the rest of the family by wrapping Carrie in a blanket and pretending she had drowned – a stupid joke, but one that many people, including the police, found highly significant.

Nell's body was of course examined by the county coroner, Irving Fearing, together with two doctors from Elizabeth City. Their report was inconclusive. Nell was dead, but she had not died from drowning – there simply was not enough water in her lungs. It appeared that she had been killed by a blow to the temple with a padded instrument, but none of the medical men could be absolutely sure. It also seemed that the body had been stored elsewhere before being dumped in the river – her clothes were not sodden enough with river water for it to have been there for any length of time. Where could it have been hidden, though? Every inch of the riverbank and every house in the town had been searched. Apart from the suggestion of a bruise on her temple, there were no other marks of violence on her body. They also speculated that Nell Cropsey's death had only recently taken place, and that she could well have been alive when the townspeople were searching for her – but where had she been?

Faced with a seemingly insoluble mystery, coupled with rising tensions throughout the countryside, the local authorities eventually gave in to pressure and formally charged Jim Wilcox with Nell's murder. The trial got under way with the long and tortuous selection of the jury. There were few in Elizabeth City who could be considered 'impartial' about Nell's death and the selection process went on for several days. Solicitor George W. Ward, acting for the prosecution, attempted to show that James Wilcox had, with malice aforethought, killed Nellie Cropsey when he had tired of her attentions. He poured scorn on the idea put forward by Wilcox's defence that Nell might just have committed suicide. There was no reason for 'a healthy, happy girl' to take her own life. He also sought to show that Nell had not been drowned but had actually been murdered elsewhere. With evidence stacking up against him, Jim Wilcox is reported to have made a startling offer to his own counsel. He said that he would reveal something to the jury which would exonerate him – something to do with the Pasquotank itself, and something which might explain where Nell had gone. However, he was unaccountably never called to the stand and nothing was mentioned about a 'mish-mash of old Indian legends and nonsense'.

The prosecution case was built around the notion that Jim Wilcox was the last person to see Beautiful Nell alive, and the trial soon achieved widespread attention. Reporters arrived from out of state in order to hear the jury's verdict. After several days, the jury delivered its verdict – Jim Wilcox was found guilty, and was sentenced to death. However, this was almost immediately overturned on a technicality, and a new trial was ordered and given to him in another county, where he was convicted once more – this time for second-degree murder. Once again, strangely, he was not called to give evidence and this time he received a prison sentence.

Jim Wilcox remained behind bars at the State Penitentiary until 20 December 1920, when he was released by pardon. He had made several attempts to get the State Governor, Locke Craig, to meet with him in prison – he claimed he had something to tell the Governor that was so secret and so astonishing that he could not have stated it in open court. It would reveal where Beautiful Nell had gone on that fateful night.

Craig always refused these invitations, on the grounds that the boy had never taken the stand to clear himself. However, when he stepped down from the post, his successor, Thomas W. Bickett, eventually did go and meet with Wilcox. At the prisoner's insistence, the two men met in a prison room with only one witness present – an armed guard, named Preston White, who had been sworn to secrecy. Guards were also posted outside the doors of the room and Wilcox was thoroughly searched before he entered. What passed between the two men is unknown, but the Governor emerged from the encounter pale and shaking. He made one trip to the banks of the Pasquotank himself, in a horse-drawn carriage, and then issued a pardon for Wilcox. Three days after the meeting, Preston White – the sole witness to the revelation – cut his throat with a razor and bled to death.

What had Jim Wilcox revealed in that closed room? No one ever knew, for the two men – Wilcox and Bickett – took the secret to their graves. A newspaper editor from Monroe, Roland Beasley, who had covered the Wilcox case in Elizabeth City, said: 'He must have told the Governor the real truth of that night and the Governor believed him. He never told exactly why he granted the pardon. Perhaps Jim Wilcox saw something at the time which revealed to him where Nellie Cropsey had gone and why her body was never found until it was seen floating in the Pasquotank. There are old stories about that place which don't bear repeating. Maybe some of them are true.'

A day after Jim's release, Beasley found himself travelling on the train bound for Elizabeth City on Christmas Eve, 24 December 1920. He did not know it at the time, but Jim Wilcox was on the same train heading home. When it stopped at the station, he saw Wilcox climb down. 'There was nobody there to meet him,' Beasley reported, 'and other passengers seemed to shun him and hurry to get out of his way.' Wilcox, he went on, was dressed like 'a mountain man', wearing rough, old-looking clothes and with a squirrel-tail dangling from his hat-band. He was dragging two large and ferocious-looking dogs on a chain-leash. Hoping to get an interview with him, Beasley approached, but Jim Wilcox simply passed by as though the reporter was not there. 'He had grown a beard and looked extremely gaunt, haggard and haunted-looking. And there was something about his eyes that was frightening – as though they were fixed on other things. There was little trace of the dapper, good-natured young man that I remembered calling on the Cropseys 18 years before.'

On his release from prison, Jim Wilcox more or less lived the life of a hermit. His father was now dead and his brother had moved away from the area, but the Wilcox house was still standing. With the little money which had come to him from his father's will, Jim set himself up as a lumber trader working well away from the Pasquotank. He tried to have minimal contact with the folks around Elizabeth City, and perhaps it was just as well. Many of them still thought of him as a murderer. 'They don't want me around them,' he would sometimes say. 'They know that I know too much – I know about things which would frighten any sane man to death.' However, he never explained what these 'things' might be. Much of his time was spent reading his Bible or visiting the river-bank, near to the little cove where Nellie's body had been found. Some people said that he was revisiting the scene of his crime, but there appeared to be some other motive for his visitations there.

Then, about ten years after his release, in 1930, Jim Wilcox unexpectedly blew his own head off with a shotgun. There was no reason given for the suicide and few people cared. Latterly, he had become even more wild and bizarre in his dress and manners – he now refused to wash himself and had taken to shouting and swearing at the Pasquotank River – and recently had told a neighbour that he had heard Nell's voice calling to him more and more frequently, telling him that something was coming for him, something that he believed to be both monstrous and inhuman. The neighbour had simply put it down to a deteriorating mental condition. Jim's death was reported briefly and curtly, perhaps because nobody around Elizabeth City wanted to be reminded of the mysterious circumstances that surrounded Nell Cropsey's murder.

The Cropseys themselves continued to live in the area, and even with them there was a mystery. From time to time, they would receive sporadic letters, all postmarked 'Utica' in New York State, all written in a peculiar, shaky hand, and all purporting to come from the dead Lucas Vance. All of them allegedly came from a non-existent address. They came at six- to seven-monthly intervals for two years, and then they stopped completely. What they said remains unknown, for they were turned over to the local police (the last two were turned over unopened) for further investigation. They are probably lying somewhere in police files to this day.

With the death of Jim Wilcox, the Cropsey affair more or less came to an end. Much remains unanswered. If Wilcox did not murder Nell, as Governor Bickett appeared to believe, then who (or what) did? Who (or what) disturbed the Cropsey animals on that fateful night? Who did Caleb Parker see apparently comforting Nell at the gate of the family home? What did Jim Wilcox know and what dreadful secret did he tell the Governor – a secret so terrible that it caused both himself and a guard to take their own lives? Most importantly of all, where did Beautiful Nell Cropsey go when she walked through the screen-door of her own home on the night of 20 November 1901? What happened to her? Could it be that she stepped through a tear in the reality of our own existence and into a realm which lies just beyond the reach of our own limited senses – an unseen world which still waits along the swampy banks of the Pasquotank River?

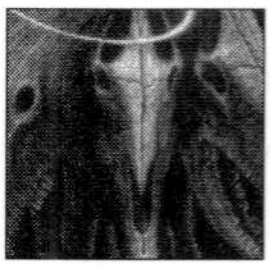

# THE HOLLANDALE WAGONS

Death held a fascination for the ancient Celts – not only what lay on the 'other side' (after one was dead) but also how one was literally transported there. Like many other ancient civilizations – the Egyptians, the Greeks – the Celts wondered how the souls of the dead actually travelled from the mortal world to the Beyond. For the Egyptians, it was a sacred boat (many representations of this have been found in their tombs), while for, say, the early Semites, it was a fiery chariot (the prophet Elisha was borne aloft in one of these and was therefore 'translated' – taken up by God without actually dying). In every case, travel into the Beyond was counted as a journey which the spirit of the dead person undertook by some means.

The Celts too, viewed death in this way. Funerary items – food, clothing and so on – were left in many Celtic tombs as provisions to sustain the spirit on its journey to the afterlife and these were consistent with the notion of travel between one sphere and another. Vehicles were also left, particularly in the tombs of high-ranking Celtic nobles, to ensure a safe and comfortable journey. In the Marne region and in East Yorkshire, for example, some individuals were buried with two-wheeled carts and chariots. Archaeologists and Celtic historians, such as Miranda Green, have stated that during the Hallstatt and La Tene Iron Age (the earliest Iron Age of non-Mediterranean European culture) Celtic nobles were buried in wooden mortuary chambers beneath earthen barrows, accompanied by four-wheeled wagons, sometimes partly dismantled. At some burial sites, three sets of horse-harness or similar trappings have been found, representing a wagon team pulling the dead chieftain into the afterlife. The so-called 'Arras culture' which flourished in western Europe around the 4th century BC is characterized by the interment of wagons and chariots together with their owners and provisions for a long journey. Evidence shows that the practice of vehicle-burial was widespread during the Iron Age right up until the 1st century BC and extended from northern Italy into Dejbjerg in Denmark. Here, even funerary urns containing the ashes of the dead were placed within wagons for transportation into the Beyond. Carvings sometimes show these vehicles being accompanied by a funeral procession, consistent with the rank and position of the interred chieftain.

The notion of supernatural processions and vehicles gradually found its way into the vernacular folklore of many Celtic regions. In Ireland, for instance, the notion of the 'fairy funeral' was at one time particularly common, while in Wales stories regarding 'phantom funerals' were legion. Contained within this belief was the central idea that the spirits of the recently dead were conveyed to either Heaven or Hell by supernatural beings – fairies or ghosts. In many parts of Ireland, the spirits of the dead were guided to Heaven under escort from the fairy host who were forbidden by God from entering the gates of Paradise themselves. Those who met with the 'fairy funeral' on the nightbound roads could be carried off with them into the afterlife by bad-tempered fairies. As a boy in the North of Ireland, I personally remember the body of a dead tramp found at a local crossroads who was deemed to have been carried off by the 'fairy host'; in actual fact, he had probably died of exposure. At certain times of the year, the rural Irish roads were packed after nightfall with wailing ghosts all in transit into the Beyond. In parts of Wales, such phantoms were under the direction of other spirits who guided them invisibly across the countryside. The only sign of their passing was a peculiar, chilly wind, which passed in an instant. In some areas of the Celtic world, certain people were 'gifted' to see the funerals passing. The 'gift' usually had prophetic overtones and the 'seer' often beheld those who were about to die passing in the supernatural procession. (It was also believed in parts of rural Wales that other 'ungifted' persons could 'see' the funeral simply by making physical contact with the 'seer' – by touching their arm or, more commonly, by standing on their foot.) The notion of the 'funeral', therefore, took on all the features of prophesy, one of the common facets of Celtic druidism.

It was in Brittany, however, that the notion of the wagon prominently appeared. Here, Ankou, the Breton lord of the dead, prowled the midnight countryside, driving a creaking cart into which he gathered the spirits of the dying or of the recently dead to convey them to the afterlife. With a skull-like face, he peered in at the windows of those houses that he was to visit, summoning the spirit with a knock or rap to join him in his nightmare vehicle. None save the departing person was to look out to behold the cart; to do so was to invite the most hideous penalty. However, the conveyance could frequently be heard creaking unsteadily along the roads after the light had failed, sometimes accompanied by the eerie wailing of the spirits which it was carrying. The grim lord sat at the very front of the vehicle urging on his black, almost skeletal, horses with a long and fiery whip.

The idea of the 'dead cart' resonated in other parts of the Celtic world and became translated into even more elaborate funeral conveyances. A phantom coach driven by the Devil, and a black, horse-drawn hearse, sometimes accompanied by spectral hounds, both feature in vernacular folklore from Ireland, through Scotland and into Wales and Cornwall – all important centres in the overall Celtic sphere of influence. The image also gained an especial prominence in Dublin during the late 18th and early 19th centuries, when body-snatching was rife in the city. In order to convey freshly exhumed bodies through the darkened streets, body-snatchers ('sack-em-up men' or 'Resurrectionists') had to load their grisly cargo onto carts and take them to the houses of their surgeon 'customers'. To keep curious eyes from viewing their activities, stories were spread about supernatural vehicles conveying the departed through the Dublin alleyways. Thus tales regarding the sound of the 'dead carts' was quite literal. Doubtless, similar stories were circulated in Edinburgh, which had just as high an instance of body-snatching as did Dublin. In rural areas of the Irish countryside, the conveying of poteen (illicit spirits) by cart was frequently covered by similar legends.

In rural Ireland too the terrifying 'coach-a-bower' (coiste bodhar – the dead coach) rushed through the countryside inspiring tales in County Tyrone and providing the inspiration for the Black Coach of Killeshandra in County Cavan. In Edinburgh, the Devil was sometimes believed to drive a diabolical coach down the Royal Mile at certain times of the year and always under cover of darkness. A number of Highland warlocks were said to own coaches which travelled across rivers and lochs. Even on Dartmoor, the spectral Lady Mary Howard rode in a coach of bones, pulled by four headless horses, gathering up those who neglected their prayers or who did a bad turn against their neighbours. Similar stories regarding 'phantom coaches' are to be found all over England. The tradition of 'three raps' on the door or window as a signal of impending death is strongly associated with such vehicles – a tradition which is to be found in many countries of the Celtic west.

In Ireland, just as the banshee was associated with certain families, so the 'death coach' became attached to others. Members of the old 'aristocratic' Irish families, such as the Fitzgeralds or the Butlers, often claimed to have heard the wheels of an invisible (or partly visible) vehicle approach their houses or overtake them on the road, when another member of the same clan was about to die. Gradually, the 'visitations' of the phantom coach percolated down from the aristocracy to the common people, so that the dread carriage visited rural districts, warning and spiriting away those who were about to die. Thus the 'coach-a-bower' became an infallible death warning in the Irish countryside, with the appearance of the carriage itself acting as the actual harbinger of impending doom. However, they still continued to be associated with certain local families.

So firm a grip did the idea of the 'dead carts' have on the Celtic mind that it travelled with many of the Scots-Irish planters to the New World. In developing frontier and rural communities in the American West, both horses and wagons were a fundamental and essential means of transport. It is therefore only natural that they should feature in the folklore of the pioneer countryside and that such tales should become imbued with traditions which had been brought with the pioneers from Celtic countries. Phantom carts, coaches and wagons began to fill frontier tales just as surely as they had done in Ireland, England and Scotland. Some of these appearances also warned of death or misfortune for those who saw them and, in an environment where hardship and danger were always present, it is hardly surprising that at least some of these 'spectral prognostications' appeared to come true.

Like their Celtic counterparts, some of these vehicles were associated with specific family units. In some cases, members of certain families saw the carriages prior to their deaths and, in other cases, the vehicles were simply foretelling death or communal catastrophe in a general sense but were driven by the ghosts of members of certain families who were long dead. Gradually, too, the vehicles became associated with families and areas who were not of the original Celtic tradition – although many of the Celtic folkloric aspects remained – but who reflected the pioneer families. These were German, Polish, Russian, Scandinavian people who built their own racial mythologies around the central Celtic theme. The phantom wagon as the embodiment or prognostication of death invariably became the stuff of rural American legend. One of the most enduring of these tales comes from Hollandale in southwest Wisconsin.

The legend of the Hollandale wagons is well known, even beyond the borders of Iowa County where it is said to have originated. Localized variations of it have been found all over Wisconsin, even as far as South Dakota. With each passing recountal of the tale it has become more and more complex, and so many different elements have been built into it that it has easily adapted to the region in which it is told, thus becoming a 'local legend' in many areas. The central story, however, comes from the farming country in the south of Wisconsin and, although many inhabitants of Hollandale nowadays profess not to know the legend, it appears to have once been a central part of their mythology.

The legend revolves around four brothers and a runaway team or teams of draft horses. The brothers are given various names – Kemps, Kamps, Camps, Von Kemp, or sometimes even Ryan or Donnelly – and, as the legend developed, were said to come from a variety of backgrounds – Dutch, English, Irish, German and Danish. They lived in the days long before the advent of the automobile when carts and wagons were the common modes of transport. High-spirited and greatly competitive young men, they were descended from generations of cavalrymen and teamsters, and every one of the four had reputations as fine horsemen. In some variations of the legend, they had reputations for other things. Although little mention of their father is made in any version, he is thought to have been some sort of 'witchy man' who had done a deal of some kind with the dark spirits dwelling in the countryside around his home. Exactly what that deal entailed was never specified; but it is believed that it had something to do with mastery over animals, especially horses. Whatever uncanny powers he acquired were passed onto his sons and created a rather sinister reputation around them. More than once the boys were denounced from the pulpit of the village churches, not that they took much notice of what the local pastors said.

They were reckless and devil-may-care in their ways, but all four of them were handsome and were good workers. All were unmarried and had caught the eyes of many of the local girls. Jake, the eldest, had smouldering, dark, good looks and a neatly trimmed moustache, and was considered to be the best-looking of the four. Sam, the second eldest, was a natural athlete, quite at home at an arm-wrestling contest or on the dance floor (he was said to be the finest dancer in Iowa County). George, the third-born, was a renowned horseman but he was also skilled as a wood-turner and as a musician. Luke, the youngest, was the most reckless and rowdy of the four, and yet he had serious, dark grey eyes and was counted as an exceptional singer. All four brothers worked together, driving wagon-teams between the settlements of Moscow and Dodgeville and were much sought after as hauliers in the local community, despite a somewhat dubious reputation. Even in their business they were wild and reckless, dashing through the streets of Hollandale at top speed and scattering the citizens who happened to be in their path. Such behaviour only added to the stories about them. Yet no others could deal with horses the way that the brothers could. Even the most dangerous, most unbreakable, horses seemed to obey them without hesitation –

perhaps it was a gift passed down to the boys from their father. Outwardly, the four brothers seemed extremely close. However, this appearance was not strictly true.

Luke, the youngest, suffered the indignity of being the last-born, and was the butt of constant jokes from his brothers. He was also tired of living in the collective shadows of the others and was always trying new, more outrageous, feats of daring in order to get himself noticed and to elevate his position in the family pecking order. Many of his 'feats' were athletic – skilfully diving into shallow pools, walking across the barn roof on his hands – but, to make an impression on his brothers, he had to do something with horses. So he began 'showing off', trying to outdo his elder brothers with 'daring' displays of horsemanship and wagon control. For example, he would routinely take corners in a loaded wagon on two wheels without shedding any of the load; he would work his way forward by walking along the wagon tongue, while the team was on the move, with the dexterity of a tightrope walker; he would start the team and, as they achieved a gallop, he would run along behind the wagon, catch the wagon-gate just at the last minute, haul himself on board and across the load to the driving seat; or he would drive a team at full gallop with the reins clenched in his teeth. Soon, his exploits were the talk of Iowa County, but his brothers appeared unimpressed. Then he hit on a master feat which would leave them open-mouthed.

Buffalo Bill's Wild West Show was travelling through Kansas, Dakota and Wisconsin. One of the acts, John S. Parker, a former Wells Fargo coachman, performed a trick that had everyone talking. It involved a spirited team pulling a heavy Wells Fargo coach which Parker was driving. With the team at full gallop, he would suddenly leap from the driving seat and land on the flanks of the back horses. Urging them on with a whip, he would balance himself with one foot on each animal, gradually inching himself forward for a leap to balance himself on the lead horses and slow the team. It was an extremely dangerous trick and Parker himself did not perform it very often (he was actually killed while attempting it during a show in Denver, Colorado); however, it inspired Luke to attempt to outdo his brothers.

He worked at the stunt in secret, practising almost every day. Like the others, he was intuitively skilled at handling horses and the animals responded well towards him. For effect, he chose as his lead team horses two young and powerful grey roans, one of which had more than a hint of Percheron about him. Both steeds were known for their quickness and spirit and would add to the overall impact of the feat, and both of them seemed to enjoy the trick and co-operate in the synchronized gait which was essential to its success. After much training, he felt he was ready to attempt the stunt and awaited his opportunity. It was not long in coming.

One afternoon, there was a delay in loading one of Luke's wagons. Four wagons had to go to Dodgeville as soon as possible, and so, with their own wagons loaded up, Jake, Sam and George set off without their younger brother. Some time later, Luke's own wagon was loaded, and he too set off along the trail. He knew that he would meet his brothers on their way back, probably around Dodge Branch Creek. There he would stage his exhibition of horsemanship for them and win their approval. He flicked the reins and the two grey roans responded with a lively and practised gait, setting the pace for the other two horses of the team. Further along, the old road dipped down along the Creek bottom towards the rolling hills beyond. About half way along was a stand of white oaks, and it was here that Luke decided to wait for his brothers.

As expected, he soon heard them coming, shouting and laughing with each other as their now-empty wagons bumped and jolted over the uneven ground which characterized this area of trail. He eased the team forward and tensed himself for the jump to the back of the drag horses. Tightening his grip on the special pair of trick reins that he had made specially for the occasion, Luke made ready. The team began to pick up speed. Round the corner ahead, the other three wagons came into view with Jake out in front followed by George and then Sam, calling playfully to each other. Seeing the approaching wagon, they stopped – their faces a mixture of puzzlement, then anger and then delight. As they saw what Luke was going to do, they laughed and whooped their approval, laced with obscenities.

With his team now at full stretch, their younger brother climbed up on the driving seat and jumped. As he did so, the wagon bounced on a rut in the track and one of the drag horses missed its step. Luke landed awkwardly, missed his footing and fell between the horses. He first bounced on the wagon tongue and tried to hold on. The startled team, however, bounced the wagon through a ditch and across a litter of rocks. Luke lost his grip and somersaulted under the hooves of the grey roans. He tried to roll clear but a flailing hoof caught him on the side of the head. Somehow, an iron end-hook caught on his shirt and he was pulled after the runaway wagon for almost 100 yards. The cloth ripped free and the outer wheels of the laden wagon passed over Luke's head and chest, killing him instantly. It was all over in a matter of minutes. The other three brothers watched in horror, too far away to do anything. Their screams echoed from the nearby white oaks. They organized themselves to capture the runaway team. Jake started home with Luke's twisted and mangled body, while Sam and George tried, rather unsuccessfully, to calm the team, especially the two grey roans. Finally they transferred the load to Sam's wagon and managed to tie the horses behind it. Then they, too, started for home.

Luke was buried shortly afterwards in a corner of the family farm. For some reason, there was no church funeral, and yet his interment was well attended – it was said that there were over 50 wagons and buggies from the local community. Perhaps everyone wanted to see that the reckless young man was finally in the clay! Afterwards, the other brothers tried to use the two roans for hauling, but they were always skittish and spooked and were of no real use at all. Finally their father, Eli, took his rolling block rifle, walked out into the barnyard and shot both horses. That seemed to be the end of it all – but it was not.

About a year after Luke's death, some of the people of Hollandale thought they heard a wagon pass by their houses, very late at night. It was an eerie sound – the creaking and swaying of the vehicle itself and the steady plod of the horses as they pulled it. Several homesteaders went to their doors and looked out to see who was travelling abroad at such an unearthly hour, but the road seemed empty and no trace of a passing wagon could be seen at all. Then, a travelling harness salesman stopped in a local tavern and told a peculiar and rather chilling story. Standing at the bar, he enquired if there were any 'young hotheads' in the neighbourhood, as one had almost driven him into the ditch.

He had been travelling towards Hollandale from Dodgeville and, at a place where the road ran into an old creek bottom, he had slowed his horse. He remembered the place distinctly because several white oaks grew nearby, their branches stretched wide and menacingly against the late evening sky. Suddenly, out of the gloom, a wagon approached him, going at full speed. The salesman pulled his horse over to the side of the trail as the vehicle thundered by. Two grey roans led the team and were driven by a young man who almost stood on the driving seat as if he were about to jump onto the backs of the drag horses. Even in the brief moment that he passed, the salesman went on, he had seen the wild gleam in his eye and the strange contortions of his face in the gathering dusk. He assumed that the boy had been on a visit to one of the local distilleries and was madly drunk. One of those drinking at the bar looked up in astonishment for, in the admittedly hazy description, he recognized his own dead brother. Sam laid down his drink and went home in great fear.

For several more years, sighting of the strange wagon continued, sometimes on the road between Hollandale and Dodgeville, but also on the Waldwick road. It was always seen late in the evening and always appeared to be travelling at speed. On some occasions, the sighting preceded a misfortune or disaster in the local community: once a child was drowned in a creek; another time a house was burned down in a sudden fire. However, as automobiles began to venture along the roads, these sightings became less and less common. The other brothers continued to work as hauliers although they had now become more staid and sober in their ways. All of them remained bachelors.

Around the beginning of World War I, Jake died after a prolonged illness. On the night he died, the sound of a wagon was said to approach the door of his house, shortly before the actual moment of death. It drew up and stopped – and Jake died. Afterwards, two wagons were seen on the road between Hollandale and Waldwick (Jake's old hauling trail) and once again they were usually seen before some local misfortune.

A few years later Sam died; on the night of his death, a driverless team, pulling an empty wagon, rushed past the door of his house and off into the dark. Now a third wagon joined the other two on the local roads around Hollandale. They seemed to be going at full speed as if racing each other, and local wisdom said that it was as well to keep out of their way. Even though cars now travelled along these roads, the sightings of the wagons now increased, and on several occasions drivers reported swerving to avoid their madcap dash.

George died a mere six months after Sam and a fourth wagon made up the phantom company. They were now to be seen along Highway 191, which had been constructed over some of the old hauling trails. Sometimes they were seen as men and teams, travelling along the centre of the highway; at other times, they were seen simply as insubstantial silhouettes, travelling over the ridgetop trails. They appeared to delight in pursuing travellers, particularly those on horseback, who were out late at night. No two encounters with them were the same. Sometimes the wagons appeared driverless; sometimes horseless and moving under their own power; at other times, the brothers were seen, in their Sunday finery – dark coats, white shirts and black Derby hats – driving their teams along ferociously; at other times still, they were seen as four skeletons, driving rotting wagons which were falling to pieces and were drawn by skeleton horses. Sometimes, the ghosts were even accompanied by other spirits who often sat beside them on the driving seats or who ran along beside the wagons, travelling faster than any mortal. One is described as a pretty young girl with coppery red hair, who gazes adoringly at either Luke or Sam. The origin of this female is unknown. At other times, the wagons seemed crowded with wailing spirits – those recently dead in the countryside round about, their cries sounding like the moaning of the wind. In some cases, these visions preceded some sort of local disaster or a personal misfortune for the viewer.

Time has not decreased the sightings of the Hollandale wagons, for stories relating to them appear in recent folklore. Even the recent tales vary from the ghoulish to the relatively benign. The descriptions of the brothers still differ, too. One account, given by an elderly Norwegian-American gentleman, is as follows.

I'd heard of the Hollandale wagons and of the brothers since I was a little boy, growing up in the hills. I knew many people who'd seen them at night and I'd heard dozens of stories. Most of them were pretty straightforward tales, about ghostly figures driving wagons or phantom teams. I never saw the brothers when I was a boy but I heard them plenty of times. Sometimes, in the winter, I'd hear them just before dawn – whips cracking, drivers shouting, horses whinnying all along the roads. I'd check down in the snow but there'd be no tracks at all. This was always on stormy nights and on snow-closed roads when even birds would have left a track but no sane person would be out and about. Then, in summer, I'd hear them up along the ridges above the main roads – the same noises and the rumble of wagon wheels over stony ground. There would sometimes be shadows, moving and rolling about under the trees too, but never anything that was clear. But the stories about them would go on, all over Iowa County.

When I was a young man, I finally saw them for myself. I was driving back from Dodgeville in my first car, from a band concert in the town. I should have been home well before dusk but a young German girl had kept me in the town. It was very dark and I wanted to get home before Dad got up for milking. I turned the car onto a side-road which was a shortcut back to our farm and went bumping and rolling over heights and hollows in the trail.

About two miles or so out of Hollandale, something caught my eye. There was a big, looping curve in the road and, as I brought the car round it, I chanced to look back towards Dodgeville and I saw a row of lights moving which seemed like moving and weaving lanterns. These lights were gaining on me and something made me speed up a little towards home. Even so, these strange lights seemed to come on, drawing closer and closer. Soon the car was going at its top limit but still I somehow couldn't manage to shake those lights. They got close enough for me to see them in the glow of their lanterns – four wagons and four drivers, driving as though the Devil himself was after them.

Foolishly, I tried to escape, pushing the poor old car to its limits on that rocky, rutty road. All I heard was a loud and growling laughter which rang all around the vehicle and seemed to be coming from the wagons themselves. Then they were alongside of me and what a sight they were! A sight that I'll take with me to the grave! Each wagon was lit up with a faint brilliance like St Elmo's fire hanging all around it. Each rider was dressed in his Sunday best and sat on a driving seat made from a coffin with his high-polished boots on a footrest made of human skulls. Snakes of all kinds made up the harness, the collars and the reins and the manes and tails of the horses were also made up of rattlers and coachwhip serpents. And the drivers carried snake whips. Each wagon carried a load of horse-bones – skulls, ribs and legs – and every one of them had skull-lanterns lining its sides. As I said, the drivers were finely dressed in night-black suits and, as they passed by me, each one looked down and smiled and gave me a tip of his hat. The last one rushed past and gave me the biggest smile and seemed to tip his whole head! That one had to be Luke!

When they passed by, they seemed to go even faster, as if they'd just gone up a gear. Showers of sparks winked from the wagon wheels, seeming to leave a trail of flame and smoke behind them. It seemed as if none of the wagons would take the big bend which was coming up fast for they didn't seem to slow down at all. And, instead of attempting that bend, they just went straight on and off the road, with the horses still at full stretch. And, suddenly, a great and flaming black hole opened in the side of the hill in front of them and the wagons went straight in. In an instant, the hole closed over again and they were gone. There was nothing but the bare hill in front of me in the moonlight. Some time later, a relative of mine unexpectedly died over beyond Waldwick – she died slowly and horribly and her death had been foretold by the wagons that I saw on that awful night. I never saw or heard them again but I still know plenty who have.

Everyone says that you have to be careful out on Highway 191 late at night. Especially on those moonless, overcast nights when there is a bit of a fog in the hollows and around the creek bottom. Your eyes will suddenly start to feel heavier and the fog will seem to get thicker, like breath coming from the nostrils of the Devil's horses. Then you'll be surprised to see wagons on the trail, just where it gets curvy and goes into sweeping bends. When you see cars piled up by the side of the road, you'll know that those drivers have met with the Hollandale wagons and been scared into the ditch. Don't laugh at them, for you never know what awaits you around the next turn of the road. Anyway, that's what I know about the dead brothers and the Hollandale wagons. Just pray that you never meet up with them.

# SELECT BIBLIOGRAPHY


Baring-Gould, Sabine *Book of Cornwall* Methuen, London, 1906 edn.

Botterell, William *Traditions and Hearthside Stories of West Cornwall* Penzance, reprint 1996 .

Brown, James *History of the Highlands* Edinburgh, 1838.

Brown, Theo *Devon Ghosts* Jarrold , Norwich, 1982.

Bourke, Angela *The Burning of Bridget Cleary* Pimlico, London 1999.

Cahill, Robert Ellis *Olde New England's Strange Superstitions* Old Saltbox Publications, Salem, Massachusetts, 1990.

Calef, Robert *More Wonders of the Invisible World* Gloucester, Massachusetts, 1700.

Ceitinn, Seathrun *Foras Feasa ar Eireann* Dublin, 1631.

Crofton-Croker, T. *airy Legends and Traditions of the South of Ireland* John Murray, Dublin, 1825.

Drake, Samuel *New England Legends and Folk-Lore* Castle Books, reprint 1993

Emory, Sarah Anna *Reminiscences of a Nonagrarian* Boston, Massachusetts, 1897.

Gregory, Lady *Visions and Beliefs in the West of Ireland* London, 1920; reprint 1992.

Hardin John *Tar Heel Ghosts* University of North Carolina Press, 1954.

Harland, Edwin Sidney *The Science of Fairy Tale* London, 1891.

Hogg, James *Private Memoirs of a Justified Sinner* Edinburgh, 1824.

Hughes, Marion & Evans, W. *Rumours and Oddities from North Wales* Carreg Gwalch,1986.

Jones, K. I. *Seven Cornish Witches* Oak Magic Press, 1998.

Jones, K. I. *Folklore and Witchcraft of Devon and Cornwall* Oak Magic Press,1997.

Lovecraft, H. P. 'The Shunned House' *Weird Tales* magazine, October, 1937.

Mann Mather, Cotton *Wonders of the Invisible World* Harvard, Massachusetts 1693.

O'hOgain, Dathi *An Encyclopaedia of The Irish Folk Tradition* , Dublin & London, 1990.

Owen, Elias *Welsh Folk Lore* Felinfech , reprint 1996 .

Perley, M. V. B. *A Short History of the Salem Village Witchcraft Trials* Kessinger Publications, Montana, 1911.

Rodina, C. *Vampire* Covered Bridge Press, Massachusetts, 1997.

Scot, Reginald *The Discoverie of Witchcraft* London, 1584.

Scott, Sir Walter *Redgauntlet* Oxford University Press, 1998 edn.

Seymour, Reverend St. John *Irish Witchcraft and Demonology* London & Dublin, 1911.

Stevenson, Robert Louis*Dr Jekyll and Mr. Hyde* Edinburgh, 1886.

Stewart, Duncan *History of the Stewarts* Edinburgh ,1739.

Summers, Montague *The Vampire* Kegan Paul, Trench, Trubner,. London, 1928.

Taylor, L. B., Jnr. *The Ghosts of Virginia* (privately printed in 4 vols.), Progress Printing, Virginia, 1995-98.

Wilson, A., Brogan D. & McGrail, F. *Ghostly Tales and Sinister Stories of Old Edinburgh* Edinburgh, 1991.

# INDEX